# Caribbean Calling

## Great Comments about <u>Caribbean Calling</u>

Jimmy Gordon paints an honest picture about the challenges of being a firefighter, he captures the laid back tropical feel and spins a tale of action and adventure all at the same time. ~ *Alex Liest, Vice President of Parrothead in Paradise*

Get Ready for a wild ride. Jimmy writes a non stop action adventure that will leave you wanting more. ~ *Marianna Boylan, founder and moderator of the Bookmasters reading cub.*

# Caribbean Calling

by
j. d. gordon

**Red Engine Press**
**Key West, FL**

Published by Red Engine Press

COPYRIGHT © 2006 by Jim Gordon

All Rights Reserved. No part of this book may be reproduced or transmitted in any form or by any means, electronic or mechanical, including photocopying, recording, or by an information storage and retrieval system (except by a reviewer who may quote brief passages in a review to be in a magazine, newspaper or on the Internet) without permission in writing from the publisher.

All characters and events in this work are fictitious, and any resemblance to actual persons, living or dead, is purely coincidental.

Library of Congress Control Number: 2006924022

ISBN – 10: 0-9745652-8-8
ISBN – 13: 978-0-9745652-8-6

Cover Art by Shannon Benna

Printed in the United States of America

Quantity discounts are available on bulk purchases of this book for educational institutions or social organizations. For information, please contact the publisher:

**Red Engine Press**
1107 Key Plaza #158
Key West, FL 33040

**Dedicated to my wife and daughter**

# Acknowledgments

First and foremost, I would like to thank my wife, Kim, for her unending support and patience while I spent hours away from the family clicking away on the keyboard. I'd like to thank my editor and very good friend, Patricia Hernandez, for her meticulous attention to detail, and her guidance with both content and the literary world in general. Thanks to Tom and the crew at Curly's for putting up with me at all hours, typing away at the end of the bar. The same goes for Sue, who is the best bartender at Shannon's Pub. Joyce Faulkner, I am full of gratitude for all of our late night chats and the reassurance and advice you so kindly offered. Thanks to Marjorie Spoto for all of her support. Finally, thank you to the rest of my family and friends. You all patiently listened to my stories long before anyone had the chance to read them, and you gave me hope. To my readers, it's all for you!

j. d. gordon

## Prologue

In the corner of a cracked asphalt playground, under the cover of shade provided by an old gray stone building on the corner of Grace and Laramie, in the city of Chicago, two boys squared off, face to face.

Comfortable old brick bungalows and large brick apartment buildings lined the streets that surrounded the school grounds. A group of children huddled together, shoulder to shoulder, circling the two boys. The miniature prizefighters, both fourth graders, occupied the center patch of the only grass, marked by tall iron fences that grew within the boundaries of the school. The two stood toe-to-toe, their eyes narrowed and their fists clenched. They were peers preparing themselves for combat. It was a showdown that had been brewing for some time.

It had all started during a child's game -- a game referred to as "Jonny Tackle." The kids didn't know how, or why, or even who had invented the game, or where it had gotten its name. They knew that each and every student had always played the game for as long as anyone could remember.

The unwritten rules of the game went like this -- Mister Tackle would start off each game standing alone in the middle of the field. Akin to medieval soldiers, the rest of the students would line up on one end of the playing field. A cry from the student in the center -- "Jonny Tackle!" -- slicing through the confines of the schoolyard, began the game.

## Caribbean Calling

Like a herd of buffalo in a wild frenzy, the kids would bolt, the goal being to reach the other side of the playing field without being dragged to the ground by Jonny Tackle. Tacklees were made Jonny's teammates, and would then assist in pummeling the remaining runners. Eventually, the tide would turn. A single runner would remain, staring down the field, picking the best route. Tacklers focused their attention on the runner. If the final runner could make it through the mob, he would be the glorious victor, and could designate the next "Jonny Tackle."

At one point, a cold war of sorts developed when one of the boys playing "Jonny," a boy named Bartley, fell into a skirmish with one of the runners, who thought that Bartley was playing too rough with the smaller kids and called him on it. Over the course of the next few weeks, the rivals targeted one another. The competition intensified daily, though an actual "coming to blows" most of the kids were expecting never happened. Instead, there were glares, whispered threats, and a sense of impending confrontation.

On the last day of school before the summer break, the recess bell rang and the children went through the usual democratic process for selecting the session's first "Jonny Tackle." This game was important. Those who were interested raised their hands. The rest would vote.

On this day, one boy raised his hand. It was Bartley. He was a tough and rugged boy -- the proverbial playground bully. He was the one kid who relished starting off as the lone tackler. Taller than most kids his age, his brown hair was buzzed down to a prickly crew-cut, and he had one blue eye and one brown eye. His nose was crooked, and he was one mean son-of-a-gun, for a nine year old. Bartley's father called him the Red Baron German Fighting Ace (Baron, for short), a nickname inspired by his penchant for slamming his Big Wheel into the other kids on his street, knocking them off of whatever it was their own parents

# j. d. gordon

had provided as transportation. The nickname stuck.

It was the first round of play. Bartley took some time to scan the line of runners and to pick his target. Then, he hollered the appropriate phrase, "Jonny Tackle!" The children took off. Like a great white shark, Bartley stalked his prey -- a small boy, a year or two younger. The kid was easy pickings for a beast like the Baron. Bartley lined up and dropped his shoulder, ready for impact. The two bodies crashed like a big rig into a Volksie, leaving the small boy pinned to the ground, the Baron's weight upon him. The other runners continued to the safe zone on the other side of the field -- safe, for the moment, from the Baron.

Bartley wasn't finished with his catch, though. The child lay still on the ground. Bartley stood above him, his foot on the boy's chest, the heel of his dirty, old, beaten tennis shoe digging into the child's ribs, one hand raised in triumph. The boy began to cry and plead, but Bartley showed no mercy. He refused to release him. Soon, a single runner left the sideline pack and made his way over the parched earth in the direction of the Baron.

This boy's build was similar to that of the Baron's. They were the same age, and about the same weight and height. This boy was different, though, and the other kids looked at him with admiration, not fear. He had a smile on his face. He'd been known to intervene, often, on behalf of the less physically imposing kids in these types of situations -- like the one that had begun the tension between him and the Baron several weeks ago. He had short brown hair, like the Baron, but both of his eyes were blue.

This boy was one of the guys, a good athlete and joke-teller. The girls liked him, too. He didn't tease or chase or pinch. A good student, this boy strapped on his orange patrol belt and proudly affixed his white hat every morning and afternoon to assist his fellow students on their way home. He considered it a great privilege. Everyone knew and liked him, except for Bartley.

# Caribbean Calling

"Get off of him, Baron!" he ordered, approaching at a run.

The Baron sneered. "Who's gonna make me?"

"I am, Bartley! Now move! Let the kid go!"

The Baron paused for a moment, then stepped down off of his prize. A cloud of dust rose from the ground beneath his feet as he shuffled toward the patrol boy until there were twelve inches of space between them. While they stared each other down, kids gathered around like Roman spectators watching gladiators in the Coliseum. The Baron threw the first punch. The schoolyard cold war was getting hot.

The patrol boy ducked beneath the Baron's swing. He could hear the swish of air as the Baron's heavy limb swung overhead. Then he counter-attacked, his tight fist connecting with the Baron's already misaligned nose. There was a crunching sound, and then small drops of blood began to slip from one of the Baron's nostrils. A few tears ran down his cheek -- and then Bartley began to sob.

The patrol boy stood still, waiting, not the type to hit a man when he's down. Suddenly, he felt his collar yanked hard by some unknown force. His feet slipped out from under him and dragged on the asphalt as his abductor carried him away. Small stones popped and flew as the patrol boy's rubber heels tried to grab ground. He could see Bartley being hoisted to his feet and hauled off in the direction of the principal's office. His own captor, a teacher assigned to monitor the playground during recess, paused long enough to extract a ring of keys from her pocket so that she could open the detention room. That's when Bartley turned toward him, before being forced through the principal's door. He wiped the blood from his nose, made a fist and raised it in the air in defiance, and said, "I'm gonna get you one day, Eddie Gilbert! There'll be a day, and I'm gonna get you!"

j. d. gordon

## Chapter One

Dr. Elaine Keller stepped out of the environmentally-controlled first class section of a Boeing 747 and into the warm and humid air of San Juan, Puerto Rico. It had been a few short months since she had earned the credentials to be a full-fledged medical practitioner. She'd broken her old man's heart when she'd chosen Northwestern University in Evanston, Illinois, rather than the University of Michigan. Her father, a prominent surgeon, was an alumnus of the latter.

Her father, as any good father would, eventually came to support her decision. As regarded this current choice she'd made, though, Elaine could still remember his reaction, word for word:

"You're going to…have you lost your mind? You're going to do what…and where?!"

"I'm going to spend my first year volunteering, Daddy, down south," Elaine replied calmly. It was her decision and she was going to stick by it.

"What will you do there? Where the hell are you going? When are you leaving? Why the hell are you doing this?" her father had interrogated as Elaine moved back and forth between her walk-in closet and her four-post, canopy-covered bed.

One large canvas duffel bag lay open on the bed, surrounded by heaps of clothing and other personal items. That which would fit in the bag was all that Elaine would be allowed to bring. On

## caribbean calling

both sides of the duffel, stenciled in large block letters, the words 'CARIBBEAN RELIEF CORPS' appeared.

Similar to the Red Cross, Doctors Without Borders, and the Peace Corps, the CRC was not as well known as its peer organizations, and funding was beyond modest. The volunteers spent their nights living in run-down, old buildings, sleeping on rusty army cots dug up out of military surplus stores, and surviving on simple meals. Despite the discomforts, Elaine had chosen the organization because it seemed to need the most help. It was in her nature to be drawn toward the underdog. In the end, and as usual, Elaine's father relented, and gave his blessings to his only daughter.

Elaine completed the first half of her journey when the wheels of the airliner touched ground in San Juan. After exiting the American Airlines terminal and heading for a gate operated by the Gulf Stream Airline Corporation, she saw the tiny plane which would serve as her transportation for the final leg of her trip.

It was the smallest aircraft she had ever traveled in. After boarding the aircraft she sat down in one of the six passenger seats.

The plane vibrated as the pilot increased the power to the engines of the puddle-jumper. Elaine glanced out the small round window. The spinning propeller blades were barely visible. As the plane began to gain altitude, she gazed down on the landscape below. She had already reviewed the paperwork the CRC had sent several weeks ago describing all of the details about the island nation she would call home for the next year. According to the CRC report, the island was small and depressed, with a very weak economy. Most of the island's citizens lived in small shacks or grass huts. This last, brief survey of San Juan would be her last look at modern civilization for quite some time.

## j. d. gordon

Throughout the flight, the young sawbones studied her materials while sipping on a cola provided to her by the flight's sole attendant, she also happened to be the aircraft's co-pilot. Eventually, the aircraft's tires touched down on the dirt runway of what might be called an airport in some circles. She was the only passenger to exit the plane. Like a bus company, the airline made regular stops in different locations throughout the Caribbean. After crouching through the small hatch at the side of the plane and descending the six short steps that led to the runway, Elaine was surprised to find her duffel lying on the ground. Apparently, some unknown individual had dug it out of the guts of the plane's limited cargo hold and disappeared. She took a look around.

She hadn't noticed the dark storm clouds rolling in during the flight -- but now, in the distance, she saw a black line gobbling up the blue sky. The air had that certain sweet smell that precedes a heavy storm, and streaks of lightning flashed about the clouds intermittently.

The single runway was riddled with potholes, which, she surmised, would force any incoming pilots to do a little creative dancing in order to avoid catastrophe. As if to provide warning, several smashed-up planes lay on their sides and tops on the spotty grass field that lined what amounted to a gravel road. Apparently, some pilots had not been creative enough.

To her left was a small, worn, two-room wooden building. A weathered sign fixed above a single door read 'Terminal' in large yellow letters. There were no taxis waiting for fares, no relatives waiting for travelers to return home. There was, however, one lone person standing in front of the dilapidated terminal building. Elaine figured him to be somewhere around thirty. His hair was sun-bleached to a light blonde, and a dark pair of sunglasses shaded his eyes as he watched the newest member of the team sling her duffel over her shoulder. Clad from head to toe

## caribbean Calling

in khaki, he resembled, Elaine thought, some rich guy on safari.

An old jeep parked next to the building, its original green paint faded and cracked, identified itself as being property of the CRC in bold letters on its door. Obviously, this was her ride. Elaine readjusted her duffel and headed in the man's direction.

"Let me grab that for you, Doctor!" The man trotted toward her, relieved her of the bag, and tossed it into the back of the jeep. "You're Elaine, I assume? The new doc, right?"

"Elaine Keller, MD, at your service," she replied. The trip, though uneventful, had been exhausting.

"Let's get hopping!" The young man was brimming with energy. "As you can see, there's a storm brewing."

Elaine assessed the vehicle. It would be a wet ride -- there was no top for the jeep. "Looks like something a World War II general would be chauffeured around in... like something out of an old war movie," she commented with a weary smile.

"It is World War II surplus. It's tough to find parts for, but hell, it was free! It's got character, too, doesn't it?" The handsome man extended his hand. "By the way, I'm Billy, Billy Stang." Elaine noted an East Coast accent.

The two made small talk as the jeep cruised along the island's primitive roadways. The streets were narrow, and the few cars Elaine spotted shared the roads with carts towed by donkeys, mules, and oxen. The island's citizens seemed to go about their daily business, paying almost no attention to the two Americans cruising past their homes and places of business. Old wooden shacks and open-air tents lining the road were manned by peddlers selling various goods. Occasionally, the scent of unfamiliar spices wafted past and mixed with the smoke from cooking fires.

"I don't think I'll be eating any meat while I'm on the

## j. d. gordon

island," Elaine remarked, after passing an open meat stall. Creatures of all types hung from hooks attached to large metal racks, all covered by a variety of insects buzzing around the hanging flesh. A butcher was going to town on a bloody carcass with a rusty machete. Elaine couldn't make out what kind of animal was being prepared for someone's dinner, but it sure looked like a dog to her.

Billy laughed. "No problem, but we do only eat local products. It's supposed to help the economy, albeit in a small way, I guess."

Bushes and trees appeared to be non-existent until the duo were a good distance from the town, where the barren fields were replaced by lush tropical foliage.

"So, Elaine, if I may call you that, what's your story?" Billy asked.

"Well, I just gradu........Whoa, there, man!" Elaine screeched as she was nearly bounced out of the vehicle. One of the front tires had slammed into a Grand Canyon-sized crater in the middle of the road.

"Oops, sorry," Billy smiled. "I guess I didn't catch that one in time."

"That's okay," Elaine tightened what sufficed as her seatbelt. "I finished my residency not too long ago. I guess I'm not ready to become a full-fledged adult and enter the job market. I guess I wanted to get away for a while, do something different." She paused. "And your story?"

"Me? I suppose you could say I'm one of your assistants."

Thick tropical plant-life now encroached upon the vehicle. Occasional large drops of rain smacked Elaine in the face, as Billy raced to beat the downpour. The wind began to pick up, lightning streaked overhead, and thunder echoed nearby. "I'm a

## Caribbean Calling

RN. I worked in the emergency room of a Boston hospital. After some time there, I decided to head down here. I felt like life was getting a little too complicated back home." Billy was shouting now in order to be heard above the surrounding wind.

When he offered no more information, Elaine couldn't tell if he wanted to concentrate on the road, or if he wanted to avoid expanding on the subject. Volunteers had their own reasons for being there, she figured.

"Hang on, Doc, and enjoy the ride. We should be there pretty soon."

Twisting the wheel hard, Billy stomped on the accelerator to avoid hitting an animal that was scurrying across the road. Ten minutes and a few miles later, the jeep plunged out from under the canopy of the rain forest and back out into open space. Not as barren as the more populated real estate they had passed through after leaving the airfield, Elaine found the countryside much more picturesque. Rolling hills of thick grass were covered with occasional plots of dark green foliage, amongst which unique and beautifully-colored flowers now waited for the impending drops to fall from the sky. The rain came down in a steady drizzle now as the jeep crested a large hill. They had been on the road for almost an hour. There, in the foreground, Elaine had her first glance at her new home, at least for the next year.

The village was a cluster of small buildings snuggled in a valley between two impressive rocky mountains. A tall metal-framed tower stood on the crest of the higher of the two peaks. The jeep followed the winding roadway next to a stream of clear water that wriggled through the center of town. On either side, farming fields surrounded the settlement. Elaine was unfamiliar with the types of crops that sprouted from the lines of tilled earth, and the fields were now abandoned, the villagers readying themselves for the approaching storm.

# j. d. gordon

For the most part, the village consisted of small, wooden, one or two room structures, most with tin roofs, though a few were shingled. Children waved at the passing vehicle as their parents beckoned them to come inside, safe from the storm. A wide variety of animals -- dogs, cats, chickens, goats, and sheep, and burros -- shared the village streets. It wasn't clear to her whether they were pets or livestock. At the center of town, an open-air market where the townsfolk and visitors from other villages on the island bought, sold, and traded their goods, was preparing to close. The aid station itself was a short distance out of town, and within minutes Billy pulled the topless jeep up in front of the compound's main building. The stick-built handsome building boasted a large, covered, and screened porch, and the long panels of wooden siding were painted a gleaming white. Windows, evenly spaced along the building's sides, were covered with sturdy dark-green storm shutters. The building was nowhere as run down as Elaine had expected.

Surrounding the structure, several other buildings of various shapes and sizes stood. The largest was a pole barn set out behind the main building. Elaine figured this to be the station's main storehouse, but she would have to wait before familiarizing herself with the grounds. Billy ushered the young doctor under the protection of the main building's front porch, and then inside, without further ado. Elaine's first impression was that she had stepped onto the set of the African Queen.

A pair of screened double doors provided entry to what appeared to be a reception room. Several benches upholstered with dark-green canvas lined the walls. Farther along, a wooden counter painted bright white separated the waiting area from whatever lay beyond. Behind the counter, filing cabinets shared space with an old desk chair, which sat unoccupied. A large-blade ceiling fan stirred the moist air, keeping the room cool enough to be comfortable. The space was spotless and smelled of

## Caribbean Calling

disinfectant. Elaine recognized that this main building acted as the medical center for the village, as well as for other nearby towns.

"Hello, Mom! We're home!" Billy called out, Elaine's duffel slung over his shoulder. The rain now pounded outside and the wind whistled and banged the shutters open and shut. It sounded like Jack's giant was spilling a never-ending bag of marbles onto the wood-shingled roof of the hospital. "I've got some introductions to make, folks," Billy shouted as he dropped the duffel onto the polished wooden planks on the floor behind the counter. Six individuals rushed out to greet the newest team member. Billy made a grand gesture. "Here they are, one and all!"

Though she hadn't expected an overabundance of volunteers, Elaine's first thought was that six staffers didn't seem sufficient somehow. Billy motioned to a large woman with tanned skin wearing a knee-length dress decorated with huge red flowers. Her gray hair was bundled and pinned up beneath a red bandanna. A pair of cheap flip-flops did their best to protect her gargantuan feet. She was holding a glass pitcher, half filled with ice and a light colored liquid.

"This is Batilda, she does all our cooking. You'll find she's a real whiz in the kitchen. We call her Batty," he said with a wink.

"You betta not calls me Batty! That ain't my name, you skinny little bugger!" Batilda laughed and swung the pitcher. Elaine took several steps backward.

"E's the only one that dun't get a rap about the 'ead when 'e calls 'er that, lassie!" Elaine presumed the hearty, tall, tanned man was an Australian.

"Never mind him, honey. You call me Batilda and you'll be fine. I got some fresh Key limeade here. Made it myself earlier today. May I pour you a glass, dear?" Batilda's tone as she addressed the newcomer shifted to that of a kindly grandmother.

"Batty's from Chicago," Billy interrupted before Elaine could answer. "She spent twenty years running the Salvation Army's disaster canteen." Batilda shot Billy the evil eye, but a smile was hidden in the creases of her mouth. She loved Billy like a son.

"Oh, I went to college in Chicago. It's like home to me," Elaine offered. "My father would have preferred Michigan...but, well...uh, yes, I'd love a glass of, uh...limeade." She suddenly felt awkward and flustered.

"I'll be right back, honey, let me go refill this pitcher." Batilda shuffled along toward the rear of the building, out of sight behind a canvas partition.

A huge boom of thunder echoed about the canyon, shaking the windows and walls. Elaine jumped at the report.

"Aw, you'll get used to that, little lady. We get 'bout one a these 'lil bastards a week," the Aussie boasted.

"Well, since the Kangaroo's feeling so friendly, we'll move on to him next." Billy motioned with his head toward a big man, over six feet tall. A tight denim shirt with frayed, torn-off sleeves covered his torso, revealing much of his muscular chest, little tufts of garment hanging from the seams. His arms were solid. A faded tattoo of a great white shark was displayed on his right forearm. A pair of cut-off blue jeans with a greasy red rag jutting out of his back pocket showed off his impressive legs, and his feet were stuffed into a pair of old, faded, tan work boots. Elaine accepted his outstretched hand. It was rough as sandpaper.

"This is Kangaroo," Billy said. "At least that's what we call the big fella. His name is Jonnie Stillwater, or Tillwhether, or something like that."

"That's Jonathan Tillwater there, mate," the Aussie shook

## Caribbean Calling

his head in mock disgust.

"The Kangaroo is our resident fixer-upper. He's the maintenance department around here," Billy continued. "That there is Reggie, she's our teacher. Reg is from the West Coast." A girl of no more than twenty-five years stood up and offered her hand.

Reggie was a slight gal, the top of her head was no more than five feet above her ankles and she weighed in at less than one hundred pounds, soaking wet, Elaine imagined. She was sporting a pair of khaki shorts and a cream-colored polo shirt. Her brown hair was cut short, but left long enough to be wavy. She reminded Elaine of Velma from the old Scooby Doo cartoons, right down to the black, plastic-framed glasses. She was barefoot, a braided multi-colored combination of string wrapped around her left ankle.

"That gentleman there is the only true islander among us. Manhattan Island, that is. Believe it or not, he is our agricultural department."

"How in the world did you end up here?" Elaine smiled as she shook the man's ebony-colored hand.

"Seemed like the only way to get the heck out of the city. My old man was a lawyer. He about lost his head when I decided to go to school for agriculture." He let forth a throaty laugh. "I'm Martin, by the way."

Decked out in a pair of unpressed blue jeans, but looking pretty sharp, Martin reminded Elaine of a character out of Magnum PI. A flowered Hawaiian shirt with a red background was tucked under his belt, and a pair of blue tennis shoes, while scuffed, wouldn't have looked out of place in the lobby of a good hotel. The only thing that revealed his profession was the mud stuck deep under his fingernails.

# j. d. gordon

"And this here is Pastor Tom." Billy pointed to a man sitting cross-legged on the floor, reading a book. The pastor marked his place with a scrap of beat-up paper and rose to meet the new doctor. A short man with a slight build, Elaine was struck by how his clothing hung from his frame. Unlike the rest of the workers, who wore shorts, Pastor Tom was outfitted in a pair of olive chinos and a crisp white tee shirt under a lightweight knit cardigan sweater. Even the tropical weather was not enough to keep his slim body warm, she mused. The Pastor's head was covered by a horseshoe pattern of short graying hair, and a pair of wire-rimmed glasses slipped down to rest on the tip of his nose.

"It is a pleasure to meet you. It'll be nice to have a doctor around here again." The Pastor shook Elaine's hand with a gentle touch. "Now, if you'll excuse me, I'll brave the weather and head back to my quarters." Though surprised by his initial comment, Elaine accepted his hand with a simple nod.

"And, finally, this is the boss, Robert." Elaine noticed that this was one member of the group that Billy didn't seem to have a pet name for. Billy moved in close to her, putting his hand next to his mouth as if he were about to reveal a secret. He whispered, but loudly, "Robert can be a bit cranky at times, but generally he's a pretty good guy."

The "boss" stood up and offered Elaine his hand and she noted that he was the only one dressed in the standard uniform dress proscribed by the Organization's handbook. She even recalled the specific passage, "All of our members will wear lightweight tan pants, cuffed above the knees. Footwear will consist of below-the-ankle work shoes -- unless specified by one's job description. Our members will be provided with standard olive cotton socks. The shirt will be of white cotton, short-sleeved and buttoned down, with a collar. A white cotton tee shirt will be worn beneath the collared shirt. In times of inclement or cool weather, long pants, sweatshirts, and jackets may be worn. These

## Caribbean Calling

items must be approved by the site manager." It didn't appear to Elaine that her teammates were too hung up on the dress code.

"Welcome, welcome, Doctor! We've been awaiting your arrival. It's been some time since we've had a physician around here."

Elaine's smile disappeared. "Pardon me? No doctor? Do you mean that I'm the only doctor here? Aren't there supposed to be two doctors?" She was, after all, a brand new MD, without much experience.

"Well, doctors are difficult to come by in these parts. The Peace Corps and other larger organizations have so much more to offer. It's hard to get qualified physicians to come out our way," Robert explained.

"Pardon my asking, but how do you run a clinic without a doctor?"

Robert stopped and stroked his chin in thought. "Well, we've been pooling our resources as best as we can. Billy here has been picking up most of the slack." He smiled and nodded his head in reassurance. "Don't worry, Doctor, we're not doing open-heart surgery...at least not every day," he said with a short bark of a laugh.

Elaine was rendered speechless, looking to Billy and then to Robert with questioning eyes. "Well," the chief officer added, eyeing his watch, "it's late. Perhaps Billy could provide you with a dime tour and save the scheduled orientation for the morning?" Nodding, Elaine watched as Billy retrieved her duffel.

"Ya'll tryin' to sneak out on me?" Batilda demanded, pushing the canvas partition aside, fresh pitcher of ade in hand.

"Oh, Batilda, yes...or no, really. So sorry. The doctor will take that in her quarters," Robert nodded towards the back door.

# j. d. gordon

Batilda rolled her eyes behind the boss's back. "I'll be along with it in a jif, dear," she answered, smiling at Elaine.

Billy led Elaine to the rear of the building. Along the way, they passed several of what Elaine assumed were patient treatment rooms. They looked almost like photos of Civil War hospitals in tents she recalled from her high school history books. Ancient cots lined each side of the corridor. Tall screens made of white canvas and supported by aluminum poles served as privacy partitions.

At the end of the line of cots, a long desk stretched across the expanse of the back wall, above which were shelves filled with paperwork and medical books. A computer, circa 1990, sat on the desktop. Everything was clean as could be. Fresh white paint covered all surfaces, and the wood floor planks were polished to a high sheen. After a small storage room, where shelves held various medical supplies, the exit led out to a large yard. The storm was beginning to subside. Warm drops of fine rain still fell, but the violent thunder could be heard now in the distance. The air was fragrant, sweet, fresh, and clean. The rich plant life was in full release of its various aromas.

Walking a few steps out into the yard, Elaine was better able to view the spacing of the other buildings. Billy pointed to the pole barn. "That's the main storehouse as well as the maintenance shack and garage. We have a few vehicles here. There's the Jeep, and an old brown Ford Bronco, which we use as an ambulance, and then there's a good old-fashioned school bus. I like to call it the Partridge Family-mobile. You'll understand when you see it. We use it as a supply wagon and as a group transport vehicle. The compound generator and fuel supplies are in there as well.

"There's the john and showers," Billy continued, pointing to a small building standing no taller than six feet. No roof was evident. As they approached the facilities, Billy exhibited the two stalls built side by side with a paper-thin partition between them for privacy. Each stall contained a makeshift toilet and shower.

"So, then, we share the washrooms?" Elaine asked, trying very hard to sound as if this wasn't cause for alarm.

"Yeah, but that was all in the brochure, right?" He looked at her and cocked an eyebrow. "Don't worry, milady, we won't peek. There's also a small sink in your cabin for washing hands or brushing teeth, you know. There's electric, but please run everything past the Kangaroo before you plug it in, to make sure you're not going to pop something else around here." Elaine remained quiet, digesting the reality of her new accommodations. "I am your humble servant ma'am," Billy gestured with his free hand in the direction of the team's quarters.

As she passed in front of him, Billy's eyes focused on her form, and the slight scent of freesia or juniper crossed through the air. The boy from Boston was already developing a crush on the young doctor. Her short pair of tan overalls, with a white ribbed cotton tee underneath, complimented her tanned and toned calves. Her strawberry blond hair hung beneath her neckline in loose curls pulled through the back of a NYPD ballcap. On their ride to the aid station, he'd become captivated by her ice-colored blue eyes once she'd removed her trendy sunglasses. Her attractive figure, especially her firm and perky round breasts and petite waist had put a permanent smile on his face.

Down a short path, a row of six buildings provided shelter for the camp workers. The cabins seemed sturdy enough, built on short stilts about a foot above the ground, with three steps leading to a wood door framed with screens to protect the interior from bugs and other critters. Canvas sheets could be drawn for added protection from the elements or prying eyes. Billy stepped up and opened the screen door of the third house. The spring used to prop the door open moaned as it swung, and the sound reminded Elaine of her father's hunting cabin back home in Michigan. She pushed the thought out of her mind. It was way too early to be homesick.

Her new home, sweet, home had a musty scent and was modestly equipped. A camp cot sat in the far corner next to a small nightstand, on top of which stood a small lamp with a plain wicker shade and a sweating pitcher of the greenish liquid Batilda had left, though she hadn't crossed their path. Across from the cot, a stained sink sat under a plain square mirror. To the right of the door, a small desk and filing cabinet were accompanied by a worn director's chair. A short couch, more like a futon, and a low coffee table provided a resting area. A dresser and freestanding armoire completed the furnishings.

"It's plain, as you can see, but we call it home. Most of us have picked up items here and there to spruce our places up." He looked at her expectantly. "It'll take a little time, but you'll get settled in, you'll see."

An uncomfortable pause followed after Billy set the duffel down. Elaine turned around in a circle and appraised her new habitat. Finally, she broke the silence. "Well, okay. Thanks, uh, Bill. I'll work on, um, getting settled in, then."

"I'm two doors down, if you need anything at all. Just holler. We're pretty casual around here, so don't be shy. Batilda will make sure you get up on time. We only have one alarm clock. Tomorrow should be a busy day." Billy tipped an imaginary hat as a silent good night, turned, and opened the door.

"Hey, Billy?" He turned and waited. "Uh...thanks. I'll see you in the morning, then, at breakfast." He smiled and retreated into the dark.

Finally alone, Elaine began a survey of her room. Batilda had turned down the fresh sheets on the cot and had even left a

## Caribbean Calling

foil-wrapped mint on the pancake-like pillow. She dragged the duffel over to the cot then poured herself a glass from the pitcher. Chunks of Key lime floated around in the concoction, and the sweet and tangy cool drink was refreshing. It wasn't quite like the traditional lemonade from home, but it hit the spot after a long day of travel and surprises.

Removing and sifting through the contents of her bag, Elaine paused when she located a small black item from one of the inside pockets -- a satellite telephone. It was the one item her father had insisted she bring. As promised, she activated the phone and connected. As she lay back on the cot, light rain pattering outside, she related the story of her first day so far away from home to her relieved father. Ten minutes later, she fell into a dreamless sleep.

j. d. gordon

## Chapter Two

The comforting aroma of freshly brewed coffee hung in the air of the kitchen. Outside the small window above the sink, bright-colored leaves skipped along the ground, propelled by the day's crisp autumn breeze. Two shifts of Salt Creek firefighters milled about the kitchen, half of them waiting for their shift to begin, the others waiting for the clock to strike 7:30 a.m., so that they could head home. Eddie Gilbert selected a chair near the kitchen's television. A young woman reporter updated viewers on the previous evening's third World Series game.

"Alright, guys, time for roll call," the lieutenant declared, poking his head through the kitchen door. Roll call was a daily ritual for firefighters everywhere. The time was used to report assignments for the day, and to impart any important information from the previous day's shift. Eddie made a feeble attempt to listen, his attention monopolized by the sports report.

"Ed, says here you're up for vacation. A month, huh?"

Eddie had worked under Lieutenant Tim Roucka throughout his entire career with the Salt Creek Fire Department. He turned away from the television screen. "Yup, taking a little trip." Eddie scooted his chair closer to the kitchen table.

"You're not heading south again, are ya? After that last fiasco, you'd have to be nuts." Tim was referring to Eddie's

## Caribbean Calling

extended vacation less than a year before. The account of his adventures was still fresh in everyone's mind. According to the now legendary tale, Eddie had found himself, during what was supposed to be a relaxing vacation, in battle with a pair of Caribbean crime lords who had kidnapped a wealthy Congressman's daughter for ransom. He'd played it down at the station, but it had been a dangerous and breathtaking adventure. All he'd wanted was to wander about on the open seas of the Caribbean for a while. Heroics hadn't ever been part of the plan.

"Well, yeah, actually, I am. I don't know, for some reason the Caribbean calls to me. I can't seem to get it out of my system. I've kept in touch with a couple of the girls and their families. I'm heading down to visit and hang out. We're staying at some kind of winter retreat or something like that. Should be pretty safe. They're loaded, or at least their folks are," Eddie responded with a sly smile.

As the rest of the crew settled around the table with steaming cups of joe in hand, a loud tone screeched from a speaker overhead. "Salt Creek Fire Department Station One, please respond to a possible overdose at 155 West Candlestick Parkway. Ambulance 1238 and Engine 1222, you're due to respond." The female voice belonged to a dispatcher working in the town's central station.

"Couldn't even get in one cup of coffee," Hank Brickman complained in regards to the crew's first run of the day. He stood and placed his half-filled cup on the counter. "We taking the box today, Eddie?"

The 'box' was what rescue workers referred to as an ambulance. Firefighters rotated vehicles -- one shift would be spent riding on an ambulance, the next on an engine, the next on the truck, and so on. Eddie had worked with Hank since his first day on the job, over seven years ago. Though there was a gap in their ages, the two men got along famously, their work styles blending well.

"Sounds good, Hankster," Eddie replied, downing what he could of his coffee on the way to the sink.

Five firefighters headed out to the apparatus floor where the department's emergency vehicles waited. Three of the men threw their gear onto the engine, and Eddie and Hank jumped into the ambulance. The diesel engines roared as the large overhead doors rose. Emergency lights flashing and sirens screaming, the vehicles pulled out into heavy traffic -- nine-to-fivers, mostly, heading to work. Only some had the common sense to move to the side of the road.

"What a picture-perfect day," Hank mused as he rolled the driver's side window down, lit up a cigarette, and flicked an ash out the window. He offered the pack to his partner.

"No, thanks," Eddie declined.

"I didn't think so. But it would've been rude not to offer, at least." Hank knew that Eddie occasionally indulged in the vice. Eddie reached over and turned up the volume on the radio, stopping his search for a suitable station when he heard the familiar notes of Dire Straits', Sultans of Swing. The song conjured up memories of his childhood years in Chicago.

Eddie had been born and bred in the Windy City. He hadn't relocated to the burbs until he'd been picked up by the Salt Creek Fire Department. He missed the urban lifestyle, but he didn't mind living in Salt Creek. It was a prosperous town, and he could walk to the trains, restaurants, and trendy retail shops from his mid-rise condo located in the quaint downtown section of the village. It had struck him funny at first. Most towns have a central business district, commonly termed "downtown," but most suburbanites associated the word "downtown" with the entire city of Chicago.

## Caribbean Calling

Eddie had been raised in an area of the city known as Lakeview, four blocks from Wrigley Field. Hence, he was a big Cubs fan. Generally, Hank and Eddie saw most things eye-to-eye. Their opinions on most subjects were similar. There was one thing that they disagreed on -- Eddie loved the Cubbies and Hank was a fan of the White Sox.

With the ambulance's diesel engine growling away like an old dog, the two men, casual, calm, and confident on the surface, pulled over to the side of the road in front of their destination. Grabbing their medical equipment, they headed for the front door of the home where a teenager stood waiting. The engine pulled up as they scaled the front porch stairs and disappeared into the dwelling behind the kid. On their way to assist the medics, the engine crew stopped at the ambulance to grab the rest of the gear.

The house reflected the typical style of Salt Creek homes -- hardwood floors, tall ceilings, and copious skylights allowing the sun to bathe the interior. The furnishings were top-notch. Eddie noticed a stainless steel Viking range in the kitchen as he passed by. One fine day, he thought to himself. The kid led them down a stairway to a basement, where two more teens stood waiting.

In the center of the room, a police officer knelt over a still form lying on top of a mattress, beneath a mass of sheets and blankets. The basement looked like it belonged in a frat house, nothing like the upper floors of the house. The place was a mess. Dirty clothes littered the floor, and empty beer and liquor bottles were scattered everywhere.

"Looks like somebody had a little party here last night. Parents gone for the weekend, huh?" The officer directed the question to the two young men standing. Both looked sick and nervous. Mute, they stepped out of the way, allowing Eddie and Hank to pass. Eddie and Hank approached the officer and the body on the mattress. While Hank went to work, Eddie began to question the teens.

"What happened here, guys?"

"I don't know, man," one answered in a shaky voice. "We were hangin' out, you know, with the guys. Jason showed up around midnight. He was pretty wasted already. Like, drunk, you know."

Eddie knew that speaking gently to them would result in more information. He wasn't a cop, after all. "Were you guys doing anything else? Were there any drugs around?"

The smaller of the boys looked at his friend. "You better tell him, Scott. You better tell him."

Scott hesitated, looking down at his feet. "Yeah, well, it wasn't mine. I mean, it wasn't here, but I think Jason was chasing the dragon before he got here."

Eddie knew what he meant, but asked anyway. "You mean he was smoking heroin?"

Hank interrupted. "His pressure is 162 over 88, pulse is weak and at 122." Eddie turned his attention from the boys and recorded the stats on his clipboard. As Hank continued his assessment, the engine crew thundered down the stairs with more equipment and a "stair chair," an old contraption used to carry patients up and down narrow stairwells.

As the firefighters began to assist Hank with the preliminary patient care, an intravenous line was established, sticky pads from a heart monitor were affixed to the young man's chest, and a hollow tube was placed in one of his nostrils to assist with breathing. An oxygen mask was placed over the teen's face, covering his nose and mouth. Hank prepared the intubation tube, which was used to secure an unconscious patient's airway by being inserted through the throat and into the trachea. "We'll need some Narcan, Ed."

## Caribbean Calling

Eddie began to prepare the medication when the form lying on the mattress began to shake violently. "He's seizing," he called out. "Let's get some Valium into him, too." One of the firefighters handed him a small cardboard box. Eddie ripped the top of the box off and extracted a syringe. After removing any air bubbles, he swiped a rubber port on the hub of the intravenous line with an alcohol pad, inserted the needle into the soft rubber, and depressed the plunger on the syringe. Seconds later, the patient's body became still.

Hank removed the plastic mask from the teen's face, allowing the hiss of escaping oxygen. He then manipulated the kid's tongue and jaw with the blade of a laryngoscope and guided a tube down his throat. After securing the device, a firefighter attached a bag-valve mask to the protruding end of the tube and began to squeeze the bag in order to facilitate the patient's natural breathing.

The remaining rescue workers strapped the limp form onto the stair chair and carried him up the basement stairs. Upon reaching the top, the patient was transferred onto a regular stretcher.

Eddie and the rest of the crew collected their equipment while Hank and another firefighter maneuvered the stretcher out to the waiting ambulance. With the patient secured in the back, Hank jumped into the vehicle's driver's seat as Eddie dialed the emergency room on the radio. A female voice answered.

"Hey, this is Salt Creek Ambulance 1238. We've got a run for you," he reported. "I've got an unconscious seventeen-year-old male patient, possible overdose. He seized at the scene and was administered two mg. of Valium. We're about four minutes out." After disconnecting, he continued to monitor the kid's condition.

Three minutes and 42 seconds later, the two paramedics pushed the stretcher through a maze of hallways, hospital employees, and patients. As usual, the emergency room was in a state of organized chaos. The overworked staff, clad in loose-fitting scrubs, darted about with purpose. Providing the best care to the most people in the shortest amount of time was their primary goal.

"Salt Creek, here," Eddie bellowed to announce their arrival.

"Is that the overdose?" a short, slender nurse asked as she exhaled and pushed her red hair away from her face. Eddie nodded in the affirmative and the woman waved them down to the other end of the hall. The young man on the stretcher remained motionless.

As the trio made their way, they passed treatment room after treatment room, each one full. A concerned young mother caught Eddie's eye. A small boy lay on the bed beside her, a doctor sewing up a gash on his noggin. He smiled at her, knowing that it looked a lot worse to her than it was.

Near the back end of the ER, Hank and Eddie rolled the stretcher into a room and transferred their ward over to an empty bed. Several people were already in the room waiting. A nurse scribbled the details of the patient's condition on a form while Eddie related the specifics, and a woman from the Admissions Office typed the patient's personal information into a computer mounted on a mobile tripod. Even while a nurse's aide changed him into an examination gown, the teen remained silent.

"Hey, Ed! Whatcha got for us today?" A doctor who looked a few years past retirement age strolled into the room to check out the new patient.

"Hey, Doc! What we have here is a young man who had a little bit too much fun last night." Eddie related the story for the third time. He'd known this particular physician for several years now. He was a levelheaded man in his early seventies, a little gray at the temples, but with a runner's build. The gray

## Caribbean Calling

lab-coat and Armani suit underneath lent the aged saw-bones a distinguished air. At over seventy years on the planet, Eddie couldn't imagine why the doctor hadn't retired years ago. Rumor had it that the doc had laid the first brick back in the '20s when the hospital was built. The rumor, of course, was false. That would've made the doc nearly one hundred years old.

"We'll take good care of him. Thanks for the report." The doctor issued orders to the staff fluttering about the patient.

Eddie pulled off his latex gloves and tossed them into the appropriate receptacle while Hank wheeled the stretcher in the direction of the linen closet. Clutching his clipboard, Eddie planted himself in front of one of the paramedic's computers provided by the hospital for preparing run reports.

Down the hall, he watched Hank tuck a fresh sheet onto the stretcher, crisp and clean for the next customer of the day. Both hired and trained at the same time, the pair had become as tight as brothers after so many years together, and Eddie had something on his mind he wanted to share. He'd bring it up on the return trip to the firehouse. That was always the best time for a private conversation. As he got back to typing, a young nurse interrupted him with a tap on the shoulder.

"Hey, Lu, what's up?" Ed smiled with genuine pleasure. "When did you get back in town?" LuAnn was a longtime friend. She'd left the nursing profession a little over a year ago claiming to be burned out. She'd made plans to take a new job "flying the friendly skies." They'd kept in touch on a semi-regular basis, via e-mail.

"I came back last week," LuAnn answered, with a 'aw-shucks' look. "I'm glad to be back. It's been awhile. I decided that nursing is my true calling."

Eddie had always found her attractive, but she'd been involved with some guy or another. Though he wanted to, he didn't ask whether she was single, but he did end the conversation by promising to call and set something up, lunch, or dinner, maybe.

The ambulance was packed up with fresh supplies and the paperwork had been submitted. Hank and Eddie climbed into the cab of the ambulance, Hank slipped the transmission into drive, and the two men ventured back out onto the road. Eddie picked up the radio microphone and reported to dispatch,

"Salt Creek Fire, this is 1238. We're returning in service." A friendly female voice responded, acknowledging the message. Hank pulled a pack of smokes out of his shirt pocket and stuffed the end of one between his lips, then offered them again to Eddie. Eddie waved him off at first, and then accepted it, along with Hank's lighter, which was emblazoned with an *Aerosmith* logo, giving Eddie a short case of the giggles.

"Man, you never cease to amaze me," he said with appreciation. Then he took on a serious tone. "So, Hank, can you keep a secret?" he asked, already knowing his buddy's answer.

"Of course, Ed, what's up?"

"I'm not going on vacation," Eddie blurted out.

"What the hell does that mean?"

Eddie sparked his cigarette and took a long draw, then exhaled away from the sign plastered in front of him warning NO SMOKING. "Well, you know that mess I got into last year?"

"Yeah, that Crow guy, or whatever his name was, the one who almost killed you after you saved that girl? Duh, I remember."

Eddie laughed. "Right, Jennifer Klein. Well, her dad's a pretty big deal down in Florida. He lost his campaign for re-election as a Congressman, but he's got a hell of a successful

## Caribbean Calling

business in shipping. Anyway, he offered me a job. Some kind of security position."

Hank looked at him, astonished. "You're gonna take it?"

"I'm going down for a month to check things out. You know, see how it is."

"You're gonna leave the fire department? Man, that's sacrilege!"

Eddie sighed and took another drag. "Hank, it's a big, big decision. I've been doing this for what seems like forever. It's a part of me."

They sat silent for a minute or two. "Is he gonna pay ya well?"

"That still has to be worked out. He's gonna give me ten grand for the month, plus traveling expenses. I have the tickets already," he grinned. "First class."

The radio blared, interrupting any further conversation. "Salt Creek Fire, you have a code one for an unknown illness at 225 Archway. 1238 and 1222 are due." This time it was a gruff sounding male dispatcher who repeated the order before signing off. Eddie didn't recognize the voice.

Hank put on the emergency vehicle's lights and siren while Eddie picked up the radio hand-set and informed the dispatch center that they were now en route to the call. A code one meant a citizen had requested an ambulance. Two vehicles were assigned to most calls. The ambulance carried the stretcher and medical equipment, and the engine provided a crew to assist.

Hank made a U-turn. "Unknown medical? I hate these kinds of calls. I hate going in cold."

Minutes later, he was backing the ambulance into the home's driveway. A police car screeched to a halt behind the ambulance.

# j. d. gordon

Hank flipped his cigarette butt onto the ground near the curb as he walked around back. Considering the fact that the situation inside was unknown, they grabbed the full compliment of gear -- an oxygen tank, face masks, medications, plastic tubes, blades for intubations, scalpels, and forceps. Eddie slung a bag over his shoulder. Hank followed behind after retrieving the main drug supply box and the cardiac monitor/defibrillator.

The three-man engine crew spilled from the truck and followed the ambulance crew through the front door. A police officer, a young guy, new to the town's police department, entered last, his trusty pen and pad of paper in hand.

The home was located in an older part of town still populated by good old-fashioned, blue-collar workers. Quaint, neat houses sat on fair-sized lots on the narrow tree-lined streets. Most of the homes were occupied by retired folks or tradesmen and their families. An old and frail woman wearing an Edith Bunker house dress and a concerned look on her face met them at the door.

"Fire department, ma'am," Eddie declared. Emergency personnel were trained to announce themselves even if the fact was obvious.

"Oh, my, there are so many of you." The elderly woman's voice cracked as she spoke. As five firefighters and a police officer entered her home, she continued, "I'm sorry I had to call 911. I'm not sure this is an emergency."

"Don't worry, ma'am. We're always happy to help," Eddie assured her. The woman led them down a dark and narrow hallway. The walls, painted white, maybe forty years before, were aged to a yellowish hue. A worn green carpet covered the floor, so thin in places that the wood showed underneath. Photos on both sides of the hall displayed brides standing with their arms around various family members, graduates, and men in different styles of military uniforms, many in sepia tones. At the

31

end of the hallway were two doors. The woman pointed to the door on the right.

"He's in there...my husband is in there. In the washroom," she directed.

Eddie opened the door and couldn't help himself. He grinned from ear to ear and let out a chuckle. "Well, what the heck happened here?" he managed.

"What the hell does it look like to you?! I'm stuck, for crissakes!"

With his skeletal frame, the poor guy had slipped, ass first, through the commode seat, leaving his lower cheeks brewing in four inches of cold water. His torso protruded from the rim of the toilet and his knees were pressed up against his ribs. He had been attempting to free himself by pushing on the seat with both hands, but his arms were too weak to beat the hold of the seat. His wife had tried to help, but it was useless. They'd tried calling their children, but no one had answered. They couldn't bear calling the neighbors. They'd had no choice but to dial up 911.

After listening to the long story, Eddie spoke in a kind and casual manner. "We want to get you out of there and make sure you're not hurt, okay, sir?"

"Okay, then! Quit yapping and get me out of here! My ass feels like a goddamned sponge!"

"Okay, okay, sir. What's your name, sir?" Eddie inquired as he and Hank set down their equipment and clipboards and took a position on either side of the gent's throne.

"Frank!" he barked.

Securing a grip beneath each of the old bird's wings, Eddie nodded at Hank. "Ready, Frank? Here we go!" In one quick motion, the two men lifted the fellow out and replaced him on the seat properly.

"Ahhh...thanks boys. Now get the hell outta here and let me finish my business!" Frank released a maelstrom of gas.

"We will, Frank, we will." Every time Eddie and Hank caught each other's eye, it was a struggle not to bust out laughing. "We need to take your vitals, sir. We need to make sure you're alright, and then we'll get your signature on a piece of paper and we'll leave you alone, okay?"

Eddie motioned to the engine crew and the police officer that they could go ahead and clear out. The firefighters gathered up their equipment and exited the home. Frank pencil-whipped his signature on the bottom of a liability release form and kicked the men out of his washroom. They could still hear the man complaining as they retreated from the home.

Eddie was looking forward to giving the nurses back at the hospital a light moment in their day. They'd get a hoot out of this one when he called in the release. After a few guffaws over the radio, Eddie changed channels and contacted the dispatch center. "Salt Creek dispatch, ambulance 1238 is now in service and returning to quarters." A female voice responded an affirmative.

"So when are you heading out?" Hank asked as they headed toward the station.

"Tomorrow afternoon. They're sending a limo to take me to O'Hare, believe it or not. My flight's at four p.m. I figure I'll have to get there around one in case security is backed up."

"Shit, I've never been in a limo or flown first class, ya lucky bastard," Hank complained. "Well, I don't care for flying anyway, as you well know."

Eddie knew all about Hank's fear of flying. In fact, he knew about everything about Hank. In the fire service, living with coworkers, depending on them for your life sometimes, it was like having a second family. There might have been particular individuals Eddie didn't care for, but he learned to live with them. When the shit hit the fan, these guys needed to trust each other. There was no question. You could always count on your brothers and sisters.

"What do you guys think you're doing?" The shift's Battalion Chief met the men as they exited the ambulance back in the station's bay.

"Why? What's up?" Eddie thought he and his partner had somehow found themselves in some unexpected trouble.

"It's almost eleven o'clock!"

"Yeah...so...what?"

"So what! It's almost lunchtime! Get to the store! I'm starvin' here!" The Chief was grinning.

Eddie relaxed. "Hank, we better follow orders! Timmy's tummy is talkin' back."

At the Salt Creek Firehouse, Eddie had the honor of holding the position of shift chef. It was a bit of an extra effort, but it got him away from the regular chores and house duties, and even got him out of the building for a while to hit the local supermarket, which he'd done during almost every shift since the beginning of his career. One of the old-timers working in the checkout line knew Eddie so well, she'd asked him to be part of her daughter's wedding ceremony.

The rest of the morning and afternoon were uneventful. The firefighters went about their day in typical fashion. If they weren't responding to calls, they spent their time sharpening their skills through training, they maintained the vehicles, they cleaned the equipment, or they tended to the daily housekeeping activities.

## j. d. gordon

After dinner, the crew settled down in the day room. One of the guys had brought in a DVD that he'd rented. Eddie had seen "Road Trip" once before. It was geared toward the youth market, but Eddie enjoyed the story line. It brought back memories of trips he'd taken with his childhood friends during his college years. Summers consisted of working a million hours during the week, and then blowing all that hard-earned cash by partying away the weekends. A few of his friends' parents had summer homes in Wisconsin, and they'd capitalized on being away from watchful eyes. They'd raised some hell, all right. Watching the movie made Eddie feel like he was getting old. Over thirty years now he'd walked the planet. Nothing was new anymore.

Recliners kicked back, the firefighters' digestive systems were working hard to break down the recently-eaten meal. Eddie had put together a pan of lasagna roll-ups and a tray of sausage and peppers for dinner. It would be, perhaps, his final night acting as chef. That made everything sink in. The decision he would soon have to make was beginning to hit him hard. Could he really leave the fire department behind -- the camaraderie and the pride and joy of helping folks out when they needed a hand? Feeling a bit shook up, he figured he would take it as he had taken most things in his life -- he'd roll with it, see where it all went. After all, nothing was written in stone.

Hank was snoring loud. Eddie checked for saw dust beneath his feet, but Hank's own unique melody ceased when a sharp tone pierced the comfort of the day room. "Salt Creek Fire, you're to respond to a code three activated fire alarm at 333 Trailway Drive. Truck 1225, Engine 1222, and Ambulance 1238 are due to respond."

The day room emptied as the firefighters abandoned their Lay-Z-Boys and sprinted out to the apparatus floor. These calls often turned out to be false alarms, usually due to a malfunction in an alarm system's equipment, or someone 'accidentally'

## Caribbean Calling

activating a wall-mounted pull-station. But the firefighters had to respond to every call as if it was the real thing. Mounds of gear lying around on the floor took shape. Standard uniform footwear was discarded, replaced by rugged pairs of rubber boots. Heavy fire-resistant pants were pulled up to the waist, secured by red suspenders. Protective jackets covered torsos. Hoods and helmets completed the outfit.

Assigned to the ambulance again, Hank keyed the ignition while the diesel engines came to life with a roar as the garage doors receded, lights flashing and sirens wailing.

Eddie glanced at his wristwatch. "I can't believe it's already nine o'clock. The minute the sun drops, it starts getting chilly now."

"Winter's right around the corner. Where the hell does the time go?" Hank shook his head.

"You recognize this address, Hankster?"

Hank looked at him and raised his eyebrows. "I don't recall anything significant about it."

"Memory's disappearing right along with the nice weather, huh?" Eddie kidded his partner. "This was the site of our first fire together. You remember now?"

Hank paused and then nodded. "That's right. I remember it well. It was arson."

j. d. gordon

## Chapter Three

Hank and Eddie had only been assigned to shift for three days before that first job. Although they'd been employees of the Salt Creek Station for over twelve months, their first year hadn't been spent working in the station running calls. The first year was considered probationary and was a continuation of basic training. The training process began with six weeks at the Fire Academy, eight hours a day, five days a week. Academy days started in the wee hours of the morning with physical training -- sit-ups, push-ups, running up and down the training tower dressed in full turnout gear. It reminded Eddie of his days in the military.

The rest of the morning was spent in the classroom, where the students focused their attention on their instructors who were crusty, old, retired firefighters. Lessons were imparted on the principals and extinguishment of the different classes of fire, along with a variety of rescue techniques from burning buildings, busted-up cars, and all of the other various places people could find themselves in danger. Instruction in how to operate the various types of hoses, hand tools, and power tools, including the jaws-of-life, was offered. Each afternoon was spent developing practical training evolutions, and classroom knowledge was applied to simulated real-life situations -- not once or twice, but over and over again, until the recruits could perform the functions in their sleep.

## Caribbean Calling

After the first six weeks, the recruits continued on to another week of specific instruction in how to pump the fire engines and the pressures used for the different types of hoses, or 'lines,' as they're called in the service. They learned how to draft from natural water sources, how to pump water from one engine's tank to another as part of a relay, which was used when a water supply was too far away from a fire for a single engine company's supply line to reach it.

Before returning to their assigned departments, the recruits spent a final week of instruction in Hazardous Materials. Dangerous stuff was out there everywhere -- in trucks, trains, boats, and planes, to name a few.

After eight weeks, Eddie and Hank had bid their farewells to their classmates, instructors, and new friends, and had returned to Salt Creek, only to spend the remainder of the year going through paramedic training, which covered all areas of emergency medicine -- heart problems, strokes, traumatic injuries, childbirth, gunshot wounds -- the list went on and on. Finally, after a little over a year, Hank and Eddie were placed on shift as full-fledged firefighters. On their third shift, the two men had experienced the first real fire of their career. The tone had sounded over the speaker, followed by:

"Salt Creek Fire, you're to respond to an activated fire alarm at 333 Trailway Drive."

The two probies had scrambled for the rigs while the veterans, knowing these alarms were usually false, had reacted in a more relaxed manner. Some even took the time to scratch their asses or stomachs as they emerged from a nap in one of the recliners. Hank and Eddie were riding backwards, it being back in the day when fire engines were still made with open-air jump-seats placed behind the cab where the engineer and officer sat. A headset equipped with a microphone and earphones allowed for communication between the four individuals.

## j. d. gordon

The sirens had wailed and the air had bellowed through the small opening where Eddie sat. He caught the reflection of the red and blue lights whirling away in his peripheral vision as he fumbled with the straps of the air-pack placed in the back of his seat, mounted to allow for quick application while en route to a call. Connecting the waist strap, he'd felt the click of the connection and tugged it to ensure it was fastened. He'd then rechecked all of his other connections, as he'd been taught to do back at the Academy. Running his hands over his shoulder and chest strap, he checked the regulator and hose line. Finally, he switched his flashlight on and off to make sure it was working. Whether it was night or day, a light would always be needed in a burning building.

The officer on the scene had ordered the skid load to be used as the first line for attacking the fire. This option allowed for the fire engine to remain away from the building, while at the same time allowing firefighters the best advantage while entering the building.

Eddie had dropped the bundled up hose near the doorway. He could already feel the heat coming from behind the closed door. Dark puffs of smoke escaped from around the door frame. A young police officer stood nearby. As the fire engine moved away from the building's driveway in the direction of the fire hydrant, Hank had followed behind, stretching out the skid-load's length of supply line. When the engine came to a stop in front of the hydrant and set its air brakes with several loud hisses, Hank removed more of the large canvas hose until he found a break -- a brass coupling used to bind two lengths of hose together. He separated the coupling and attached one end to a port on the back of the engine. Then he signaled to the driver that the task was complete. The driver was now responsible for hooking up the engine to the hydrant, and working the pumps housed within the engine. Ed, the officer, and now Hank,

## caribbean calling

counted on this man to provide them the water needed to dowse the fire.

Eddie and his officer had flanked out the skid load's one hundred and fifty foot long attack-line. The nozzle was lying in front of the doorway. The two men fit their air masks to their faces as Hank ran up to them.

"Hank," the lieutenant shouted through his face gear, "get your mask on and open this door up. And keep the line coming... this is a big place! And watch out for other companies in there. I'm sure Command will have people all over this place soon." Indeed, other emergency vehicles were showing up on the scene as the words exited his lips.

After a signal from the officer to charge the line, a veteran firefighter, Brian McMurphy, worked the levers and valves on the fire engine's pump control panel. Water pressure began to build up within the confines of the canvas and rubber hose line and it became rigid and heavy. Eddie and the lieutenant dropped to their knees, ready to advance into the building. They needed to enter low, beneath the heat and the smoke. Hank moved to the side of the door and tried the handle, hoping the door would swing open. His hopes were answered -- the door had been left unlocked.

Smoke and heat blasted Eddie around the head and shoulders immediately. Although protected by heavy flame-retardant gear, the heat still made its way down through the thick layers to his skin. Eddie crawled forward, deeper into the building, with the lieutenant trailing behind. Eddie could feel him occasionally bump into the tank of his air-pack as they struggled with the heavy hose-line. Eddie was moving along by touch and feel alone, as well as a novice's instinct would allow. The thick smoke almost obscured his vision.

Suddenly, he was stopped in his tracks by the heavy thud of

a solid object connecting with his helmet. Stunned for a second, he paused. There was still no sign of the source of the fire, and Eddie looked back at his lieutenant for direction. He could barely make out the man's form through the heavy smoke.

"Let's head to our right," the officer hollered, his voice muffled by his mask. Eddie had ultimate faith that Carl Boutin, a twenty-year veteran near retirement, was making the right choice.

Using his left hand for direction in moving past a wall that blocked their path, Eddie shifted and began to move to the right. The heat was intense. Eddie wasn't sure, but he thought he could make out something in the distance. His vision obscured, he assumed the fire was closer than it appeared. The team reached the end of the wall, and then turned left, trying to move deeper into the building. That's where they found the source.

What looked to be a mammoth stack of pallets, consumed in flames, stood not more than ten feet in front of the firefighters. It was hot as Hades, and Eddie could feel the sweat dripping down his back. Temporarily paralyzed, he watched as smoke and flames raged towards the ceiling, accompanied by loud crackles and pops, almost as if the fire was taunting him.

"Ed!" Carl grabbed Eddie's shoulder to get his attention. He pointed at the fire. "You see that?"

"Yeah," Eddie responded, in a daze.

"That's the fire." Carl pointed at the nozzle in Eddie's hand. "The idea is to use the water from the hose to put out the fire."

The spell was broken. Eddie came to and unleashed a powerful stream of water in the direction of the fire, diminishing the flames into glowing embers. It wasn't long before a cloud of white steam replaced the dark smoke and the temperature dropped.

## Caribbean Calling

The cause of the fire turned out to be arson, as the State Fire Marshall announced after an investigation. The culprit still hadn't been apprehended. Throughout the night, over thirty firefighters from four different agencies had needlessly risked their lives. Eddie was pissed. It was one thing to risk life and limb in order to save the property or the life of honest citizens, but it was an ugly thing when some bastard placed firefighters in danger over love, money, or vengeance. Arson often turned out to be the perfect crime. The evidence was usually destroyed and fire always did plenty to get the criminal's point across.

"I never told ya, but I was pretty hacked off that night." Hank was making a right turn onto the call's street.

"What? Why?"

"One word, Ed, jealousy. I wanted to work the nozzle. I was stuck humping hose in for you glory boys."

"Someone's gotta do it." Eddie clapped his buddy on the shoulder, and they laughed.

The alarm turned out to be false. A janitor working the night shift had thrown a frozen pizza into the oven in the company's break room. Evidently, the appliance hadn't been scrubbed down for quite some time. Droppings from countless past meals had begun smoking as the oven heated up. The janitor had tried to get the smoke to blow out the window, and had fanned it vigorously, but the smoke detector in the center of the room had already gotten a whiff. The fire alarm had sounded and a light at the alarm company had gone off. Some unknown person, most likely in some other state, had received the alarm and then called the Salt Creek dispatch center.

The firefighters assigned to the truck and the ambulance waited with lights flashing in front of the building while the

j. d. gordon

engine crew toured the building, confirming the false activation. A burnt-toast smell still lingered in the break room. A few minutes later, all three emergency vehicles were returning to their assigned quarters. It was twenty minutes past nine. The rest of the night was uneventful.

The silence of the bunk room in the early morning was invaded by the tones set off each morning at the firehouse. The beeps and buzzes were set off as a test for the system. They did double duty, though, as an alarm clock. The tones were set off at seven a.m. Change of shift was at seven-thirty. One half of one hour, long enough to rub the sleep out of the eyes, brew a pot of coffee, clean up the kitchen, and toss out the trash.

Eddie stretched out on his bunk for a moment or two, and then sat up in bed. He pulled up his socks, then his pants, tucking his shirt in and securing his belt around his waist. The firefighters and paramedics of Salt Creek had enjoyed a quiet night. It was an unusual luxury. He cleaned his area up, folded the sheets and blankets, and stashed his toiletries on the top shelf of his locker. He'd forgotten his morning duties, letting the other guys pick up the slack. He was already on island time.

Intending to finish off the last few minutes of the shift batting the breeze with the guys in the kitchen, Eddie shuffled off. Hank had a fresh cup of coffee waiting. It sat steaming on the tabletop in front of Eddie's usual seat.

"Hey, don't worry, Ed, we got the morning duties covered. You sit down and relax. I made ya some joe." Obviously, Hank would have to give his buddy a little shit before he left for Florida -- but it was mixed with a hint of sentimentality. He was the only one who knew Eddie might not be coming back. The others assumed Eddie was taking another one of his long vacations.

43

## Caribbean Calling

"So, Hank, you made the coffee yourself, did ya?" Eddie sat down and set his palms around the cup.

"Yup. I got up around six-thirty. I couldn't sleep. Thought I'd set you up on your last day."

"I'm sure it's gonna be a real treat," Eddie smirked. Hank wasn't known for his talent in the kitchen, unless you counted his talent to shovel food in his mouth with both knife and fork. As guys from the incoming shift began to mill about, Eddie took a draw on the mug. He laughed inside. The coffee was brown-tinted water. "Thanks, Hank, it's great." Eddie took a couple more sips, to spare his friend's feelings, then stood. "Well, boys, I'm all packed up. I guess I'm outta here."

As the kitchen door closed behind him, he could hear one of the guys bitching about the coffee. Eddie smiled as he exited the building. As he drove away, he stared back at the building in his rear view mirror. It was hard to believe he might not come back. He hadn't chosen the job for a mere paycheck. He had chosen it as a lifestyle -- for its history, for the brotherhood. It was a deep bond.

For a moment, though, Eddie doubted he would return. This new gig was too much like a dream come true. It wasn't the money, and the fact that it was security work for a successful businessman and ex-Congressman, it was also -- Florida. But deep down, he was struggling with the decision.

His mind raced. I'll head down, check things out, see what Klein has in mind, then make my choice, he thought. What have I got to lose at this point, anyway? Nothing. I can still come back after a few weeks if things don't work out. The Cubbies are in Chicago, but the Tampa Devil Rays aren't so bad. But Wrigley Field, man, Wrigley Field! And then there's the Bucs! But what about the Bears!

Finally, Eddie put an end to his inner debate. He needed to

### j. d. gordon

concentrate on the matter at hand. He had to pack. He had to shift gears. He'd loaded up everything prior to leaving home for his last rotation. A couple of personal items and that was it. Waiting for a red light he checked his watch. The limo would pick him up in a few hours.

Eddie lived close to work in a condo in the center of town. It was pricey, and Eddie had been forced to take on an extra job, but he liked the location. It made him think of Chicago proper. The train ran by the building, and while it wasn't the EL, it was comforting somehow. Everything he needed was walking distance, including his side job as an athletic trainer for the local college's sports teams. His boss there had been pissed when he'd heard about yet another long vacation, but Eddie assumed the institution would do fine without him.

In Ed's little home in the sky, up on the tenth floor, the town below hid beneath waves of orange and yellow. Soon, those beautiful colors would fall to the ground and the landscape would be dotted with snow-covered buildings, steam rising from smokestacks billowing warm air into the winter sky. Autumn in the Midwest was incredible, but it was short. Piles of snow and frigid winds would soon replace the crisp days. Eddie didn't even like to ski.

He had a couple of messages waiting for him on the answering machine -- one from his mother expressing her love and her wishes for him to be careful. He'd have to return that one or he'd never hear the end of it. The second message was from Mr. Klein, confirming the travel arrangements his secretary had sent via e-mail. Klein ended the message by instructing him to "hit me up on my cell phone if there are any problems."

The final message was from Marci, a woman he'd met on his last excursion into the Caribbean. She was a close friend of Jennifer Klein's. They'd remained in touch, speaking on the phone often, and she'd visited him while she'd been in town for a

## caribbean calling

wedding. They were from different worlds -- she was rich, he wasn't. She was in her twenties, he wasn't. In her message, Marci said she had a surprise planned for him. Hell, he thought, maybe those weren't such big issues after all. He was a red-blooded male, after all.

By the time Eddie finished reassuring his mother, checking his e-mail, and tidying up, the doorman in the lobby was on the phone announcing the arrival of the limo. He took another glance around. His gold fish had died over the summer, so no worry there. The tank still sat empty on top of the television. He closed the door, and struggling with his luggage, made his way to the elevator.

Outside, both the chauffeur and the doorman tried to grab Eddie's bags, both jockeying for a tip. The car wasn't a limo, just a tricked-out black Lincoln Town car. Eddie enjoyed the struggle. When they were done, and the trunk of the fancy car was closed, he handed each man an Abe Lincoln.

Eddie took his seat in the back of the car. As the driver made his way along the streets, he watched out the window. A jogger trotted past a mother pushing a stroller. The car turned onto Main Street, where a group of ladies sat in front of a coffeehouse. Fallen brown leaves lined the avenue and fluttered about in the breeze. Soon, these same women would be darting from car-door to store-entrance, bundled in heavy coats.

The car moved beyond the city limits and onto the expressway and Eddie and the driver began to chat. As it turned out, the driver had gone to the same high school as Ed's dad in Chicago -- Lane Tech. Eddie searched his mind for the names of some of his father's long-time friends, but the driver didn't recognize any of them.

The driver had the classic Chicago accent. "Yeah, well, Mistah Gilbert, it was a big school, ya know."

## j. d. gordon

He pulled up in front of the American Airlines terminal at O'Hare airport, and Eddie fished around in his pocket for more tip cash. He gave another five to the driver and ten to the sky hop for taking care of his luggage and issuing the electronic tickets.

The line through security was short and the staff seemed efficient. The federal employee-thing seemed to be working out well. Eddie made a quick stop in one of the airport's gift shops to grab a pack of Juicy Fruit and a novel. He chose something written by a former paramedic named Devin called "EMS: The Job of Your Life". He figured it would make for good travel reading.

By the time he reached his gate, they were already boarding the first class passengers. Eddie made his way to his large, leather window seat. There was plenty of room to spread out. A fine looking young attendant was already serving cocktails while the rest of the passengers made their way to the back of the plane. Eddie ordered three mini bottles of rum along with a cola and two glasses of ice. Those damned cubes always melted so fast in those little cups. He poured the clear liquid over the rocks, and then added some of the sweet stuff. Slipping on his headphones, Jimmy Buffett filled his ears. He stuck his nose in his book and let the pilot fly the plane.

caribbean calling

## Chapter Four

Three men toiled in the darkness beneath a thunderous night sky. The intensity of the wind was picking up and the workers felt the first few heavy drops of water fall from the dark clouds above. An occasional streak of lightening flashed, reminding them that they needed to get their job finished, and quickly.

A man standing hip deep in the water snarled. "Son-of-a bitch, it's gonna start comin' down. Are we gonna have to work through this shit?" Another man worked in a clearing on the shoreline stacking the wooden crates that the other two unloaded from a boat. It was a sandy clearing, but thick foliage surrounded the area. A narrow stone road vanished into the blackness beyond, where insects buzzed about and the jungle's birds squawked in anticipation of the storm.

"Keep your mouth shut. Let's get these things unloaded before the heavy stuff starts coming down. The truck should be here soon." This man spoke with authority as he handed down another wooden crate to the man in the water, who then struggled with the box, eventually handing it off to the man waiting on shore. A stack of the same long, narrow wooden boxes sat a few yards away.

"How much're we makin' on this job?" the middleman asked. His greasy brown hair was soaked with sweat and plastered to his forehead. All three were dressed the same, in dark military-style

# j. d. gordon

uniforms. Side arms hung at their waists. Long arms, assault rifles, and sub-machine guns were all stashed nearby.

"Enough," the leader yelled. "You'll be getting more than the usual rate. Keep quiet, now. We're almost done, and we need to listen for the truck." As far as his underlings knew, he was an independent contractor, picking up jobs in dark, dirty corners of seedy saloons and in the back alleyways of depressed banana republics. In truth, his tentacles reached far deeper than the other two could ever imagine.

The weather turned ugly as the last crate was stacked. The wind howled through the trees and thunder crashed overhead. The rain fell in thick sheets. The expected truck hadn't arrived.

"Separate the crates into two stacks! Leave a space in the middle!" the head honcho ordered as he jumped from the boat into the salt water. A large vinyl tarp was cradled in his arms. "Spread this over the top!" He threw the bundle over to waiting arms on shore. The other two struggled like keystone cops. "No, you idiots! Use rocks to hold it down! And keep all the crates under the tarp!"

Once the cargo was covered, the three men gathered under the excess vinyl. It was crowded, but they were somewhat protected from the rain.

"Damn, Barney, when was the last time you showered? You should've brought a bar of soap."

The man with the greasy hair lowered his head in shame. "Um, it's been a while." He was a thin man, not very good in a fist fight, but he followed directions and didn't talk back.

"Kick him back into the rain, Mr. Crane. That'll clean him up a little bit." The third man had a grin on his mug, but it wasn't a friendly one. He was a muscular man with an even build, his brown hair shaved to within an eighth of an inch from

49

## caribbean calling

his scalp. With his engaging blue eyes, he was the most handsome of the crew. He'd worked for Crane once before.

"Well," Crane thought for a moment, "that's not a bad idea, Marty, but the wait shouldn't be much longer. We wouldn't want Barney here to melt now, would we?"

Crane had met Marty in Key West at a place called Captain Tony's. By the end of the night, they'd picked up a couple of young tourist girls, stolen their honor, cheated them of their vacation dollars, and capped off the night by robbing a Circle K. A week later, Crane had recruited Marty as a henchman. His employer had assigned him a drug-run and he needed some help. He'd found him tending bar at the Rum Bugger, like he'd said. Marty jumped at the opportunity, happy to oblige. Slinging drinks and selling homegrown to Northerners wasn't turning the profits he had hoped for. Marty had behaved solidly during the job with Crane, and he'd remained steady when a small arms gunfight had erupted with local law enforcement.

The wait turned out to be much longer than the three men had expected. The storm had passed and the sun was breaking through the clouds when the sound of an approaching vehicle breached the makeshift shelter. A battered two-and-a-half ton truck backed into the small clearing, its canvas top flapping in the morning's sea breeze.

"Where the hell have you guys been?" Crane demanded.

"Sorry, mon, da truck broke down. We were stuck in da road, mon." Two Black men dressed in the tan uniforms of the local police got out of the truck, pistols hanging at their sides.

"Help us load this shit up and we'll get on our way," Crane growled in way of response.

"No problem dar, mon. We load it up 'n' be on our way, mon."

## j. d. gordon

The five of them worked quickly to load up the back of the truck, leaving enough room for Crane and his cohorts to ride in back, beneath the canvas. The local officers fired up the truck and the crew and cargo were on their way.

"So what all is in those boxes, boss?" Barney asked, feet dangling out of the back of the truck, back propped up against one of the crates.

"A surprise, Barney, not exactly what our friends are expecting. That's all you need to know," Crane replied.

The men watched the landscape as the truck moved along the rough roadway, Barney's eyes fluttering with sleepiness. For the most part, it was wide and green, littered with large boulders, hills, and low mountains. It was also, for the most part, uninhabited. As they approached one settlement along the way, the vehicle pulled to the side of the road by a large open-air market and stopped. Crane poked his head out to see why. Hoards of people milled about, trading all sorts of local produce. One of the officers came around to the back of the truck.

"What the hell's going on? We're not supposed to make any stops!" Crane shouted.

"Da commandant make a few changes, mon. Dees road winds tru doze hills. You pass a aid station, mon. Stay on dat road and go about ten more miles, mon. You find what you lookin' fo', mon. Da commandant want de guvment to keep eets nose clean of doze folks out deer, mon."

"Goddamned amateurs," Crane cursed. "Barney, stay back here. Marty, come on up front with me." Barney resumed his nap almost immediately. Not a soul glanced at the men dressed in combat gear, carrying weapons, making their way to the truck's cab. These people had lived for years under martial law.

The market was noisy, crowded with livestock and produce.

51

## Caribbean Calling

Shoppers filled makeshift carts and sifted through merchandise while haggling with merchants. Marty's eye was caught by a woman on the other side of the market. She was being led around by fellow wearing a Boston Red Sox ball cap. It seemed as though he was giving her some kind of tour. Marty studied her for a moment, nodded his head in a silent farewell, and then joined Crane in the front of the old truck.

"It's better we're on our own. Things might get sticky." Crane fired up the engine. "Listen, I want to let you in on something. Maybe I shouldn't, but I think I can trust you." Crane didn't trust very many people. To him, everyone was an enemy, except for the man offering him the best price for his services. His employer paid him very well.

"You can trust me, man. What gives?"

Crane eyed Marty again for a moment, almost reconsidering. "Like I said, things might get a little sticky here. We're about to pull a fast one."

Marty wondered if this was some kind of test of his confidence, to find out whether he could keep a secret. Crane continued. "These crates contain weapons...assault-rifles and a couple of rocket launchers." He paused to wipe some sweat from his brow. Beads of moisture dripped from his bald head and down along a deep scar on his right cheek, settling in the whiskers of his goatee. The stub of a cigarette stuck out of the corner of his mouth. His tall, bulky frame added to his imposing appearance. "Here's the thing, though. Each crate holds six weapons. The two on the top of each crate are the real deal. The rest are fakes."

Marty sat silently, unsure of how to respond to this information.

"I'm tellin' ya this because I need you to be prepared. You're not gonna get any extra compensation or nothin' like that.

## j. d. gordon

You're still green and you can chalk this one up as a learning experience, ya know? Barney don't know about it, so keep your mouth shut."

A loud, crunching noise came from beneath the truck. Crane had slipped while shifting into a lower gear for climbing one of the many hills they had to ascend. As they crested the hill and began their descent, they passed through tended fields, and then a small settlement of several wooden buildings. A group of local citizens gathered around the front of the largest building. Some leaned on crutches, some were bandaged, and others appeared frail from illness or injury. An old brown Ford Bronco was parked in front of the main building, and a large woman in a flower-print dress was serving beverages and snacks on the front porch. She looked up as the truck wheeled past.

"That's the aid station, so it should be another ten miles or so," Crane broke the silence. "And you oughta keep this place in mind. You never know."

"Never know what?" Marty questioned.

"You never know with these jobs. One of us could get wounded...we may need that truck out front...you just never know." Crane spoke impatiently, as if Marty should know better.

"I was seeing if we were on the same page, big guy," Marty tried to recover.

The truck continued rambling on, making slow progress in light of the road's condition. The landscape remained the same -- dry fields, high hills, and occasional patches of vegetation. Men by the side of the road surrounded a large collection of burnt and smoldering debris, mostly felled trees and chopped logs. Dense gray smoke floated far into the distance.

"What're they doing there? Some kind of controlled burn?" Marty questioned, thinking out loud.

## Caribbean Calling

"They're making charcoal, for their cooking fires." Crane answered. None of the locals took notice as the truck bounced past.

At the top of yet another large hill, Crane stopped the vehicle and surveyed the area, looking down over a large, wide valley flooded with shallow plots of muddy water. Hundreds of people were tending the fields, which looked to be rice paddies, or something similar. It reminded Marty of the Vietnam documentaries he'd seen on the History Channel. The workers were of all ages and both sexes, and were dressed in light-colored long robes -- clean, considering the work. It was like a scene from days long ago. Some plodded along leading donkeys attached to carts, while others moved the earth with wooden hoes and rakes.

In the center of the expansive fields, a rather large village seemed to be designed in the style of a fortress, or perhaps a prison. A compilation of several large buildings were surrounded by smaller structures, and a big, flat field of very thick green grass spread out from the front of the largest structure. A sand road encircled the entire area, with walking paths spiking off at intervals, leading to the other buildings. A ten-foot-high brick wall enclosed the entire area into a neat box. Two gates at either end of the settlement were marked by small guard stations, similar to those found at military or government installations. The only thing missing were guard towers.

"This is the place," Crane motioned to the scene below. "Hey, Barney, look alive back there," he yelled toward the rear of the vehicle. It was a wasted comment -- drool was running from the corner of Barney's mouth as he snored. Crane engaged the beast's transmission and a trail of dark exhaust trailed the vehicle as it moved forward in the direction of the installation.

"What kind of place is this?" Marty asked cautiously.

"I'm not the kind of guy who needs a bunch of useless

## j. d. gordon

background information, but from what I understand, the place is the headquarters for one of those international cults. It's fuckin' amazing to me what some people get themselves into, givin' up all their shit to plow fields for some guy who thinks he's got God's private cell phone number. They make themselves out to be fuckin' peace-niks, and then they order up a bunch of killing machines. I don't give a fuck, anyway. I play the game as well as I can." Crane tossed a soggy cigar butt out the window. "And by the way, what I told you back there about the fakes? I meant it when I said it's between you and me. Barney's like a kid brother to me, but he's not too swift, and what he don't know is better for everyone, got it?"

The road ran straight through the flooded fields and ended in front of one of the gates blocking the entrance to the yard beyond. A carved, polished, dark-wood sign read The Plantation. A lone man with tan skin and stubble covering his misshapen head exited the guard shack and walked around to the driver's side of the cab. Dressed like the field workers, he carried a long wooden staff in his hand.

"How may I be of assistance, strangers?" he asked politely.

"We're here to see the Caretaker. We have a shipment for him," Crane answered.

"Speak the word," the guard instructed.

Crane glanced at his partner with amusement. "Vesuvius," he said.

"We've been expecting you, sir." The guard smiled, exposing teeth the color of an old lemon. "Take the road to the right and follow it around to the back of the main building. You'll find a set of large wooden doors. Pass through them, and you'll be in an open yard. You'll see an overhead garage door. Wait there." He nodded at another man in the guard shack and the gate swung open. Crane proceeded through, following the guard's directions.

## Caribbean Calling

The road traveled along the edge of the perimeter wall, past rows of buildings. Robed people gardened, painted and chopped logs. All wore blank, yet content, expressions.

"This is pretty wild," Marty commented. "How often do you come here?"

"This is my first time. It's a new account." Crane was done talking. Now it was time for business.

Just as the guard had said, the doors to a pair of large swinging doors waited open. Crane pulled the truck into the yard, where several pull carts stood next to stacks of crates, and up to a modern overhead garage door. A short, chubby man with a bald head, dressed in the same light robe, entered the yard. Two others followed him, both over six feet tall. Both with large, muscular builds -- one white and one black. The pudgy fellow motioned to the garage door, while his sidekicks re-secured the gates with chains and a padlock. Then they disappeared. The overhead door began to rise, and the pudgy man indicated that Crane should pull the truck into the garage.

As soon as they entered, the door lowered and they found themselves in pitch dark for a second before bright overhead lights blazed on. The space was about the size of a football field, with ceilings at least thirty feet high. Smooth concrete lay beneath a collection of some twenty vehicles, most military in origin, along with two trucks similar to Crane's. Another twelve were small, fast-attack vehicles built of metal framing and intended for a crew of two -- a driver and a gunner. The vehicles' large heavy tires were designed for all land conditions.

Four other vehicles were throwbacks from the 1940s, most likely World War II surplus half-track jeeps, with open tops. They were armed with dual, large-caliber machine guns set in the rear of the vehicles in rotating turrets. The only other vehicle squatted like an ugly beast, far in the back corner, partially hidden. It was a modern U.S.-issue main battle tank.

"Holy shit, they've got quite an arsenal here," Crane mumbled under his breath. The same two men that had secured the gate now led Crane and his truck to the center of the floor. The pudgy man motioned for Crane to shut the motor down and then approached the front of the truck.

"Are you Mr. Crane?" He didn't wait for an answer. "Please step down. We're pleased to have you here."

Crane opened his door and exited the truck. "This is quite an operation you have going here. I didn't expect to see this type of hardware, considering your security at the front gate."

The man chuckled. "That's a bit of a facade." He extended his hand. "I'm the Caretaker's assistant. You may call me Mr. Pusser. The Caretaker is in service for the moment. He should be here soon. Our men here will assist you in unloading your cargo. I notice the officers didn't finish the trip?"

Crane didn't feel any need to make excuses for the absent officers. "Yeah, they bailed out back in town."

"They're a little uncomfortable with our operation here," Pusser cocked his head and smiled.

"Yeah, well, to each his own, right? I've got two men with me to help out. Barney, Marty, let's get this shit unloaded!" Two of the compound's staffers appeared to assist in unloading the crates.

"It is what we like to call a preferential living arrangement."

"Whatever you want to call it is fine by me. I'm a delivery man." Crane didn't bother to look up. "So, where'd you get the rest of this machinery?"

"Unfortunately, thanks to the government of the United States, our previous suppliers are no longer in business. Your

## Caribbean Calling

organization came highly recommended from the commandant of our local police force."

"Oh, yeah?" Crane said, keeping his eyes on the unloading process. "That's interesting. You mentioned they were uncomfortable with your setup here."

"The soldiers, or, um, the officers, don't quite know what to make of us. They avoid our members. The commandant is well aware of our activities."

"Well, that's great, then." Crane was tired of talking and wanted to take care of business and get the hell out. Watching as each package was unloaded. He made a mental inventory as to what was in each box. He was to collect payment at time of delivery. Marty, Barney, and Mr. Pusser's crew made quick work of it, and in a short time the crates were spread out on the floor. This worried Crane. He had hoped to pile everything in one bunch, collect the cash, and head out.

A silence hung in the air for a moment once the task was complete. Pusser spoke first, "I realize you're waiting for payment. We'll need to wait until the Caretaker has inspected the goods. He should be here shortly. Some refreshments, perhaps?"

Crane looked at his partners. Barney was wet with sweat, but Marty remained cool and collected, as if he'd never raised a hand.

"Sure, we could use something," Crane answered.

"Why don't you follow me? We'll move to a more comfortable area, better suited for conversation." Pusser was sweating profusely. It was cool in the garage and he hadn't exerted himself, yet streams of sweat ran from his bald head. He dabbed at the drops with a small towel retrieved from an unknown pocket within his robe.

"Yeah, well, no offense, Mr. Pusser, but we'll stay here for the time being," Crane objected.

"Whatever suits you, sir. I'll return in a moment. Perhaps the Caretaker will have finished his business by then." Pusser excused himself, leaving his two assistants behind. They stood silently waiting, even as Crane tried to strike up a conversation.

Ten minutes or so later, Pusser reentered the area, followed by three others all dressed in the same garb. A tall thin man with short gray hair set the pace, walking across the space of the garage. The two others looked every bit as large as the boys that had been keeping Crane and his cohorts company in Pusser's absence. One was a white guy with a thick tuft of black hair covering his forehead. The second was a mountain of a man, black, with cropped hair. His expression was bright, and his dark eyes appeared to observe everything going on around him.

"Gentlemen, I'm Reese. My disciples call me the Caretaker. Welcome to The Plantation. A cart is on the way with refreshments. Why don't you show me what you have for us?" The Caretaker's voice was soft and pleasant, but his stare might lead one to believe that he could see right into their soul.

"Alright, then. Let's get started." Crane directed Barney to grab a crowbar he had stashed in the back of the truck, and the still sleepy man went to work prying the lid off one of the crates. When the lid popped off, he set the broken piece of wood next to the crate and pulled out a clump of hay used as packaging.

Crane walked over to the crate and removed an AK-47 assault rifle. The metal barrel of the Russian-designed weapon glistened with a thin coating of protective oil. The red stock and front handhold were polished and almost completely smooth. A tiny nick or scratch was the only indication that the weapon had ever been used. Crane rummaged around in the crate and withdrew a canvas carrying case. He unwrapped the leather strap that bound the case together and displayed three curved magazines. "I went ahead and loaded up these magazines. All three are ready to go," he said.

Reese turned to one of the large silent members of his party and motioned for the man to examine the goods. Accepting the weapon from Crane, he worked the mechanism, checking to see if the chamber was clear. After his inspection, he slammed one of the magazines into the bottom of the rifle and worked it again, sliding a round into the chamber

"Why don't we step out into the yard and give the weapon a test drive?" Reese suggested. He headed for the door without waiting for an answer. The rest followed. Outside, two servants moved a large pull cart away from one of the stockade walls. Hidden behind the cart were two human-sized targets made of thick, heavy padding. The forms were riddled with bullet holes. The man shouldered the weapon. With his close-cut hair and flowing cotton robe, he looked like something out of a Middle Eastern terrorist training film. He pulled the trigger several times, sending multiple rounds to echo between the tall walls of the yard. The slugs slammed into the target, heavy thuds reporting upon contact.

Next, the big man manipulated a selector switch on the weapon and again placed the stock of the rifle against his shoulder. He depressed the trigger and the rifle fired off on full automatic. The remaining shells in the magazine erupted from the weapon's side. Brass shells clattered as they dropped to the ground around the shooter's feet. The Caretaker, Reese, clapped.

"What do we think, Baron?" Reese questioned.

Finally, the man spoke. "We're happy. Excellent performance," he smiled.

"Well, then. Let's head back inside and see what else you have for us, Mr. Crane."

# j. d. gordon

A cart with several glasses and a moisture-beaded pitcher of clear liquid waited back inside the garage. A servant offered each of the guests a glass. Crane waited to drink. He wanted the Caretaker to take the first swallow, in case. Then he drained the glass in one long gulp. The drink was cool, with almost no dominant taste, a little sweet with a light citrus tone.

"Thank you. Very refreshing," Crane offered prior to getting back to the matter at hand. "There are three other rifles in that crate. The crates marked with the red 'A' on the side contain the rest of the rifles." He moved with authority over to another box, marked with a black 'R.' After direction from Crane, Barney wrenched the top off with the crowbar, and again rummaged through the straw, removing a short olive-green tube.

"These are the rocket launchers you ordered. There are twenty in all, four to a box. They fire one time and then you toss it," Crane explained with all the patience he could muster. "You want to try one out?"

The Caretaker instructed the man he called Baron to examine the apparatus. The Baron grabbed the tube from Crane and extended the unit to twice its length with ease, as if he'd done it a hundred times before. He collapsed the launcher and looked to his boss. "Looks good, sir."

For the next hour, Crane and his boys went through each box, displaying the items to the Caretaker. Crane was nervous, but he didn't show it. He was counting on this scheme to set him up for an early retirement. He'd been dreaming about it for years, since after he'd been hired by his current employer's organization. If it didn't go well, it wouldn't mean the end of his dream, it would mean the end of him, too.

## Chapter Five

Crane had started out his path in life on a legitimate and honorable course. His father had been a middle-class worker, a deputy for a small county's sheriff department in the Midwest. Robert Crane had been a rising star on the football field -- an all-star quarterback. His grades had been the one thing standing between him and a free ride with a prestigious university.

After graduation, the university had been a no-go, the first big disappointment of his life. So, Crane entered the military. He'd barely scored high enough on the ASVAB test to qualify for entry into the service as a military police officer. Passed over several times for promotion, it wasn't long before Crane had been discharged for accepting kickbacks and bribes. An embarrassment to his family, Crane had then moved south to try and start over. That was another story entirely.

In an attempt to win back his father's respect, his admiration even, Crane had tested for several of Florida's law enforcement agencies. Unfortunately, his dishonorable discharge from the service had quashed those hopeful intentions. Crane had eventually found himself in Key West, working as a doorman -- a bouncer, really -- in one of the island's seedier establishments. In time, he'd started peddling small packages of drugs and hustling low-class hookers. That was when he'd run into this fellow named Hector.

## j. d. gordon

Hector was a low-level gangster working for a large crime organization. He checked Crane out by hiring him for small jobs here and there -- smuggling Cuban refugees into the country, making drug drops on isolated beaches or shady docks, being a body guard for high-priced whores. After a while, Hector's confidence in Crane had increased and the gangster had introduced Crane to his employers -- Blackwell and Lester Crow.

A father and son team, the Crows ran a large-scale crime ring operating out of a private island in the Caribbean. The Crows dabbled in all areas deemed undesirable by decent folks -- prostitution, slave-trading, pirating ships and reselling the goods, drugs. If it was shady business, the Crows were avid participants.

Five years later, when Blackwell Crow had suffered an untimely death, the organization had seen a change in its leadership. Lester Crow, who had once been the second dog, now acted as leader of the pack. Hector became his right-hand man, and Robert Crane was promoted to a project leader position. This level of authority within the organization allowed Crane some flexibility in regards to the planning of operations.

This current job had started out at a bar, The Schooner Wharf, in Key West. He'd met Hector for a couple of cocktails, and to exchange the cash and information for the purchase and delivery of the arms. Crane had only made it out to Crow Island a couple of times. Very few people were given that privilege. As the waitress served cold beers and a band played in the background, the hand-off was made. Hector set a soft, brown leather bag under the table at Crane's feet. The two smoked and shared a few drinks, as old friends would. They'd even stuck around to hear a couple of old Clapton tunes -- both were fans. After the third glass had been drained, Hector lay a wad of cash on the table, taking care of the waitress very well. The two men had nodded farewell and gone on their ways. Hector, Crane assumed, would be going back to Crow Island.

## Caribbean Calling

Crane returned to his rented room at the Hibiscus Motel, a few blocks off of Duval Street. He opened up the leather case and examined the materials inside -- a stack of greenbacks, a list of the materials to be acquired and where to acquire them, and instructions on when, and to whom, the materials should be delivered. Crane had contacted Barney and Marty and arranged a midnight meeting at the Iguana Café, across the street from Captain Tony's. Next, he'd made arrangements for the purchase of the materials. The ratio of real weaponry to imitations would leave a large sum of cash left in his pocket.

His scheme had taken a little imaginative coordination. Using an alternative contact in the weapons industry to purchase the legit items, he'd greased a few palms to ensure that mouths were kept shut concerning the size of the purchase. He wanted to keep that information from the Crows as long as he could. As regarded the fakes, Crane had found a company over the Internet willing to ship the replicas overnight to a dock where his boat was moored. He'd used a credit card number he'd lifted off the street earlier in the day.

Waiting at the Iguana Café, sipping on a Piña Colada blended with 151 rum, he chowed down on a plate of deep-fried alligator bits dipped in a spicy Cajun bar-b-que sauce. He knew the Colada looked a little fruity, but he didn't care. It tasted good, it was refreshing, and who was going to fuck with him, anyway? Marty showed up around midnight with an old canvas duffel slung over his shoulder. Barney was late, as usual, eventually strolling up in a pair of filthy white cutoffs and a greasy old tee shirt, a red-sauce stain marring the front of his shirt.

The three men shared a couple of cocktails as they watched the late-night party crowd bounce from bar to bar, up and down the Duval strip. The night air was warm and moist, carrying the scent of spicy cooking from the back of the café. That, mixed

# j. d. gordon

with the smell of old booze-soaked planks, wandering cigarette smoke, and sea air made for a strange but pleasant aroma. The sound of a blues band playing at Captain Tony's drifted across the street. Once the tab was settled up, the crew returned to the Hibiscus to stage out the plans for the next day. Forty-eight hours later, they were unloading their cargo on that dark, lonely beach, beneath the thunderous sky.

Crane figured this current plan to rip off both his employer and their new client to be his last. He would have to duck and hide for some time from the Crows, but he knew he would have the funds to do so. Between the money he had already stashed away and the take from this job, he figured he would do fine.

Things finally squared away, the weapons, for the moment, were back in their wooden shipping crates. The Caretaker waved one of his assistants up. The large man set a black briefcase down on the ground in front of Crane. He reached down and picked up the case, then held it out for Marty.

"Do you mind?" Crane asked.

"I would expect no less." The Caretaker understood the need for Crane to check the contents of the case. After all, business was business. Crane flipped through the bundles of greenbacks. A moment later, Crane secured the lid of the case, satisfied.

"Well, that should do it. It's been nice doing business with you folks. What do you want us to do with the transport?" Crane asked, as Marty and Barney took their places in the truck.

"Leave it where you were picked up. I'll notify the commandant. Please," Reese smiled warmly, "have a good evening, gentlemen."

Crane watched his rear view mirror as he waited for the

## Caribbean Calling

overhead garage door to rise. The door wasn't moving fast enough. He wanted some distance between himself and the compound before his customers became aware of the fact that they'd been had. He'd already made out figures behind the vehicle digging into the crates and removing items.

Crane let the door open to its full height and then engaged the truck's transmission. The vehicle moved out into the yard. The stockyard gates were still secure. Butterflies tickling his stomach, he hit the center of the steering wheel to sound the horn. All he heard was the sound of his palm pounding on the cracked vinyl. The horn was broken. Flustered, he opened the door and stepped out onto the running board of the truck. "Can we get this gate opened!?" he yelled.

One of the Caretaker's men ran over, the hem of his robe flapping around as he made his way. A moment later, the chain securing the door was released and the man swung the gates open. Crane gave the man a wave as he drove through. Following the path back around the same way he'd come in, he noticed that there weren't as many people out and about. He hadn't realized it until now, but the meeting had turned into a half-day event.

"So, Marty, how long do you think we have before they figure it out?"

"Not long. They were already going through the crates when we pulled out."

"Maybe you should jump in back with Barney."

"Um, pardon my asking, but if you don't trust the guy, why do you bring him along on your jobs?" Glad to be on the move, Crane still couldn't help checking the rear view.

"Don't trust him? I trust him. I trust him not to screw me over. He's got tight lips. Barney's not great in a fight, but he's a crack shot with a rifle."

# j. d. gordon

"No shit?" Marty asked in a doubtful tone. "Military?"

"No, not military. He'd never make it in the military."

"Then where did he learn to shoot?"

"He says his father taught him. Used to hunt a lot, I spose."

"So, where did you pick him up?" Marty asked.

"I used to work the door at a bar in Key West. Sort of a shit hole. I used to sell to him. He overheard a conversation I was having one time about a little side job the owner of the club had hooked me up with. He approached me and offered his services, and it turned out he did a good job. He's been following me around like a puppy dog ever since. To tell you the truth, I kinda felt sorry for him. I cleaned him up, got him off the drugs...for the most part, anyway."

Crane stepped on the brakes, stopping at the top of a hill. The aid station they'd passed on the way was visible in the distance. "Go ahead and jump in the back with Barney. Tell him to get ready."

Marty exited the truck's cab, slamming the door behind him. He flipped the canvas flap aside and jumped in, expecting to see Barney crashed out again. Instead, Barney looked up, wide-awake. He was sitting Indian-style on a thick woolen blanket, holding his most prized possession -- a vintage M-1 Garand. The weapon, used during World War II, had been handed down to his father by his grandfather. He'd smuggled the weapon home after the war rather than turning it in. Barney had inherited the rifle years later, after his own father had passed. Grandpa would've been rolling in his grave if he'd been aware that his grandson was using the rifle for such dishonorable business.

The stock was a deep cherry red and highly polished. The barrel was gunmetal blue. A thin layer of oil had been applied with tender care and it gleamed, even in the dull light of the

## Caribbean Calling

cargo hold. Barney was busy polishing each individual thirty-caliber shell prior to inserting the round into the magazine. A bandoleer of ammunition clips sat next to him. Apparently, he'd been busy during the ride so far. He had ten magazines for the rifle, and he was loading the last one. A disturbing grin was plastered on his skinny face.

"Crane said to hang back here with you. He doesn't think we're gonna make it to the boat without some unwanted company." Marty felt a little wary, considering Barney's current disposition. Barney looked up again and nodded and Marty moved to the back of the truck's bed. A couple more arms were hidden under an old wool blanket. Marty picked up his weapon of choice -- one of the AK-47s, like the ones they'd sold to the Caretaker. Two of the same tube-style rocket launchers remained under the blanket.

Crane sent the vehicle forward down the hill and rounded the road in front of the aid station. A few people remained in front of the main building. One of the workers, a young woman, waved. Crane smiled, lifted a finger, and continued on. The sun was beginning to set and the landscape took on an eerie glow. It was a little cooler now, but just a little.

After passing through a village, Crane noticed two vehicles parked on the road ahead, blocking the way. Both looked to be older model 4x4 Broncos or Blazers, or something similar. An official seal of some sort was painted on both the driver and passenger doors. There were four men, dark skinned, two of them brandishing rifles. Crane glanced at the side mirror. He couldn't see any sign of trouble approaching from the rear, but he now knew for sure that the word was out.

His mind raced. He needed a plan of action, and one of his finer talents was thinking on his toes -- grace under pressure. He decided to play it straight. As the old truck rumbled along, he yelled back to give his partners a head's up on the situation, and

## j. d. gordon

then he stopped the truck a few feet in front of the roadblock. The two armed officers lowered their weapons, pointing them in the direction of the truck.

"Is there a problem, Officer?" Crane posed the standard question, like a drunk getting pulled over for weaving in traffic. The young man approached the driver's side of the vehicle with his pistol drawn.

"We got orders to stop all transport trucks and search for contraband. We need to take a look at your cargo."

Crane knew that this was a stalling tactic. "I'm gonna be honest with ya, fella. We both know we're the guys you're looking for, and we both know why. Now the question is, what's it gonna take to get you to look the other way?"

The officer crooked his neck, a questioning look on his face. "What you have in mind, mon?"

"Well, let's see what I have here..."

"Now watch it, mon! Nuttin' funny, now, mon!"

Crane reached over and released the clasps securing the briefcase, exposing stacks of cash, each wrapped with a thin paper strip. He grabbed four of the stacks and waved them at the officer, spread out like a hand of playing cards. Motioning for another officer to move forward, the man grabbed the wads of cash and handed them over to his commander.

"Andrew Jackson, hey! But I always liked Grant the best of the old presidents, mon."

Crane returned to the briefcase and grabbed another bundle of currency, this one loaded with fifty-dollar bills. He displayed the wad. The same soldier came over and took the bundle, then offered the bills to his boss. The officer flipped through the stack.

"Let's go boys! Dis ain't de truck we lookin' for." The

## Caribbean Calling

soldiers lowered their rifles, jumped into their vehicles, and cleared the way. Another four by four stopped next to Crane's window.

"You might want to move quick, mon. De boys from de compound are not very fah behind." The vehicle sped off into the distance.

Crane jammed his foot on the gas pedal. Up ahead, the path led into the rain forest. Crane thought about setting up an ambush, but decided against it. He figured his best chance was to get into the populated town beyond the jungle. The drive to the beach, and the boat, wasn't far beyond the town.

His hopes were dashed when Marty stuck his head out from the rear area of the truck. "Looks like we got company coming, big guy!"

"What've we got?" Crane yelled.

"Well, it's hard to see. The road curves a lot, and with all the vegetation…"

"Spit it out, Marty!"

"It looks like a couple of those runabouts. You know, those quick bastards with the machine guns."

"Do what you have to do. I'll try and get us to the town."

In back, Barney was kneeling on the floor of the truck, firing off his prized possession. It wasn't long before Crane could hear the rapid cracking of the thirty-caliber machine guns mounted on the small, fast-moving vehicles. Marty knelt behind Barney, periodically taking shots with his AK-47. One of the rocket launchers lay by his side in case an opportunity presented itself.

Crane was preparing for the next turn in the road when he heard the enemy's heavy machine gun fire. A loud pop invaded his space, and he found it impossible to steer the truck. The rear

## j. d. gordon

of the vehicle swerved, and he felt himself losing contact with the road. Slowly, the truck began to tip as it careened forward. Crane could see the plants whipping over and past the truck's windshield. Finally, the truck tipped onto its side and slid along the ground. Everything seemed to move in slow motion, including the piercing of the front windshield by a heavy branch. If Crane had been sitting in the passenger seat, he would have been impaled.

Crane could hear light vehicles run past his truck, crunching through sand and dirt, then skid to a halt ahead. They were some distance beyond where the truck was lying. Suddenly, a face looked at him through the windshield. Marty smashed the window with the butt end of the Russian automatic rifle, reached in, and tried to pull Crane from the truck's cab. Barney was out of sight, but Crane could hear him firing off his rifle. A sharp pain ran through Crane's body as Marty tried to free him. He looked down and saw what looked like a pound of ground beef lying in a puddle of blood. Both of his legs had been crushed by the truck's dashboard. He was already feeling weak.

"It's nuh...no good. Take the case and go," he said feebly.

"Hey," Barney called out, "I think there's more coming around back this way!"

"Go," Crane ordered in a whisper. He shoved the briefcase out the window. With what force he had left, he grabbed Marty by the collar. "Take care of Barney. He's... he's been a good friend to me."

"I will. I promise. That's the warrior's bond, right?" Crane didn't answer as the life drained from his face. Because he had no other choice, Marty hoisted the briefcase, turned to Barney, and said, "Let's go," grabbing the skinny guy by the arm.

"What about Crane?" Barney asked, as he slammed another fresh magazine into the vintage rifle.

## Caribbean Calling

"He's dead. Let's go." Marty dragged Barney into the bushes.

Barney's jaw dropped as he let himself be led away. Once they were protected from view, he turned his head to survey the scene of the crash. Four men dressed in black combat uniforms examined the wreckage. When they pulled Crane's bloody body from the cab of the truck, he jerked away from Marty's grasp, stood to his full height, lifted his rifle to his shoulder, and pulled the trigger, depleting the entire magazine. Two of the men dropped as the slugs ripped through their bodies. The other two returned fire with small machine guns. They were skilled with the deadly weapons, and Barney was riddled with projectiles.

Marty knelt over Barney's body. His chest was splattered with blood, and he didn't seem to be breathing. The remaining two troopers were crouched and slowly making their way over to his position. He sprayed the area with the AK-47. He wasn't sure if he'd struck his mark, but both soldiers dropped to the ground.

Tightening his grip on the handle of the briefcase, Marty's right shoulder screamed with pain. He could feel warm liquid already soaking his shirt. He placed his hand on the wound and could feel the hole that the bullet had made as it pierced his flesh. He would live, but he would need medical care, and soon.

Realizing that he'd failed to grab extra ammunition, he tossed the Russian rifle to the side. He could hear other vehicles approaching. He grabbed the bandoleer of magazines from around Barney's torso and scooped up the antique rifle, sliding in a fresh clip. Then, he stripped Barney of his shirt and belt and improvised a dressing for himself. As best as he could, he made his way from the scene. He could hear still more pursuers spilling from their vehicles, along with the sound of a man shouting orders. For a split-second, he thought about the words of advice from the late, great Crane, "Remember the aid station. You never know."

# j. d. gordon

Making his way farther into the jungle as silently as possible, he had covered some distance when he heard vehicle engines increase in number. He crawled down into a low, covered ditch filled with about six inches of standing water left over from the earlier rains. He had a good view of the area where the truck had toppled over. Through a haze of mosquitoes, he could see figures moving about, searching. Headlights lit up the entire scene, and the posse used flashlights as well. In the impending darkness of the night, this was of benefit to Marty. Anything not directly in the lights' path would be invisible.

He settled down into the ditch, rifle ready, pointed in the direction of the search party. The men now mounted their chase vehicles and set off in different directions. Leaving the roadway, they circled the crash sight, and on several occasions neared his hiding spot. After some time, the fast-attack vehicles tore off down the roadway in the direction of the previous evening's drop-off point.

Marty was beginning to feel very weak. He knew he needed care, and soon. After repositioning the bandage on his shoulder, he stood up and started to walk in the direction of the aid station. He figured he had about a two mile walk in front of him, and the weight of the rifle and ammunition would slow him down.

In his business, a trusty weapon could be the difference between life and death, and rather than drag the case of money along, Marty decided to stash the item. He would come back and pick it up later. In a worst-case scenario, he could use it as bargaining chip if he were to fall into the hands of his pursuers. He found a pile of rocks near a filthy puddle and a large patch of low bushes and half-buried it there.

It was slow going for the lone and wounded hired gun. He darted from cover to cover, and occasionally had to crawl through open spaces. It was late in the night, or early, depending

## Caribbean Calling

upon one's perspective, when Marty found himself atop a hill, not far off the roadway. The small village was in sight, the aid station being at the far end. Marty glanced at his wristwatch, it was three a.m. There were a couple of hours left before daylight. He picked up his pace, lumbering along with the old rifle slung over his good shoulder. He didn't relish the idea of tromping through the town in the light of day, nor did he want to spend the day in the tropical heat hiding, waiting for a chance to make it through the town. He was thirsty, hungry, exhausted, and in pain.

As he limped his way through the town, the main road was quiet. Always waiting for the sound of vehicles, he glanced back to make sure he wasn't being watched or followed. Finally, he found himself unlatching the wooden gate that surrounded the small compound of buildings comprising the aid station. Making his way across the neatly-trimmed lawn in front of the main building, he looked at the stairs leading to the porch and main entrance as if they were Mount Everest. He reached out to grab the handle on the door. His final memory was falling down on the porch, the first rays of sunlight skipping over the hills in the distance.

j. d. gordon

## Chapter Six

Eddie stepped out into the terminal in Tampa. As with most modern airports, there wasn't much difference between the airport where he'd boarded the plane, and the one he was standing in. Well, there was one difference. The people here were tan, and wore shorts and sandals instead of jackets and gloves. Eddie searched for a hint as to where the baggage claim area was hidden.

Once he found it, no bags were present, but the vinyl belt was rotating. A flashing yellow light indicated that the luggage was soon to arrive. A large group of people waited silently, staring at the belt as if some miracle of life was about to take place. Eddie's was amongst the first few pieces to tumble through the leather flap that separated the passengers from the world of airline workers. He stepped forward to claim his bag -- an old canvas duffel he'd picked up in an army-navy surplus store.

Stepping out onto the arrivals platform, he noticed the climate change as soon as the automatic doors slid open. The crisp Midwestern wind was replaced by balmy, sweet breezes. In a few hours, he was in a whole different world. He stood around for a moment, surrounded by desperate smokers, searching for a good spot to wait for Marci. The heightened security didn't allow for vehicles to sit around waiting. Airport security and police officers moved any squatters on their way.

Setting up camp near a concrete post in the shade, he

## Caribbean Calling

relaxed. He stripped down to his tee shirt. The fire department job shirt he'd worn on the plane was too heavy for this climate. As he stuffed it into his carry-on bag, a horn sounded. Marci sat smiling in a convertible Jeep Wrangler. The top was down and Marci looked adorable, her ashy blond hair pulled back into a ponytail, stray locks hanging over her sunglasses. She swiped the hair away from her face.

"Hey, fella, you looking for a ride?" she asked, a coy grin on her face. Eddie walked over to the Jeep and tossed his duffel onto the back seat. She leaned over and gave him a peck on the cheek. She smelled like coconut.

Dressed in a light, short skirt and a white linen short-sleeved blouse, Marci's skin was smooth and tan. Eddie sat down in the passenger's seat and applied his safety belt.

"So, how ya doin'?" he asked. Unsatisfied with the peck, he drew her into an embrace before she stepped on the gas pedal. The air felt soft and the sun warm as its rays washed over Eddie's pale Midwestern skin.

The couple's last encounter had been over a month before. Marci had come up north for a friend's wedding and Eddie had acted as a tour guide, showing her what Chicago had to offer. They'd gone to the museums, both the Field and the Science and Industry. They'd checked out the Shedd Aquarium. They'd dined at some of Eddie's favorite restaurants, including the original Uno's, on Ohio, and the Chicago Oven and Pizza Grinder. They'd ended their time together checking out the Cubs from the right field bleachers and then they'd spent the evening hitting the establishments around the ballpark. Marci had never been to a Cubs' game and was impressed by Wrigleyville.

"Well, Key West has Duval, New Orleans has Bourbon Street, and Memphis has Beale Street. Here in Chicago, we've got Wrigleyville," he'd explained.

# j. d. gordon

Before her flight back to Tampa, the two had shared some private time.

"I guess you don't have much time before you have to start work," Marci mock pouted. Eddie was scheduled to meet with Bruce Klein the next day. He had wanted to take a few days with Marci, but hadn't been able to work out the time off with the fire department. He didn't want to burn his bridges back home. This job with Klein was a trial run, after all. "I figured we'd hang around my place for today, if that's okay with you."

Marci lived on Harbor Island, across the bridge from downtown Tampa. It was her parents' place, but she was shacking up there while she looked for work in the Tampa area. A recent college graduate, Marci was an up-and-coming interior designer. She'd finished her education months ago, and her search for employment was moving along rather slowly. She'd said it was because she was picky, looking for the right firm. Until the right gig came along, though, she was happy living on her father's bankroll. A real estate developer in Boston, her father had picked up the Harbor Island condo when Marci started at the University of South Florida.

"You're the guest, though, Eddie. We should do whatever you feel like doing," she added as they merged onto the Harbor Island Bridge.

"Well, I don't have much time tomorrow. I'm supposed to meet with Mr. Klein in the late morning."

"Oh, no, ya don't," she interrupted. "Since you couldn't make it in for the whole weekend, I told him I was keeping you until Tuesday, or maybe Wednesday, or Thursday, or perhaps Friday. We'll have to wait and see. That's the surprise I mentioned in my message."

"You did, huh?" Eddie smiled. He didn't mind Marci going over his head to get him a little more time to spend with her.

## Caribbean Calling

"Well, I'm up for hanging around the island today and then checking out Tampa tomorrow."

"Alright, then! The pool this afternoon, then Jackson's Bistro tonight. Deal?"

"Deal," he agreed.

The little Jeep cruised along the bridge. Marci's loose strands of hair fluttered in the breeze while Eddie slapped a little Banana Boat suntan lotion onto his forehead. After a quick stop at the end of the bridge to check in at the island's guard shack, they entered the town. Eddie liked the look of Harbor Island. It was clean, classy, and the roads were lined with lush tropical plant life, not the typical palm trees, but all sorts of colored flowers and bushes. Sweet scents were carried in the breeze, and Eddie was impressed to find what looked like a resort, smack dab in the middle of a city.

Marci pulled her Jeep up to the front of her building, where men in shorts and work shirts with rolled-up sleeves toiled with long hoses, watering the gorgeous landscaping. Eddie noted the sweat stains under their arms and was happy, for once, not to be the guy lugging around the hose.

After a valet jumped into the driver's seat, relieving Marci of her parking responsibilities, the couple headed into the building. The lobby was magnificent. An atrium as long as a football field sat between two twenty-story towers, and was constructed of domed glass. The sun's rays filled the space, bouncing off surfaces and plants in random patterns on the polished light wood floor. The air was cool and sweet.

The condos were situated on each side, with glass and wood elevators allowing for access. Long, open hallways that looked much like balconies ran the length of the building, allowing residents and visitors to enjoy the view of the atrium while making their way to their homes.

Marci's condo was bright and airy, comfortable and cool. Eddie drew in a deep breath and surmised that the maid had paid a recent visit. The kitchen was open with whitewashed wood cabinets and a huge island in the center. The ceramic tile floor was high quality, Eddie noted, with some marble mixed in, and gleaming stainless-steel appliances looked as if they'd never been used. "That's quite a kitchen for a gal who doesn't do much cooking," he commented.

A dining room off the kitchen was dominated by an oval teak table and a hutch filled with china, which was set off against the light cream walls with pastel trim. The living room was expansive. A plasma-screen television and high-tech entertainment center didn't look out of place. No wicker anywhere, Eddie noted. Very classy. A set of French doors allowed access to a deck that stretched the entire width of the room. As it was located on the top floor, an abundance of skylights made the condo seem almost roofless.

Three full baths and three bedrooms were similarly decorated. It all looked to Eddie like something out of Better Homes and Gardens, or Architectural Digest, even. Marci's room was furnished with a large four-post bed. Her bathroom included a wide and deep hot tub and a separate large shower with multiple jets at various heights. The walk-in closet, which could barely accommodate the clothing and shoes it contained, was almost as large as Ed's entire bedroom back home.

"Settle in and get comfortable," Marci invited. "I'll get us some cold drinks and I'll meet you on the deck."

Eddie threw on a pair of blue cotton shorts, his fire department's red union symbol stitched onto the left front leg. Traditional swimsuits had never caught Eddie's fancy, and as far as speedos were concerned, he wouldn't be caught dead in a pair of those, so the shorts did double duty as swim trunks.

## Caribbean Calling

As an afterthought, he tossed on a Boston Red Sox jersey. It had been a gift from Marci. She'd spent a little time as a ball girl for the team, a few years back, which was one of the many things Eddie appreciated about her.

Stepping from the bathroom back into the main bedroom, he dumped his carry-on bag out on the bed. Sorting through the pile, he selected a few items for poolside use -- sunscreen, a CD player and head phones, his well-worn CD pouch, a pack of Juicy Fruit gum, and his favorite beach towel -- a Ralph Lauren decorated with the image of an old bi-winged sea plane. Several old stains from spilled tanning oil and drinks were evident as well, but Eddie felt like the stains added character. He left the bag on the bed and stepped out onto the balcony where Marci was sitting on a wood and cloth director's chair.

Director's chairs always conjured up childhood memories for Eddie. His uncle had owned a lakeside summer home on the western coast of Lake Michigan's lower peninsula. One weekend each summer, he would host a family get-together. Ed, his older brother Red, and all the cousins would play in Lake Michigan's waves, while the adults spent their time on the large deck that overlooked the beach, drinking, cooking, and talking politics. Eddie had an indelible picture of his uncle, sitting there like a king in his ever-present collapsible director's chair, always with a martini, and always with a wide-brimmed fishing hat. They were good memories.

"A drink?" Marci asked. A green bottle stuck out from a bucket of ice. An empty glass sat on the tabletop and Marci held another flute filled with golden, fizzy liquid.

"Absolutely," Eddie replied, pulling the bottle from the ice. The Italian sparkling wine was chilled. He took a seat across from Marci and looked out onto the bay, Tampa's skyline looming in the background. Up on the twentieth floor, the ground floor pool looked miniature, despite its Olympic-

## j. d. gordon

regulation size. He took a sip from the glass, swirled the liquid around on his tongue, and enjoyed the bubbles tickling the inside of his mouth. The drink relaxed him almost before it hit his stomach. "Good stuff. Sweet, not dry. I like that." He raised his glass to his hostess. "That's a mighty fine pool down there."

"Yup, that's where we're headed." In a short time, the wine was gone. Marci stood. "There's a cooler in the closet in the kitchen, ice in the freezer, and beer in the fridge. Why don't you set us up, I'll change, and we'll head down."

After loading the cooler with refreshments, Eddie watched with true admiration as Marci returned from the bedroom, dressed, if you could call it that, in a string bikini and a short white tee shirt covering her upper decks.

"Damn, girl. You look good," Eddie couldn't hold back.

The swimming pool was almost empty. Only six or seven others were soaking up the sun around the cool, clear water. The couple chose a set of chaise lounges on the far side, overlooking the bay. It was a study in contrasts -- the urban landscape and sounds of the city mixed with the chirping of birds and the idyllic immediate surroundings.

Eddie grabbed some tanning oil and began to rub it on Marci's back and shoulders. He didn't know how she felt about that, but it sure was an enjoyable experience for him. With an already deep tan, her skin glistened in the hot afternoon sun. Eddie was still pasty and white. He hoped that the afternoon under the sun would help remedy that. He twisted the top off of a couple of Coronas and Marci slipped a small piece of lime into each of the clear glass bottles. When she closed her eyes, Eddie covered his ears with his headphones and let Bob Marley lull him into a catnap.

caribbean calling

## Chapter Seven

Elaine rolled over on her small bed, wishing the mattress was a little bit thicker, and then parted the hanging mosquito netting to get a closer look at the clock on her nightstand. The small hand was on the four, the big hand on the six. It was cool and comfortable in the early morning, and she didn't want to get out of bed to answer the loud knocking on her cabin door. It was much too early for Batilda to be making her morning rounds.

For the past two weeks, until today, Batilda had woken her for breakfast like clockwork. It was much busier around the aid station than she'd ever imagined, because she was the only doctor on hand, running an entire clinic. At least she had Billy. He was a real help, every bit as good as some of her peers back home, and they'd been licensed doctors. Batilda always lent a hand -- Pastor Tom, as well. The Australian -- Kangaroo, as they called him -- was always busy fixing something, up to his elbows in grease. Martin normally worked in the fields, teaching the villagers how to best manage their crops. Reggie spent most days teaching the children Spanish, English, and rudimentary math and science.

Yesterday had been the first time she'd had a chance to go out and do a little exploring of the island. Billy had fired up the old Jeep and the two had visited the market in the village nearby where citizens from all over the island bought and sold goods.

## j. d. gordon

Elaine had been awed by all of the different products and services being peddled. Meat stands, where butchered and fly-covered animals hung from metal hooks, stood alongside vendors selling heaps of fresh fruits and vegetables. Some stands offered services -- carpenters looking for work, day laborers, and folks willing to tend fields for very low wages. One stand even displayed a long row of canoes constructed from locally grown trees. Small stores rolled and sold cigars. Old women sold polished stones and jewelry. Other peddlers offered items that wouldn't be legal in other parts of the globe.

The pair spent several hours exploring the market. Elaine bought several trinkets to send home, but kept an ankle bracelet made of small polished shells, stones, and tiny gems that she didn't recognize, for herself. Billy wrapped it around her ankle, giving her foot a quick massage as the opportunity presented itself.

The day of leisure had concluded with a picnic on the beach and a swim in the ocean. They feasted on mangoes, limes, and light, buttery bread that Batilda had made for breakfast, and which Billy had smuggled from the kitchen counter. After sharing a bottle of Australian wine, they'd made it home in time for Elaine to set a broken ankle for one of the men in the village who'd injured himself working in the fields. Before bed, Elaine had called her father, as she did every evening. He was very protective, and she didn't want to worry him. He'd spent enough money on the fancy phone, and she figured it was the least she could do.

She rubbed the sleep from her eyes as she made her way to the door of her cottage, and opened it to find Batilda standing there. The front of her flower-print dress was covered with blood.

"We've got an injured man in the main building. I think he's a soldier. He was carrying a rifle. I've got Jonathan watching him now." Batilda was short of breath.

## Caribbean Calling

Elaine instructed Batilda to wake Billy and bring him along, she threw on a surgical robe over her pajamas, and then she sprinted for the main building. Back in the treatment rooms, she found the big Australian sitting next to one of the beds. A man, filthy, with crusted blood and dirt covering his dark clothes, lay there at his side. Pale and covered in sweat, the stranger was taking quick and shallow breaths. A rifle stood against the wall.

Jonathan, who'd been holding a wad of white towels against the man's wound, moved away from the bed as Elaine approached. He picked up the rifle on the way. Elaine removed the makeshift bandage, made from a soiled shirt and a belt. Most of the blood had dried, she noted. When Billy walked into the room, Elaine asked him for sterile saline, a surgical kit, and bandages. "Grab a little morphine and some lidocaine while you're at it," she ordered. Billy was gone only a moment. Elaine would have liked to place an oxygen mask on her patient, but they had run out of the precious gas.

"Can you hear me, sir? What happened to you?" She irrigated the wound with the saline solution. The crusted blood began to fall away, exposing the bullet hole.

"Where am I?" the man whispered weakly.

"You're in a hospital. We're going to fix you up, okay?"

"The aid station?" the man asked, appearing to regain consciousness.

"Yes, the aid station. What happened, sir?" she asked again.

The man hesitated. "I was shot...held up on the road."

Jonathon interrupted. "Perhaps I should call the magistrate, mate?"

"No!" The man sat up in bed, wincing with pain. "Don't call them. They're the ones who held me up."

Elaine motioned to the Kangaroo not to press the issue. She'd leave the confusing details to the boss. "Someone should get Robert up and tell him what's happened," she said.

"He's off-base in the capital arranging for new supplies. Technically, you're in charge here, lassie."

Elaine digested the information while she cleansed the wound and started an intravenous line as a precaution against shock, or in case she had to push other medications. She injected the wound area with lidocaine to numb the pain and paused to make a plan of action. Clearly, the man had been shot, but without radiological equipment, she had no way of locating the chunk of metal except by doing it the old-fashioned way -- she would need to dig for it with a pair of forceps.

Elaine found the lead embedded in the muscle of the patient's shoulder and removed it. It dropped with a dull thud into a the metal surgical bowl. After stitching and dressing the wound, Elaine let the patient rest. The morphine was coursing through his veins.

Back in the supply room, Elaine, Billy, and the Kangaroo spoke quietly, assessing the situation. "So, how do we handle this? Should we call the cops?" Elaine questioned. Her partners had been living on the island much longer than she had, and no doubt had a better perspective of the island's legal system.

"Cops?" Billy replied. "There aren't any cops. They're more of a paramilitary-type, third-world-nation-type deal. I'm not sure how straight they are."

"Why don't we wait until the bloke wakes up. We'll ask 'im what's up and go from there." The Australian walked off as if the decision had been made. "I'll take this with me while I give the old bus its monthly maintenance." He grabbed the rifle and headed for the door.

## Caribbean Calling

"Hey, Kangaroo, how about the ammo?" Jonathan turned and caught a bandoleer that Billy had removed from the visitor's torso.

"Thanks, mate."

Elaine looked at Billy and nodded her head with assurance. "I'm sure he'll be fine. And I imagine Batilda will have breakfast ready soon. I'm going to go get cleaned up. I hope people are healthy today. I'm tired."

Billy winked. "I'll meet you in the shower room, then?"

"Oh, Billy, you think so, huh? Maybe in your dreams." She left him standing there.

The dining room and kitchen were located in a smaller building behind the main clinic, separated only by a canvas awning. The kitchen was complete with a double sink, a large combination refrigerator/freezer, and a stove with four large burners and a double oven. Batilda's appliances were powered by propane. Occasionally, when the budget ran short, she'd have the Kangaroo collect firewood for the bar-b-que pit out back.

A wide doorway led to the eating area, where a couple of ceiling fans stirred the air. Batilda's Café, that's what they called it. One large table made of wood planks sat in the middle of the room, a set of benches running the length on each side. The floor was made of flat stone, light colored cement used to bind the pieces together. Like everything else at the compound, the walls were painted white and were as clean as could be. Batilda toiled from dawn 'til past dusk to keep the place shipshape and the folks well fed.

Elaine made her way back to her quarters and picked out clothes for the day. As usual, she selected items that were cool and comfortable -- cut-off khaki pants and a light green scrub shirt left over from her days as an intern. On her feet, she wore a

# j. d. gordon

comfy pair of Timberland leather shoes. She preferred sandals, but wasn't comfortable wearing them during the workday. Finally, as the mornings were cool, she grabbed an old college sweatshirt. The standard uniform provided by the agency still hung unworn in the corner of her closet.

Elaine ran into Pastor Tom on her way to the shower room. She considered talking to him about the wounded man, but decided to wait until later. She wanted to roll the situation around in her head while she showered.

The water was cool this morning. The large containers in place above the stalls hadn't had a chance yet to absorb any of the sun's heat. Most of the workers waited until the end of the day to shower, when the water was at its warmest, but Elaine needed her morning shower. Without it, she felt sticky and slimy all day long. A shower and a strong cup of coffee was what she needed to get her going. Of everything back home, it was often her morning trip to Starbuck's that she missed the most.

She pulled the chain that opened the valve and allowed the water to flow through the small holes of the large shower head. The water was cool, but invigorating, causing small goosebumps to form on her skin. She lathered herself up with what was on hand -- a plain bar of white, pasty soap. She had wanted to make a trip to the Body Shop to stock up before leaving, but hadn't found the time. Maybe she'd ask her father to put a package together and send it down, but she couldn't help but wonder if the package would even arrive before her time on the island was up.

After dressing and tying her hair up in a ponytail, Elaine headed for the dining hall. Billy hadn't shown up as he said he would, she thought. It was an amusing flirtation. Typically, she wouldn't dream of engaging in a workplace romance. This job was temporary, though. She'd known Billy for a couple of weeks, but he was so damn cute.

## Caribbean Calling

That's it, she thought, back to the situation at hand. Who was that man laying on the cot in the aid station? Why was he afraid of the local police? Why was he armed? A drug smuggler, perhaps? A political enemy of the local government, maybe? She knew that all she could do was wait to ask him those questions when he woke.

Kangaroo and Billy were sitting at the table when she walked into the dining area. The room smelled of cinnamon, vanilla, and butter. Batilda handed her a cup of coffee, and the steaming, dark liquid was a welcome site, especially after the early morning cold shower.

"Where were you, Billy? I took an extra long shower hoping you would show yourself," she teased.

"If only you were serious," he replied, lifting his eyebrows with delight at the thought.

"Okay, alright, mates. Enough of that rot. Leave the flirtin' aside, we've got somethin' else to go over 'fore the others show up for the mornin' vittles." It was true that the Kangaroo was a little jealous of the flirting going on between his two co-workers, but he was serious now. "I'm sure we've all had a little time to think about this," he continued. "I suggest we leave the rest of the folks in the dark until we figure out what's going on."

"You mean lie to them? I can't do that. Batilda knows about it, anyway. She's the one who found him," Elaine argued.

"Not lie, little girl, don't tell 'em the whole story," he retorted.

"I agree," Billy added. "That way, if anyone questions them, they won't let anything out that shouldn't be let out yet."

"What if we're harboring a fugitive? What if this guy is some kind of crazed murderer?" Elaine needed more convincing. "What would Robert do if he were here?"

"That's tough to say," Billy replied after some thought. "It would all depend on his mood. You've noticed the changes in his personality, haven't you?"

"That's an understatement," Elaine admitted. On her third day at the compound, Robert had read her the riot act for taking a seven-minute shower after a long, hard day. Five minutes was the rule. A half-hour later, he'd been as sweet as pie. "Well, let's go with what the friendly Robert would do," she suggested.

"That would be to wait and see," Kangaroo responded. The three regarded each other for a moment. "Then that'll be the plan, mates." Nods went all around.

"How do we keep the others from going into the ward and discovering him?" Billy had brought up a good point. "And how about the villagers? Sick or injured folks will start showing up any time now."

"We'll close the clinic. We'll say we've got a patient with a potentially contagious disease and he is in quarantine. We'll only accept critical patients until we can get this sorted out." As the only medical authority on the premises, the Kangaroo thought Elaine could get away with it.

Elaine thought for a moment. "What disease? Tuberculosis? That would mean the universal precautions would have to be in place if anyone wanted to enter the treatment area."

"Sounds reasonable to me," Billy answered. "But we won't be able to keep this up for long. People are going to need our help sooner or later. I'd bet sooner."

When the rest of the team began showing up for the first meal of the day, they talked about the day's projects with their co-workers. Reggie went over a new lesson plan, and Martin laid out his intention of digging new irrigation channels. Soon, platters of steaming food made their way to the table -- French

## Caribbean Calling

toast with warm maple syrup laced with chunks of coconut and pineapple, scrambled eggs, and small spicy sausages. Elaine, recalling the open air meat stands, skipped on the sausages.

During a lull in the conversation, Elaine made an announcement about a patient who had arrived during the night with a possible case of TB. She informed everyone that routine cases were not to be seen today in the clinic, and asked Pastor Tom to sideline people coming to the clinic for simple problems. The holy man wouldn't be working in the fields today. "Emergencies only, folks, we want to keep everyone away from the main building until we know everything is clear."

"If we take the proper precautions, can we be of assistance in the patient's care?" the pastor inquired of the doctor.

"I would feel better if you left it to me and Billy," she answered calmly.

"So, this doesn't have anything to with that rifle I saw the Kangaroo stash away in the garage this morning?" Reggie asked. Her square frame glasses had slipped down to the point of her nose. Elaine was silent for a moment, taken aback by the teacher's comment. When Batilda shot her the evil eye, she looked at the Australian with questioning eyes. He shrugged in reply. "Okay, folks, I don't feel right covering things up with you, anyway." Batilda smiled to herself, but Elaine noticed.

Elaine outlined the facts of the mysterious stranger, which weren't many. She had few answers herself. "We're going to take this route until he is better, and can shed some light on the subject, or until Robert comes back and makes a decision. So, everyone, please go on about your normal activities, and if anyone asks, stick to the TB story. The less said the better." Heads nodded in agreement and the rest of the meal was eaten in relative silence, with only an occasional "pass the milk." Soon, the group broke up and went their separate ways.

## j. d. gordon

While Elaine and Billy checked on the patient, the Kangaroo went out back to take care of a brake job on the bus. Pastor Tom took his seat on the front porch, rocking while reading a book. Within a short time, a mother and her daughter approached the clinic on foot. The girl looked flushed and dazed.

"I tink she got da fever, Pastor," the woman said when she reached the porch.

Pastor Tom asked them to sit down and wait. Then he went inside to find Elaine. "You'd better come out, Doctor. There's a little girl outside who doesn't look well. She may have a fever."

Elaine grabbed her medical bag and followed Pastor Tom outside. "Well, hello there, dear. You aren't feeling well?" She turned to the girl's mother as she inserted a thermometer into the girl's mouth. "We have what may be an infectious patient inside. We don't want to take any risks," she explained. After examining the girl's throat and ears, she extracted a bottle of penicillin from her bag. "Ma'am, your daughter appears to have strep throat. I'm going to give you these pills for her to take every six hours. She should rest in bed and drink all the liquid she can. Do you understand?" The woman nodded her head. "Be sure to bring her back in two days so I can check on her again, okay?"

"We do dat. Tank you, doctah. Tank you."

"Do you have a ride back to town?"

"No, ma'am. We walk. We got no ride."

Elaine looked to the pastor. "Could you find someone to give them a lift in the Bronco? Perhaps you can spread the word about the clinic being closed today? It shouldn't take more than twenty minutes or so, right?"

The pastor didn't hesitate before scooping the girl up in his arms and carrying her to the vehicle.

## caribbean calling

"Tank you, tank you, doctah," the woman repeated over and over.

"It's no trouble at all. I'm very happy to help. She'll feel better soon. Don't forget the pills. One every six hours until they are all gone. That's very important, okay?" Elaine didn't know whether the woman would bring her daughter back in two days. Many times, the islanders either forgot, or neglected to return for follow-ups.

Knowing that the pastor would run into any approaching visitors and head them off, Elaine returned to the new patient's bedside, where Billy was keeping vigil. He was sleeping comfortably. Elaine sat down next to the bed to check the sutures and the man awoke, startled by her touch. "Who the hell are you? Where am I?" he asked.

"You're feeling a bit better, I see?" Elaine asked. "I'm Doctor Keller. You're in a hospital, and you're safe, for now."

The man was still woozy from the morphine. "Right...the aid station. Good." He appeared to relax, though he looked at her as if trying to remember something. "I've seen you before...where?"

"I'm sure we've never met, sir." Elaine shook her head. "What happened to you? I hope you're not involved with something illegal, like drug-running." Billy stood at the foot of the bed, listening.

"No, no, I'm no drug runner." The man tried to sit up, but was forced back to the mattress by the pain in his shoulder.

"Those are fresh stitches there. And there are quite a few of them. You'll need to rest for a while before you get up," Elaine said.

The man became agitated again. "No, I can't. I won't be safe."

"Calm down, man," Billy interjected. "Tell us what happened to you."

The man didn't answer right away. "Look, I'm a simple businessman from the mainland. We were down here doing a deal with that plantation down the road."

"Plantation? What…" Elaine started to ask.

Billy interrupted again. "It's called The Plantation. I suppose it's a plantation, but I was under the impression it was some sort of cult. Everyone stays away from the place. The people out there look like they're either drugged up or from a different planet. They call themselves disciples."

"Yeah, it's like a cult. We dropped off some equipment, they paid us, and then we left. Everything was cool. Then, on the way back, they came after us. They chased us."

"What do you mean 'us'?" Billy asked.

"My partners. There were three of us." Clearly, the man's wound was taxing his strength and making it difficult for him to stay awake. He closed his eyes and was asleep almost instantly.

"Let's let him rest. We'll get more answers eventually," Elaine suggested.

Ten minutes later, the pastor stuck his head inside the room. "Excuse me, but there are some police officers outside asking to speak to someone of authority."

"Tell them we'll be right out, Tom. Whatever you do, don't let them inside," Elaine answered, alarm creeping into her voice.

Billy laid his hand on her shoulder. "Don't worry. We'll deal with it."

Elaine and Billy stepped out to the porch and found a jeep with the motor still running. A thin, sweaty, uniformed man sat

## Caribbean Calling

behind the steering wheel. Another similarly dressed man stood at the bottom of the porch stairs. Elaine thought they looked rather more like soldiers than policemen, which is how they'd introduced themselves. The man was squarely-built, and wore dark aviator-style sunglasses. His olive drab uniform was wrinkled, and his black boots were covered with red, sandy mud. A pistol hung at his hip in a brown leather holster. He was wearing a thick gold chain around his neck.

"I'm in charge here, officer," Elaine offered. As the camp's medical director, she was the boss when Robert was away, especially in matters concerning patients. "How can I help you?" Despite her calm exterior, she was very nervous. It was probable that these officers had been out all night looking for the man she was caring for inside the building.

"We lookin' foh a fugitive, miss. He may be injured. Dat's what brings us here, miss." The officer was friendly and respectful enough.

"We've only had a little girl with a throat infection through here today," she answered. "It's still early though. What type of person are you looking for?"

"Miss, a white male, miss, in his tirties, we tink, miss. He is considahed armed and dangerous. We shor he is injured. You shor nobody ees here, miss? You mind if we look around?" he asked.

"Oh, please, officer, I'm sorry. I should have asked you in. Please feel free to look around anywhere you want." Billy shot her an alarmed look, and then caught himself. "This is a sterile facility, though, so I'll have to ask you to remove your boots and clothing and clean yourselves up a bit. We have a shower out back."

The officer looked tired and worn out. He climbed the stairs and glanced through the open doorway. "No, dat's okay, miss, someone will check back latah. You see someone out of the ordinary, though, contact the local magistrate. And beware, dis man is very dangerous." The officer turned and retook his seat in the jeep. He waved a single finger at Billy and the pastor and then drove away.

"'Oh, please, feel free to look around.' That was a little gutsy, wasn't it, Doc?" Billy smirked.

Elaine regarded him with all seriousness. "What choice did I have? I've never made it a policy to try and keep armed soldiers away from where they want to go."

Billy turned his smirk into a smile. "It was a good move. We're going to have to do something, though, either turn him over to the authorities, or stash him somewhere else."

"Let's check on him for now. Certainly he's not dangerous in his condition." Elaine felt a trickle of sweat run down her back. The day's heat was already beginning to build.

Martin walked past the porch on his way to meet his workers. A collection of villagers clad in loose fitting shirts, short pants, and wide-brimmed hats waited in the distance, various tools in hand. "Everything okay?" he asked, indicating the official's jeep far down the road.

"No problem, Martin," Billy answered, holding the screen-door open for Elaine. "No problem at all."

As she replayed the day's events in her mind, Elaine couldn't help but think of what her father's advice would be concerning this new patient of hers. She thought, perhaps, that she would leave out the information when she spoke with him. Though he usually came around to support what he called her "crazy schemes," like when she'd convinced him that she should take a month off during her senior year of high school to travel down the Amazon with friends, she knew he worried about her.

## Caribbean Calling

Elaine had been an only child. Her parents had always wanted to have more children, but her mother had become ill soon after Elaine's birth. After she died, a nanny had been Elaine's main caretaker, and after kindergarten, she'd been sent to a prestigious boarding school in Maine, then on to a college-prep school in Chicago. Her father, who had relocated to Denver after his wife's death, had been kept busy by his career. Elaine usually came home for holidays and vacations, but there was always a babysitter around to perform the less glamorous functions of raising a child.

To make up for his lack of physical presence, her father, who did love her dearly, had kept in constant contact with her by phone or by letter from about the age of ten on. There had been several times during college when Elaine had rebelled, avoiding contact by not returning phone calls, or not visiting during vacations. Once, she had maxed out her credit cards in a fit of irritation with him. Over the years, though, they had managed to mend their fences -- and without therapy, at that.

A loud crash coming from the back of the building brought Elaine's floating thoughts back to the problem at hand. Racing toward the sound, she and Billy passed the reception desk and then moved on past the rows of neat and orderly exam rooms. The whole place seemed almost alien, without any sick or injured villagers. Elaine had already witnessed Pastor Tom turning folks away. She knew he was competent enough to know an actual emergency from a routine illness.

As they approached him, they found their patient sitting up on the edge of the bed. The tall aluminum pole that had once held a bag of IV fluid had been tipped over and was lying on the floor. The catheter on the end of the IV line, where fluid passed from tube to vein, had been pulled out of the man's arm and a slow stream of blood was dripping from the site and collecting in a small puddle on the floor. His chin was resting on his chest and he was trying to stand up. The drugs, or the pain, or both, were hampering his efforts. He seemed as if he was about to stumble. Elaine and Billy made it to his side in time to sit him back down on the cot.

"Hold on there, buddy. You're not ready to be heading out to the beaches just yet," Elaine warned. Applying pressure to the new wound in the crook of his arm, Elaine stopped the bleeding. Billy uprighted the IV pole.

"I can't stay here," the man whispered. "I'm not safe."

"Why?" Billy questioned. "You in trouble with the police?"

The man relented. "I might be. I'm not sure."

"You might be, huh? What does that mean? Like, you only tried to smuggle a little bit of cocaine off the island, and only a couple of the cops are pissed?" Billy raised one eyebrow.

The man seemed to be pulling a story out of the recesses of his mind. "Look, I was...um...I was hired by a guy to drop off a shipment. I didn't ask any questions. It was a job. Everything got out of hand, man. They tried to kill us."

"So, the businessman story wasn't the truth -- and this place. The Plantation? Why in the world would they attack you? And what happened to the men you were with? Why didn't you go to the authorities?" Elaine was trying to speak as calmly.

The man shook his head. "I don't know. I can't think straight right now." He lay back and closed his eyes.

Elaine wasn't finished with her questions, though. "So, this Plantation, what were you delivering there?"

"Lady, I swear, I don't know. Boxes and crates of shit. Like I said, I didn't ask any questions." He opened his eyes. "That's the thing, though. You wouldn't believe what I saw there. They had military equipment, guns and tanks and shit. Enough to start a

## Caribbean Calling

fuckin' war. I think that's why they tried to kill us...maybe they were scared we'd tell someone."

Billy wouldn't let up. "I've seen those guys at The Plantation, and they don't run around in military gear. They all wear white robes and tend fields and stuff like that. And they sure don't tote weapons."

Elaine waved Billy off. "What's your name?" she asked.

"Marty."

"Marty what?" Billy asked.

"Just Marty! Everyone will be better off if we leave it at that!"

Billy wasn't done, either, but Elaine held her hand up as if to say 'hold on.' "Let's let him rest now, Billy. We'll pick it up again later." She looked at the man now known as Marty. "You're safe for now. No one knows you're here. The police were here earlier, and they left. So kick back and relax. Let the morphine do its job. You must be hungry. I'll have Batilda bring something in for you."

"And thirsty," Marty added. "I sure as hell hope you're right. I'll stay for today, but I need to get off this island tomorrow."

"Leave that to us. We'll have to see. Someone will be in from time to time to check on you. If you need something, ring that bell." Elaine pointed to a small brass bell like those found on hotel lobby desktops. "You'll have to hit it hard to make it ring loudly. And please try to relax. We're here to help you. It's part of the Hippocratic Oath. There's always someone on the porch keeping an eye out. Our pastor is out there now, his name is Tom." Marty nodded and turned his head away from them.

Intending to update the pastor, and to ask Batilda to bring

the patient some food, Elaine and Billy walked out to the porch. The Kangaroo was walking across the road that separated the main building from the pole barn. He was covered in grease -- the same old dirty red rag hanging out of his back pocket. Billy called out to him.

"Well, mates, what's goin' on with the new feller?"

"Why don't you take a break," Elaine answered. "We're heading to Batty's café to talk about it. We'll have a meeting tonight with everyone."

As soon as they walked into the dining room, Batilda came charging at them. "What do you think you're doin' comin' in my dining hall lookin' like that, Tillwata'. You go clean yourself up!" she scolded. Batilda was very particular about cleanliness, and not afraid to use discipline on the Kangaroo, no matter how big he was.

Elaine came to his defense. "Batilda, hold on, dear. We need to talk for a few minutes. It's important."

"Well, just this once, I spose." Batilda glared at the Australian, and then softened her expression. "Only for the doctor. Only for her."

"And Batilda? Would you be so kind as to bring a plate of mild food to the patient? And some plain water?" If Elaine had asked her for pheasant under stained glass, Batilda would do her best to accommodate. She had taken a real liking to the young doctor.

The three co-workers sat down with their heads together. "Okay," Elaine began, "this is what we know. The guy says his name is Marty, and that he was hired to deliver a shipment of something, he says he doesn't know what, to The Plantation. He says they attacked him and his...associates. He doesn't know why, and he doesn't know what happened to the other two men."

# Caribbean Calling

"The Plantation, huh?" the Kangaroo interrupted. "Yeah, I'm familiar with the organization. Used to be they'd come around trying to recruit from the village. The local law got pissed, and from what I could gather, they made some kind of an arrangement. The Plantation could stay, as long as they didn't recruit from the locals. They said it took away from the local economy. Since then, I haven't heard much about them." The Kangaroo was one of the longest-standing volunteers at the camp. He knew most of the in's and out's of island politics.

Generally, aid workers volunteered for one year, but Jonathan Tillwater had been with the organization, and on the island, for almost ten years. No one knew why he hadn't ever wanted to return home, back to Australia, not even Batilda. On occasion, his peers had asked, but he'd avoided the subject, turning it into a joke, or just changing the subject all together.

"The thing is," Elaine continued, "he says he came across a huge stash of weaponry there. He says he thinks that's why they tried to kill him."

"Wouldn't bloody surprise me," the Aussie said with a chuckle. "Bunch of wackos, they are, I'd say. Well, we oughta get him off the island, then. I don't doubt his story. I've heard some pretty nasty rumors about that Plantation. It's likely he's telling the truth."

"I think he's full of shit," Billy said. "I think there's a lot more going on here than he's fessing up to. He's dressed in combat clothing, for God's sake. And he was armed. I don't know. I think we should turn him in to the locals and wash our hands of the whole situation. It's not our problem."

Elaine could see Billy's point, but she also agreed with the Kangaroo. "Do you have a way we could get him off the island without anyone knowing?"

The Aussie stroked his chin in thought. "Yeah, I think I

could arrange for it. It will take a day or two to set it up, though."

"Where would you move him to?" Elaine asked.

"Anywhere you want, I spose -- the Virgin Islands to start, and then to Key West, and eventually the mainland. Where's he from, anyway?"

The Pastor interrupted the meeting. "I'm sorry to barge in, folks, but we have a patient out here. He's in the front treatment room."

Elaine guessed it was serious, considering the rule of the day. "Thanks, Tom. I'll be there right away." When the pastor left, she looked at her cohorts. "Why don't we think about it until dinner? We'll pose the question tonight to the rest of the camp, and go from there."

As Billy and Elaine headed into the clinic from the back, they could hear someone moaning in pain. Elaine glanced at Marty as she passed by. He was sleeping comfortably, food untouched. Entering an exam room, they found Martin standing next to a young man lying on a cot, hollering and holding his right leg. Upon closer examination, Elaine found the boy's leg to be short and deformed. She guessed that he had fractured his femur. "What happened?" she asked.

Martin explained. "He was going to unload one of the carts. His leg sunk in the mud as he was pulling some tools out of the back. He lost his balance and his leg snapped."

"Billy, set up an IV, will you? We'll give him something right away for the pain. He'll have to be here for quite some time. He'll need to be put in traction." She turned to address Martin. "Thank you," she said warmly. She knew he cared for the island people. "Do we have any medical files for him?"

"I think so," he responded. "What do you need to know?"

## Caribbean Calling

"Well, let's see what he can answer for himself first." Elaine looked at her new patient and smiled. "What's your name, honey?"

"Fernando," the boy replied.

"Where's your pain? Can you tell me, on a scale of one to ten, how much it hurts?" The young farmhand answered the questions as best he could. "We need to set your bone back in place. But we'll wait until the medicine starts working, okay? Once the bone is relocated, it will feel much, much better."

Soon after Billy pushed the morphine into the IV line, the patient relaxed. "Do we have a traction splint on hand?" she asked. Billy nodded in the affirmative and ran off to the back storeroom, returning in a minute or so with the item in hand.

It took about thirty minutes to get things settled. After pulling the leg into a straight position by applying tension to the splint, the fractured bones were slipped back into place. Because the clinic didn't have the facilities to do more with the limb, the worker would have to stay in the traction splint until he could be moved to a more modern facility off the island. For now, they would try to make him as comfortable as possible.

Back out on the porch, Elaine, Billy, Pastor Tom, Martin, and the Kangaroo took a few moments to rest. Batilda stepped out with a tray of glasses and a pitcher of her famous lime concoction. Filling the others in on the difficult situation with Marty, Elaine got right to the point. "This is the perfect opportunity to get him off the island," she remarked.

"Not if the police are looking for him," the Kangaroo interjected. "They'll be present at any transfer we arrange. You let me take care of him, lassie. I have my ways."

Billy was still skeptical and wanted to avoid the whole situation. Elaine found herself becoming irritated by his refusal to even consider the plan, but she tried to keep an open mind. It occurred to her that he might know something she didn't, but she forged ahead. "Alright, Jon, go ahead and make the arrangements, and we'll wait to see what happens," she said, without catching Billy's eye.

"I'll set up Fernando's patient transfer," Billy offered. "We'll need to stash this Marty, though, if that's even his name. The police will be here from the beginning of the transfer all the way through until the patient leaves the island."

"Why are these things so difficult?" Elaine asked.

"We're not in the States, little lady, that's why! This is a third world nation we're in, a banana republic. Things work a might bit different around 'ere. The government likes to keep control of everyone and everything," the Kangaroo explained.

"When does Robert get back, anyway? We could use some direction," Elaine pleaded. "Why don't we send someone into town to get him?"

"That we can do. But who? You or I can't go, we have to stay with the injured, and Batty won't leave her kitchen for anything…"

Billy was cut off by the Pastor. "I'll go look for him. I know where he stays in town when he's waiting for the supplies."

"Why does he have to wait for supplies, anyway?" Elaine demanded. She was exhausted by her new and unexpected responsibilities.

The Pastor flushed before answering the question. "I believe he has a friend in the city."

"A friend! Blimey, I thought so!" the Kangaroo guffawed. "The old bird's got a squeeze, does he?"

Elaine suppressed her smile. "Regardless, perhaps we can

## caribbean calling

take Tom up on his offer to go and find him. We'll take turns keeping an eye out front." It was a statement rather than a question.

The heat of the day was building, the air sticky with humidity from the recent storms. It had been an unusually wet month. The group decided that the Pastor would head into town, Billy would work on the transfer arrangements, and the Kangaroo would lend a hand once the arrangements came through. Billy thought it would take at least a day to get through all the red tape. The rest of the crew would go on with their day as if everything was running as usual.

Elaine went inside and settled down in the office space at the rear of the clinic. She spent the next hour or so checking on her two patients and going through some of the villager's medical records. It was important, she felt, to be acquainted with the chronic conditions of as many of her new patients as possible. She wanted to do more, possibly arrange to make house calls, but the lack of personnel limited her. Finally, she set her head down on the desk for a moment's rest. It had been a long day so far. She fell asleep almost immediately.

Startled from her rest by Billy shaking her shoulder, she rubbed her eyes and glanced out the window. The sun was hanging low in the sky. Not quite dark, yet no longer light, a cooler breeze entered the space of the office. Billy addressed her quietly. "Hey, Doc, you've been crashed out for a while."

A light cotton sheet hung over her shoulders, lovingly placed there by Batilda, who'd been afraid she would catch a chill. Knowing she needed a rest, Batilda had let her sleep. She could hear voices from the treatment room and an engine running outside. "What's going on?" she asked, confused.

"The transfer. I've arranged it already. I was astounded that it went through so quickly."

"Who is it I hear speaking out there?"

"Government types, to coordinate the transfer." Billy anticipated her concern for Marty. "Don't worry," he whispered in her ear, "Jon has him stashed away in back."

"Why didn't you wake me?" she asked in a more irritable tone than she'd intended.

"Batilda said she would kill me."

"Fair enough." She shrugged and stood up.

"I was forced to wake you now, though." He backed away. "They say they need to speak to you."

Elaine stretched and went into the treatment area where the injured boy was resting. He looked good. His color was back to normal and the pain medications were obviously working. He had a happy-go-lucky smile on his face. Three other men were present at his bedside, two in uniform. The other was wearing a light-colored suit, sweat-stained and tailored from a cheap fabric.

"Are you the doctah?" The be-suited man asked Elaine in the standard island accent. Elaine introduced herself while the policemen stood shifty-eyed and silent. They were checking the place out. Dirty, and smelling bad, their olive drab shirts were unbuttoned halfway, shirttails partially untucked -- pistols at their sides. Their boots were caked with mud. Batilda would be beside herself, Elaine thought. "We are here to supervise the moving of your patient, ma'am. It's standard procedure."

One of the officers interrupted. "Dees your only patient today, doctah?" he asked.

"The only critical patient, yes. We've had a few outpatient calls, but nothing out of the ordinary."

"You may go on with your business, then, Doctah," the man in the suit declared. "I am, incidentally, the island's surgeon general. I will need some information and I will need some paperwork to be filled out."

The soldiers paced the room while Billy gave instructions on how to transfer the injured patient, along with the diagnosis and medical history. Elaine accepted a stack of forms from the surgeon general and used a tray to begin filling them out. A canvas stretcher was to be used to carry the patient to the ambulance, which was waiting outside. Old bloodstains were evident, and the stretcher's wood frame was splintered and in need of sanding and a coat of varnish. What they needed, Elaine thought, was a new stretcher.

One of the soldiers continued to walk down the row of treatment rooms, pausing to inspect each cubicle. When he reached the end of the corridor, where the desk and paperwork were located, he sifted through some loose sheets of paper on the desktop, and then rummaged through various file folders contained in the drawers under the desk. Elaine could see him, but was careful to behave as if everything was as normal as could be. Beneath her cool exterior, her mind raced, trying to recall any notes she'd left lying in open view. Small beads of sweat covered her forehead, which she wiped away with the back of her hand. "It's getting hot in here, isn't it," she mentioned to no one in particular.

"I believe, if my records are correct, that you are new to the Island. Isn't that correct, Doctah?" the Surgeon General asked.

"Yes, that's correct. I've been here a little over two weeks." It felt like an eternity.

"Well, don't worry, Doctah. By the time you're ready to leave our little paradise, you'll be accustomed to our weather."

"Right," she smiled. "Then it will be back to the frozen North."

## j. d. gordon

The Surgeon General pursed his lips and drew in a breath of air. "I can't begin to imagine the sensation of cold air upon my body. I've never experienced it. I was born and raised on the Island."

"And where did you attend medical school, sir?"

"In Mexico." He chose not to expand. "Well, I believe that should do it. We'll be on our way, then."

The officer who had been touring the facilities approached, and Elaine had to keep her fear in check. "You run a real clean hospeetal here, ma'am. You can be sure dat your patient will receive the best of care," the officer assured.

Elaine and Billy accompanied the officials as they carried the patient out to the ambulance, which looked more like a hearse. Originally painted red and white, there was a single light on the vehicle's roof. Rust ran along the bottom, stretching from front to back. A thick cloud of exhaust bellowed from the rear of the contraption, enveloping the patient and stretcher crew with toxic fumes as they loaded him in the rear. The officers sat up front and made no acknowledgment as they drove away, leaving a large cloud of exhaust and dust.

"Well, thank God that's over with." Elaine was relieved. Despite her catnap, she felt exhausted, and hungry. After a prompt from Billy, she headed to the dining room for a fruit salad made with mangoes, bananas, pineapple, and coconut.

After dinner, she went to check on Marty. He was sitting up in bed enjoying his own dinner and chatting with the Kangaroo, who had set him up in a little room in the back of his shop. An old cot had been placed in the corner, and the Aussie had swept out the place, knowing that Elaine would be uncomfortable leaving the man in a filthy space.

"Well, hello, boys," she said, glad to see that Marty's

condition had improved. "Shouldn't we move Marty back into the clinic?"

"We can if you like, lassie, but I think he's all the safer back here," the Kangaroo offered.

"Alright, I guess that's fine." She was in no mood to argue. "We'll see about getting you out of here tomorrow. Let's give you another day, though."

Marty nodded in acknowledgment.

With the sun now below the horizon, Elaine returned to her cabin. She threw herself down on the bed and thought to pick up the phone to make her regular call to her father. Seconds later, there was anxious knocking at her door. "Doctor, Doctor!" It was Batilda. "There are more vehicles coming down the road. They're armed but they don't look government troops! Come quick!"

j. d. gordon

## Chapter Eight

A heavy pour of Antigua rum chilled in a tumbler brimming with large ice cubes. The ice was beginning to melt, blending well with the caramel-colored liquor. This was how the Caretaker was dealing with the recently delivered stash of toy weaponry, and the loss of his hard earned cash. More precisely, the cash had been earned by the men and women that worked the fields surrounding The Plantation. People who lived in undeveloped community barracks built within the compound's tall stone walls.

For the most part, the workers were people recruited from some of the world's wealthier nations -- The United States, Canada, England, and other first-world countries. They were from all walks of life. The membership included poor, downtrodden individuals, looking for relief from their lives, and eccentric rich folks who had reached their maximum stress levels back at home. All of these people had fallen prey to the cool words and program descriptions presented by the recruiters from The Plantation. The poor were expected to give up all of their worldly goods, including any government assistance they were receiving, and the wealthy transferred all manner of funds to The Plantation's offshore accounts.

Once taken in, new members were indoctrinated through "self-realization," a euphemism for simple brainwashing, and through chemical therapy. It was the Caretaker's vision to create

## caribbean calling

something of a Brave New World, inspired by a novel by Aldous Huxley he'd read during high school, back in Tupelo.

Members lived in sparely-furnished community buildings and worked the Caretaker's poppy and marijuana fields. There were some legitimate, albeit less profitable, crops, as well. These were used to feed the community. The crops of the illegal variety were sold to increase the Caretaker's coffers. Control of the community was maintained through the use of medications, usually mixed into food and drink, along with some unique types of mind-control, which the Caretaker referred to as "psychotherapy." Reese held a doctorate in psychology, through an education his flock had financed during the early years.

The Caretaker had started off in life as a legitimate holy man, acting as a minister in a small town in Southern Mississippi. His flock had been devoted -- so devoted, in fact, that the Caretaker had developed alternative and very unique ideas concerning his ministry.

Today, the Caretaker was almost content. His Caribbean compound was expanding. He was a multi-millionaire. He controlled the lives of thousands of followers. While The Plantation had satellite facilities all around the globe, the majority of his followers found themselves living at the main Caribbean compound.

The earlier transaction of the day had been one part of a much larger plan. The Caretaker was collecting weapons, military equipment, and hired gunslingers. He had the intention of expanding his operation. Soon, The Plantation would encompass the entire island, not simply this little section where it now stood. Soon, the entire island of Capersdeed would be all his.

He took a long drag of rum from the tumbler, a luxury his flock was flatly denied. They'd all been called in for the day, safely tucked away from the goings-on outside. The Caretaker

## j. d. gordon

would be expecting some unusual guests in the next several days -- representatives from the Crow crime ring. Lester Crow was the head of what was called the "tropical crime syndicate," having inherited the business from his late father, Blackwell Crow, who had met his demise a year earlier during a kidnapping plot that had gone awry.

The Crow organization was to provide the merchandise that the Caretaker had been hoping to purchase. The commandant of the local police force had recommended them. After discovering the fake weaponry, the Caretaker had contacted the commandant, furious.

Now he sat in his luxurious private suite tucked away on the top floor of The Plantation's main building, waiting for reports from his troops. With twenty-foot-tall ceilings, the room was constructed from the finest imported Italian marble. In one corner, water cascaded down a twisting route, turning between small islands of bright green tropical foliage and rough stone. Large multicolored fragrant flowers filled the room with their scent. A spiral staircase ran up to a private rooftop deck where, between the skylights, grapevines twisted toward the sky, supported by lattice framework.

The main building had the look of any fine and exclusive resort. A grand reception hall greeted incoming members and visitors. In another wing of the building, a temple had been constructed for the Caretaker to deliver his sermons. A third wing consisted of administrative offices and classrooms. The fourth wing was reserved for the Caretaker, and no one entered without permission, which wasn't easily obtainable. As the largest wing of the structure, it served as his residence, as well as the living quarters for his private little army and his assistants.

Excavation had been done to provide space beneath the building for a weapons storehouse and for a garage. A second, off site location housed his private boat, as well as a couple of military-style watercraft and another small compliment of hired mercenaries.

After a knock, an officer was given permission to enter. Invited to stand before him, a dark-clad soldier made a report to his boss, "We followed Crane and his crew and overtook them in the rain forest. The truck they were in tipped over and crashed. We doubled back and were fired upon. Two of our men were hit. We brought their bodies back with us to dispose of…"

The Caretaker interrupted. "Did you retrieve the case?"

"No, sir."

"What happened? You said you found the truck," the Caretaker inquired.

"One of them got away. We recovered two bodies, Crane and the skinny, stupid one. We couldn't find the other one, though. We searched everywhere."

"Well," the Caretaker paused in thought for a moment, "It will be difficult for the third man to get off the island. I have the local police conducting a search. I don't quite trust the police, though." He waved towards the door. "You and your men clean up and get a little rest. You'll be going out again tonight if the police are unproductive." The soldier saluted the Caretaker, turned, and exited the office.

The Caretaker sat quietly, hands clasped and elbows atop his wide desk. His two bodyguards stood flanking him. Beyond their duties to provide him personal protection, the two were second and third in the ranking system of The Plantation.

"Mr. Stick," the Caretaker addressed the larger of the two. The Black gentlemen stepped forward. "I'll want you to lead another expedition tonight. Assemble a team and plan out a search. I want that man, and, more importantly, I want that case found. Find my money!"

"Yes, sir." The man excused himself from the room.

"Mr. Baron," he addressed his other subordinate. "Keep the followers on ice for now. The commandant has assured me that Lester Crow himself may come to diffuse this situation. If not him, then he will send one of his high-ranking officers. I don't know when, but he could be here shortly. He'll come by helicopter, so get someone to clean up the stockade." The Baron left to arrange for the imminent arrival of the crime lord.

The ersatz evangelist sat back in his desk chair, deep in thought, daydreaming about the future. In his mind's eye, he conjured up visions of his perfect island paradise -- thousands of drugged-up workers, an army of hired mercenaries, and his coffers stuffed with money. He decided that perhaps it would be a good idea to discuss some of his ideas with this Lester Crow. He would be a valuable ally when it came to dealing with the commandant, who would cause difficulties when it came time for the uprising. He was certain his band of hired guns could overcome the local police and military forces, which was one and the same, but the extra support would no doubt be helpful.

The Caretaker drained his second glass of the smooth rum. He set his head back against the silk-covered upholstery of his wing-backed chair and drifted off to sleep. It was some time before a knock on the door startled him from his dreams of conquest. It was light knock, most likely his assistant, Pusser. The door swung open. "Sir, Mr. Stick has assembled a team to go out. He's waiting in the garage."

"Thank you, Pusser. What time is it?" he asked.

"It's about seven, sir, in the evening."

"I can tell it's the evening, Pusser. Please, tell Mr. Stick that I will be along shortly," he ordered.

After waiting a half-hour, the Caretaker strolled into the

## caribbean calling

garage area. The bright overhead lights created round, perfectly-spaced circles on the cement floor. A line of twelve men, all dressed in black military fatigues, stood at attention in a straight line in front of a row of vehicles. All manner of gun barrels glistened in the light like naked, wet branches -- a rifle here, a sub-machine gun there, and even a shotgun or two. A grenade launcher sat towards the end of the line.

Behind the paramilitary men, a line of vehicles were prepared for the night's activities. Two fast-attack jeeps would carry two men apiece. Two more standard, old-fashioned jeeps would carry crews of four. These vehicles were unarmed, but were capable of maneuvering the tightest jungle pathways and the roughest terrain that the island could offer.

The Caretaker walked along the row of fighters, very much like a general inspecting his troops before battle. Pusser was right on his heels. At the end of the line, Mr. Stick waited. He stopped and nodded at the leader of this pack. Then, he turned on his heels and began to address the soldiers, pacing back and forth before the line.

"Gentlemen, I assume Mr. Stick has filled you in on your job tonight, and how very important it is. Whoever discovers the individual we are seeking, and the missing... attaché case...can expect a nice bonus applied to their next paycheck." He paused for effect. "In addition, you should not expect any interference from the local law enforcement. If, however, they should choose to cause any trouble whatsoever, please be sure to make them very sorry." Turning in the direction of the garage's exit, he stopped one last time. "Happy hunting, gentlemen."

As he left the building, he could hear Mr. Stick relaying orders, "The man we're looking for was wounded. We have checked the Health Center with no results. There is another option for a man needing emergency medical care -- the aid station."

## j. d. gordon

Stick went on to explain the plan. The soldiers were to split into two groups. Plantation crews down on the docks were scouring the harbor and patrolling the beaches and the waters surrounding the island. They had been hard at work for most of the day. The two land-based parties were to split the island in half. The soldiers were to check any institutions or buildings that would take in a stray and injured person. They were to search churches, schools, fire stations, private homes, if necessary, and, most importantly, the aid station.

When he gave the order, the men mounted their vehicles. The sharp sound of motors coming to life filled the garage. Mr. Stick stood up in the back of his jeep and watched as half of the team split off and exited through the rear of The Plantation compound. Stick's path trailed around the main building and the barracks, slipping between the perimeter wall and through the main yard. The guard at the front gate nodded as he lifted the barrier out of the way. Out on the road, the fields where workers toiled during the days were silent, the crops swaying in the slight evening breeze as the vehicles charged past.

The tropical air was thick and humid. The night's winds were not strong enough to draw the moisture away from the small land mass. Mr. Stick savored the sweet taste of the breeze on his lips for a moment, then directed his driver and sat down in the back of the jeep. The road headed west, and the crew followed a gentle grade that crested the wide range of tall hills. The sun was hanging low in the distance and a thin layer of clouds stretched across the horizon, casting eerie shadows on the landscape. As the sun took its final bow for the day, the two vehicles of armed men approached their first stop -- the aid station run by the Caribbean Relief Corps.

Caribbean Calling

## Chapter Nine

The cold water spilling from the multi-leveled jets in Marci's shower startled Eddie as it splashed against his sun-baked skin. Then, as the hot water began to overcome the cold, he jumped out of the way to avoid the blistering pain of the heat against his red skin. He felt like a lobster dumped into a pot of boiling water. Eventually, the water tempered, and Ed was able to prepare himself for his first day of work with Mr. Klein.

His starting day had been pushed back a week, thanks to Marci. In the meanwhile, the couple had enjoyed themselves. On his third day in town, he and Marci had taken an afternoon cruise on a refurbished genuine pirate ship. After leaving Tampa, the wooden ship headed south down the coastline. Rum punch, sangria, and cold beer flowed freely. After an hour of sailing, the chow had been set out -- burgers and dogs, mac and cheese, and a huge pot of sautéed onions simmered in a tangy bar-b-que sauce. An enormous platter of coconut-crusted cinnamon rolls followed.

Cruise guests were entertained by playing "walk the plank." There was also an old rope off to the side where folks could swing out and drop into the salt water below. It was nothing more than a wooden diving board stretched out from the port side of the tall ship, but the experience was enhanced by crew members decked out in pirate garb prodding their guests down the "plank" by poking them with cheap plastic swords.

## j. d. gordon

Eddie had a nice buzz going shortly after starting out, his brain cells immersed in a bath of rum. He'd become giddy as a schoolboy once he'd spied the swinging rope. He and Marci lined up in a row of pink-colored tourists, behind an older couple from Maine. It was the first day of the couple's vacation. They were still pasty white.

As the line progressed, Ed asked a crew member to refill his plastic mug with the tasty rum drink. Finally, he stepped up onto the port beam and grasped the line of dried hemp. The rope was frayed and stained with use. He glanced down, peering into the sea. It was an old habit. He'd seen *Jaws* one too many times as a kid.

The water below seemed to lack any sinister-looking dorsal fins, so he grabbed a hold of the rope, lifted his feet from the edge, and swung away from the ship in a smooth upward motion. As he and the rope began the return trip back in the direction of the ship, he found the courage to release his grip. The water was shallow. Ed could see plant life swaying in the currents churning near the seabed.

Seconds later, Marci had come plunging in, practically landing on top of the submersed firefighter. The two tumbled around, Eddie playfully pulling the thin string securing Marci's top, and then they frolicked in the warm water until the crew called the passengers back for the return trip to Tampa. Although the city's skyline had never been out of sight, the real world had been left behind, at least for a couple of hours.

Eddie and Marci stepped off the boat onto the pier, where a small waterside bar beckoned them. Sitting together at the end of the bar, they'd shared a Long Island Iced Tea served in a bright green child's plastic sand bucket decorated with fluorescent orange lobsters.

The bucket of tea was a bit too much for Marci. On the cab

117

## Caribbean Calling

ride back to Harbor Island, she'd taken on a pale hue. Eddie had barely been able to roll down the window before she'd stuck her head out, exposed to traffic, and hurled out the side. The cabbie hadn't been too pleased about that, but Eddie gave him an extra big tip, and he'd driven away with a smile.

The decision to take the extra time had been difficult, but well worth it. It pulled at Eddie's Midwestern work ethics to be irresponsible. In any event, the recreational part of the trip was over, and it was now time to get to business.

Ed toweled himself off and applied a light coat of vitamin E infused aloe. Klein had told him that the uniform for the first day would be casual, so he chose a crisp pair of khaki pants and a white cotton short-sleeved shirt. Marci gave him a peck on the cheek and told him she would be waiting for him as he headed out the door. He couldn't help but wondering how long the affair -- this little fantasy world with Marci -- would go on if he decided to keep the job. Did Marci think he was going to move into the condo with her? Were they now an official couple?

Questions continued to run through Ed's mind as he stuffed his bar cash into one of his front pockets. The pair had gone out last night, one last fling before settling down and getting to work, and the wad was now a jumble of crumpled five and one dollar bills. He'd have to hit the ATM, again.

Down in the lobby of Marci's building, he scanned the circular drive in front of the main door. A black sedan, a Lincoln, idled nearby. Eddie tapped on the passenger side window. The driver looked over and rolled the window down. "Are you from K and K?" Eddie inquired of the driver, who was tan-skinned, and wearing a dark suit and mirrored sunglasses.

"That depends. Are you Ed Gilbert?" The chauffeur read the name off of a small card he was holding in the palm of his hand.

"That's me," Eddie answered. The driver opened his door to

get out of the vehicle, but Eddie jumped into the back seat before he could pick his ass up off of the leather. Eddie slid up to the front of the passenger compartment, within earshot of the driver. "So, do you work for K and K, or are you from a service or something?" he asked.

"No, sir. I'm Mr. Klein's personal driver." It turned out he lived in an apartment on the businessman's estate. Klein didn't live within the Tampa city limits. He lived in a high price burb outside the city, where mansions sat on vast lots.

The drive to the office building in Tampa proper was short. When the limo turned into a circular drive in front of one of Tampa's skyscrapers, a doorman opened the rear door and Eddie stepped out and said "good morning." He wasn't sure if he was supposed to tip the guy or not, so he handed him a five dollar bill, one of a few he kept stashed for such an occasion.

Eddie entered the building through an automatic sliding glass door. The lobby was tall, with lots of plants, shiny brass, and marble. The windows in front allowed for ample natural lighting.

A uniformed guard behind a tall desk addressed him as he strode through the lobby. "Excuse me, sir, may I help you?"

For an instant, Eddie worried about what kind of organization he was getting himself into. Although the fire service was run in paramilitary fashion, with a slew of ranks and regulations, things around the firehouse were pretty laid back when they weren't on a run. Firefighters sat around in a casual manner at the station, shirts left untucked with slippers on their feet instead of boots. Eddie hoped he could deal with this change in his professional surroundings.

It was a trial run, he reminded himself. He could always return to the fire department after a month, no one would be the wiser.

## Caribbean Calling

"I'm Eddie Gilbert. I'm here for Mr. Klein."

The guard nodded and picked up a telephone handset. After a brief conversation, he hung up. "Take the last elevator on the left to the fortieth floor, that's the top floor. You'll be directed from there." The guy was all business.

Eddie entered the elevator and searched for the button for the fortieth floor. He was about to exit and ask, and then noticed one button above the fire department control labeled 'Penthouse.' He jammed his thumb into the middle of the small ring and the doors closed. The elevator ascended the forty floors in seconds.

When the doors slid open, Ed found himself in a modest-sized but comfortably-appointed reception suite. A middle-aged woman sat behind a wide desk. Her black hair was pulled up into a tight bun and she was professionally dressed. A pair of dark sunglasses sat on top of the desk, near the edge, next to a tall glass containing something orange. The woman sat, typing away on a computer keyboard, when Eddie stepped into the room.

"Have a seat, Mr. Gilbert. Mr. Klein will be with you shortly." Her fingers didn't miss a beat as she greeted him.

Eddie examined his surroundings. A corner-piece sectional wrapped around the wall to his right, and a large, L-shaped table squatted in front, covered with various magazines. To the left, in the corner, a pair of lounge chairs shared space with their companion ottomans. They looked mighty comfortable. Eddie took a seat in one and felt as if he should have a stogie in one hand and a snifter of Cognac in the other.

He watched as the woman typed away. Large doors marked with big gold 'K' stood on either side of her, and between the doors, behind the woman, a gold cursive "and" completed the decorative company initials. Eddie thought it was a little tacky, but it wasn't his office. Plants set about the place gave the room

# j. d. gordon

a fresh scent, and overhead Muzak filled the air. Eddie couldn't quite make the tune out, but it sounded like something by Air Supply.

A speaker came to life on the secretary's desk, "Mrs. Bee, please send in Mr. Gilbert." Ed recognized Bruce Klein's voice. After all, he'd spent an extended visit at the man's country house less than a year ago, after he'd rescued his daughter.

Mrs. Bee looked up from her project for a split-second. "Mr. Klein will see you now." The woman motioned to the door on the right with a nod of her head.

Ed stood up and walked toward the door. As he reached to grab the doorknob, the door opened by itself. Stepping into the office, Eddie's first thought was that it was spectacular. The thirty-foot ceiling held two enormous skylights, and Ed could see the building's twin tower stretching into the clear blue sky. One large, puffy cloud floated above.

The exterior walls were built of glass, with steel framework supporting the large sheets. Two separate glass doors provided access to a balcony, which stretched the entire length of the glass walls. A brass banister defined the patio's perimeter. The city and bay views were incredible. Eddie noticed someone standing out there, a man wearing a wide-brimmed hat and a gaudy Hawaiian shirt. He was smoking a cigar.

"Eddie, my boy! Come in, come in! I've been looking forward to seeing you again." The business tycoon stood up from behind his desk and walked across the expanse of his office, closing the distance between the two, with an outstretched hand and a warm smile. The men greeted each other with a hearty handshake, and then a quick, backslapping embrace. Klein was decked out in a pair of shorts and a golf shirt. Apologizing for the casual attire, he explained that he'd had an early golf game that had run a bit late.

## Caribbean Calling

Escorting Eddie to a desk in the center of the expansive room, Klein invited him to sit. The place looked like the big loft apartments that Eddie had seen advertised in the papers back in Chicago. A kitchen area, an entertainment section complete with a giant flat screen television, impressive speakers, deep cushioned recliners, and a wet bar completed the single man's paradise. Ed wanted to ask if he could shack up right there. A rough brick wall separated what Eddie assumed to be Bruce's partner's office on the other side.

"So, Ed," Klein had a mischievous grin on his face, "how was your week with Marci?" He finished the question up with a wink.

"Yeah," Ed smiled bashfully, "we had a nice week. I guess I'll be staying with her during my time here."

"Are you okay with that, Ed? I can set you up somewhere else," Klein offered.

"No, I think I'll be okay for now. How's Jennifer?"

"She's doing well. Thanks for asking. She's going to school out in Colorado now. She's not sure what she wants to do with herself these days. It's been difficult for her, as you can imagine."

Eddie nodded. "Hopefully, time will do its job. I still think about it a lot, myself. There were some very frightening moments."

During the next hour or so, Klein laid out the job and what he expected from Eddie. Basically, the work seemed to Ed to be like some kind of high-class courier. He'd be transferring important documents and other valuable items from place to place. He couldn't help but feel disappointed. An expensive messenger, that's what he was going to leave his life at the firehouse behind for? At least, he thought, he wouldn't be sitting behind the desk down in the lobby asking folks for their identification.

122

# j. d. gordon

"I know you're familiar with firearms, Ed. I've got something for you." Klein slid his top desk drawer out and grabbed a small set of keys. He walked over to the wet bar, where a black and white photo of Humphrey Bogart smoking a cigarette while standing at the helm of a small fishing boat. He had a long look on his mug.

"Can I get you something to drink, Ed?" Klein asked as he poured himself a tumbler of Dewar's. The fireman declined the offer. "I have something for you here...a tool of the trade."

Klein turned to the picture on the wall. Like something out of an old detective movie, he pulled one edge aside and revealed a safe. After spinning the code, he began pulling items out until he came to a brown leather case, which he set on the bar's counter.

"That's yours, Ed." He walked back to his desk. "And these are your credentials," he added, displaying a small packet.

Ed picked up the case and unwrapped the leather strap that bound it together. Inside the case was a blue automatic -- a Colt .45 automatic, model 1911A1.

"Nice pistol, Mr. Klein. Thanks."

"It's not a pistol, Ed, it's a classic firearm." He extended his hand. "Your credentials for carrying a concealed weapon are in here. You need to keep these on you at all times." Klein grabbed another leather item and tossed it to Eddie. It was a shoulder holster made of soft, tan, and well-oiled leather.

"Thank you," Ed offered, unsure of what else to say.

The businessman picked up an envelope. "Take this with you today, too. It's your contract. Take a look at it tonight, and we'll discuss everything in the morning."

Klein sat down, the morning sunlight cascading across his desk. The man out on the balcony puffed away on his cigar,

## caribbean calling

staring out at the city and bay. Whoever he was, he had a real good view. Ed decided not to ask.

"Well, it's been nice catching up, son. I'm going to send you back down to the lobby. A fellow named Rodger Clark will meet you there. He'll get you all set up and acclimated to your new environment. I hope things go well. I'd like to keep you on the payroll."

As soon as the elevator doors opened on the lobby, the situation hit him. Here he was, in a huge office building, in downtown Tampa, clutching an automatic weapon in his hands. He stepped out into the lobby and asked the man at the desk about this Rodger Clark fellow he was supposed to be meeting.

Bruce Klein stepped out onto the balcony overlooking the city. A strong breeze was coming off the bay and carried with it the scent of cigar smoke. "That's Edward Gilbert. He's around for a little while trying the job out. I was thinking of hooking him up with you if the need were to arise."

"Gilbert? The firefighter from up north?" Klein responded to the man's question with a nod. "He was with Brighton, right? On Brighton's last job?" Brighton Sparks had been one of Klein's men. He'd met his demise during Jennifer's kidnapping.

"Yes, Mario, he was."

Mario was a rather rough looking individual. His colorful shirt was wide open, displaying a scarred, hairy stomach that hung over his khaki cut-offs. A necklace of multicolored beads hung around his thick neck.

"I'm open to it, I guess. I've got no doubt you've checked him out. You think he'll stay on?"

"Maybe. We'll see how things work out."

# j. d. gordon

"Alright, then."

"Where are you headed for the time-being?"

"I'm heading down to the Keys, spend a little time on the water. You know how to reach me."

"I'll be in touch."

The meeting ended when Mario stubbed his cigar out, stepped back into the office, and headed for the elevator, leaving Klein alone with the sun and the breeze.

The guard in the lobby asked Eddie to wait while he contacted Rodger Clark. Eddie walked in circles, checking the place out. He was impressed with the luxurious appointments of the building and was lost in thought when he felt a tap on his shoulder.

"Are you Eddie Gilbert?" The man extended his hand. He was dressed in a tailored dark blue suit. His wavy blonde hair was cut short, his nails were manicured, and his shave was razor-close.

"Yes, I'm Eddie."

"Great," the serious man replied, giving Eddie the once-over. "Mr. Klein has asked me to get you situated. We're going to have to do something about your wardrobe, there. And we're going to have to do something about that pistol."

Without further ado, Mr. Clark led Eddie toward the exit, where a company car was waiting in the drive. It wasn't anything fancy -- a standard black Lincoln. The two sat in the back of the car and engaged in some small talk until the car arrived at their destination. Eddie described his background with the fire department and the time he'd spent in the navy as a

## Caribbean Calling

medic assigned to a platoon of Marine infantry. He avoided the story about he'd come to know Bruce Klein.

Rodger Clark turned out to be a wannabe lawyer turned police officer, turned security expert. He'd graduated from the University of Southern Florida about ten years before with a degree in political science. He'd wanted to go to law school, but his grades hadn't been good enough to get him his fancy piece of paper. He'd then applied and tested for the Tampa Police Department, leaving that position when his father, a Tampa politician, had arranged for a spot with the Klein security forces. He couldn't pass it up. The salary Klein offered dwarfed what the Tampa police force could.

The Lincoln pulled up in front of a Bigsby and Kruther's shop, a high-end, retail clothing store. "What are we doing here?" Ed asked.

"A benefit of the job. Uniforms."

The two entered the shop and were greeted by a suave Italian salesman in a Hug Boss suit. With his black hair greased up and pulled back in a long ponytail, Ed thought he looked like a character from The Sopranos.

"How are you, Mr. Clark? You have another member of the team, do you?"

"Yeah, but we're not going with the full boat right away. He's a temp for now."

The next two hours were filled with the trying on of different suits and shoes, and the selection of ties, shirts, and socks. Fifteen thousand dollars later, Eddie had five new complete outfits. He was floored. If Klein was working on getting him to stick around, this was a hell of a start. The salesman announced that the finery would be available for pick-up after six.

It was after lunchtime when the two emerged from the high-end men's boutique. They stopped to eat thin slices of pizza and drink cokes at a small place close to the shop. The next stop was a police supply store where they picked up a lightweight bulletproof vest. The salesman boasted that the garment would protect the wearer from most ballistics, even at close range. Eddie knew that in reality, the vest would protect him from most handguns, but anything larger, like rifle ammunition, would penetrate. He kept his mouth shut, though.

During the rest of the afternoon, Rodger bounced Eddie around the city. There were six different buildings that he would be visiting on a regular basis, transferring classified papers and large sums of cash from place to place. In effect, Eddie was an expensive, armed messenger. The longest haul was an occasional drive out to one of K and K's plants. There were three in the area, spin-offs of the company's main holdings, which, for the most part, involved shipping. K and K owned storehouses and docks in most port cities around the globe. Clark explained that the job would take Ed out to those ports of call.

For most of the local work, Ed would be using a company car, the standard black Lincoln. Black wasn't the best color in the sub-tropical climate of Tampa, but they looked good, and the maintenance staff kept the air conditioning in top-notch condition. The longer hauls would call for boats, planes, or helicopters.

The last duty of the day was to return to Bigsby and Kruther's to pick up the 'uniforms.' After that, Rodger deposited Eddie at the door of Marci's building. He bundled his new haberdashery in his arms and made his way to the elevators. When he arrived at the condo, Marci was sitting on the balcony reading a book. He set the pile down on the couch, grabbed a cold Corona, and joined her. After an alfresco dinner she ordered in, they played hide the baloney for a while and crashed early.

The rest of week was spent with Rodger, getting

## Caribbean Calling

indoctrinated into the system. Each morning, Ed would groom himself, strap on his protective vest, slip into a tailored suit, and fix himself up with his fancy shoulder holster. The feeling of the weapon at his side was one he would have to get used to.

By the end of the week, he realized that it wouldn't be long before the job would become tedious. Each morning, he and Rodger would receive a list of assignments. The list detailed the pick-ups and drop-offs that were to take place that day. At pick-ups, they would accept a standard black or brown briefcase. Some of the cases felt light, almost empty. Others were heavy, as if stuffed with gold. Perhaps they were, Ed thought, but he wouldn't dream of asking. His job was to grab the case, handcuff it to his wrist, and carry it off to the assigned destination.

He'd find himself daydreaming about getting back to work at the firehouse when a Tampa rig screamed by with lights and sirens wailing.

On his first day out on his own, he was assigned a run almost two hours to the north. His assignment was to drop a small bag off to a butler at the location's main house. The bag wasn't secured and felt almost empty. It was getting close to lunchtime, and Ed spied a small café right next to the beach, a typical gulf-side establishment. He pulled into the gravel lot, in sight of the water breaking on the rocks. Music played in the distance, an old tune by Jim Croce, *Bad, Bad Leroy Brown*. Ed rolled up the window and shut down the engine. Perhaps things weren't so bad with this position, he thought to himself. Ready to grab the bag and bring it in, his curiosity got the best of him. Almost without thought, he unzipped the bag and sifted through its contents.

Inside, he found a skimpy bikini, a tube of suntan lotion, three CD's, and a white greeting card envelope with a red and silver wax seal in the shape of a rose on the back seam. Hit with guilt, he tossed the card back into the bag, zipped it up, and dumped it onto the floor of the back seat.

## j. d. gordon

Humming along with the Croce tune as he stepped into the diner, Ed surveyed the place. A long bar looked out over a deck where a small hotel was visible down the beach a ways. The gulf waters shimmered beyond the sand. People stretched out on the beach, a few swimming in the warm salt water. Most of the café's patrons were sitting on the deck, enjoying the view. Ed took a spot at the bar.

A young girl, the bartender, came over with a menu and he asked for a Red Stripe. While he was waiting, he activated his cell phone and dialed the number for the firehouse back home. It was his shift day, and he thought he'd give the guys a shout out and see how things were going in his absence.

Caribbean Calling

## Chapter Ten

While the private phone line rang in the empty firehouse, the firefighters of Salt Creek were trying to control a blaze that had engulfed one of Salt Creek's luxury homes. Hank Brickman was riding backwards on the first engine to arrive on the scene. His position on the rig placed him on the nozzle, the first to attack the burning building. The alarm had come in as a confirmed structure fire. The police officers on the scene radioed that there was smoke apparent, and that the residents of the home had all been evacuated.

Hank stepped off the rig and noticed a couple of police officers speaking with the family, all huddled together, fending off the cold. He had some brief sympathy for the family, considering that their home was on fire, but at least they were safe. That was a load off any firefighter's mind. Then, the objective was to fight the fire, not to search for victims, or worse, charred corpses.

The officer ordered Hank to pull a cross lay. A hose line was already tied into the vehicle's pump. Three firefighters were assigned to the vehicle, meaning that only two would make the original attack. One would stay behind to work the pumps. As Hank pulled the heavy hose line from the side of the engine, he could hear his officer confirming with the family that everyone had made it out of the house safely.

One of the windows on the second floor had already been

blown out. Flames danced and smoke billowed out of the opening. The outside of a brick chimney ran up the side of the home where the fire was located. The front door was wide open. As Hank and his officer pulled the line up the small flight of stairs that led to the front door, the two could hear the sounds of other companies arriving on the scene. Placing their cold air masks on their faces, they activated the system and waited for the hose to come to life.

Once the line was rigid, the officer and firefighter switched on their hand lanterns, secured their hand tools in their belts, crouched down, and entered the structure. The smoke and the heat in the foyer were light. The men crawled in deeper toward the direction of the fire, and in a short time, they could see flames bouncing about around a corner. The smoke was getting heavier and the heat more intense and Hank's ax kept slipping out of his belt as he crawled along the floor. He took a moment to secure it.

After a few more moments and a few more feet, the men were staring at the fire. The other companies were being deployed as needed, and must have been assigned to Hank's line. Suddenly, it became easier to maneuver the rigid and heavy hose. Smoke was collecting near the ceiling, and if the blaze went unchecked much longer, the gasses would heat up and flash over, a situation no firefighter wanted to be a part of.

Hank adjusted the bale on the line and released a rushing stream of water. His first attack was directed at the smoke churning around near the ceiling. He wanted to cool the temperature of the room before advancing farther. The main body of the fire was on the other side of the room, spreading toward what Hank thought was the kitchen. The attack did the job. The firefighters could feel the difference in temperature almost right away. They crawled farther into the room.

Once they were in an effective range, Hank sat up on his knees and braced himself before letting a long stream of water

## Caribbean Calling

quench the burning material. The fire screamed and crackled in defiance. Steam filled the space of the room. The fire was checked, but for only a moment. As soon as Hank closed the bale, the flames returned with ferocity.

Hank and his officer had to reposition themselves in order to get a better line of attack on the fire. Hank ran his gloved hand over the plastic shield of his face-piece in an effort to see through the smoke and steam. He opened the bale once again, longer this time. The blaze decreased in size but didn't submit. It was almost as if this fire was determined to consume the house. Hank felt a hand pull on his right shoulder. He could barely make out the form of the officer.

"We're pulling out!" the officer hollered. His voice was muffled and sounded far away. "The second floor is fully engulfed! We have to move fast!" Hank could make out the sound of an air horn blasting three times in the distance -- the alarm was used to warn firefighters to pull out of the building.

As they began to make their way out of the room, the ceiling above the two firefighters collapsed. Hank fell forward with the impact, and was forced to the floor. The plastic shield of his face mask had cracked down the center, and he couldn't breathe. The seal of the face piece had been broken, leaving his air supply to rush through the breach. Attempting to stand, Hank could feel the heat of burning debris inching down through the fire retardant material of his protective gear. His personal alert device, which was attached to his breathing apparatus, started squawking. The unit was designed to emit a loud tone if a firefighter stopped moving for a set period of time, usually between thirty and sixty seconds.

Suddenly, Hank could feel someone pulling on his legs. One of his leather boots slipped an inch or so, and Hank could feel hands readjusting their grip. Then another set of hands joined in the struggle. A moment later, he felt his body being dragged along the floor. Charred bits of carpet and wood flashed in front of him. Then he was out on the porch, where two other firefighters helped him to his feet. Able to stand on his own, he surveyed the scene around him as his fellow rescue workers helped him away from the front of the building.

Several vehicles were on the scene now. An officer in a white helmet glanced in Hank's direction as he issued orders through a lapel microphone attached to his portable radio. Dark gray smoke drifted across the scene where firefighters ran back and forth, some toting ladders, others pulling hoses. Groups of bystanders watched as the scene unfolded before their eyes, police officers keeping them at a safe distance.

Hank was escorted to the back of an ambulance nearby, where paramedics assisted him in removing his protective gear. An oxygen mask was applied before they gave him the once over. The officer in charge of the scene glanced over to see how Hank was doing. The two men made eye contact, and Hank gave the officer a thumbs up to let the officer know he was alright.

The phone continued to ring with no answer. "The guys must be out on a run," Ed muttered to himself. The Bartender sat the Red Stripe on the counter in front of Eddie and took his order for an eggplant sandwich and Cajun fries.

He'd call back in a day or two to check up on his buddies. For now, he'd have a brewski and enjoy the sun.

## Chapter Eleven

Doctor Keller sat straight up in her cot, alarmed by Batilda's tone. "What now?" she thought to herself. She ran to her armoire and threw on a pair of khaki shorts, sandals, and a fresh scrub shirt. The old screen door creaked as she opened it and stepped outside.

"I already ran and got Jon. He and Billy should be up front already," Batilda panted, sweat running down the sides of her face.

Elaine raced to the front of the medical building. Jonathan was nowhere to be seen, but Billy was standing on the front porch with a quizzical look on his face. Elaine joined him while Batilda disappeared out of sight. Two vehicles screeched to a halt -- one a jeep carrying four mean-looking military types. A big Black guy, who took up almost the entire rear area of the old jeep, jumped out before the men in the second vehicle. All approached the two aid workers in a threatening manner.

"What's going on here?" Billy inquired calmly, considering that the men in the smaller vehicle were brandishing guns.

"We're looking for a man. He's injured and a fugitive from justice." The large Black man's tone was threatening.

"Some of your men were out here earlier," Elaine offered. "We told them, just as I'll tell you, that there is no one here who is out of the ordinary."

Her answer didn't satisfy the dark giant. Mr. Stick motioned to his soldiers to follow as he strode up the short stairway. He pushed Elaine out of the way as she attempted to protest his actions, and the soldiers still on the roadway shouldered their weapons. There was no stopping them. The gunmen entered the building.

Elaine and Billy followed as the men ransacked the medical center. Powerless, they watched as the place was ripped apart. Unable to attain any fruits from their labor, the goons then evacuated the building. Mr. Stick set about surveying the aid compound. His minions followed as he traversed the perimeter of the building. Once he reached the rear of the structure, he stopped in his tracks, Elaine and Billy right on his heels.

There, right in front of them, Jonathan limped along toward the trees, supporting the injured Marty as the two tried to make an escape. The giant pointed the tip of his Russian-made assault rifle to the sky and pulled the trigger. The entire magazine emptied in one long roll of thunder. Mr. Stick had made his point. The two escapees stopped moving and stood stock-still.

Mr. Stick stepped forward and grabbed Marty by the scruff of the neck, leaving Jonathan no choice but to step away. It was either give up the goods, or be mowed down by a hail of streaking bullets.

Stick threw Marty to the ground and he screamed in pain as the stitches in his shoulder ripped apart.

"Where's the case?" Stick screamed at him, spittle flying. Marty responded with a pathetic groan. "Where's the fucking case?" This time, he emphasized the question with a kick to Marty's shoulder, where fresh blood was soaking through a thick cotton bandage.

"I don't know, man. It was lost in the wreck."

## Caribbean Calling

"Bullshit! Drag this piece of crap around to the jeep. We're heading home."

Instantly, Elaine turned defiant. "Where do you think you're taking him?"

"None of your bid'niz, bitch! If you were a smart girl, you'd stay out of this!" His voice was thick with anger.

"Like hell! That's my patient!" Billy knocked her in the ribs with his elbow -- harder than he'd intended. She seemed not to even notice. "There must be some kind of law on this godforsaken island! You can't go around dragging sick patients off...My god!" Elaine gasped as a gunshot rang out. Mr. Stick wobbled like a Weeble -- but unlike a Weeble, Mr. Stick fell down.

The leader's associates homed in on the source of the gunfire. Two more reports echoed before they had time to react. One of the men was grazed by a rifle shell that Jonathan had loosed in his direction. With a classic M1 stuffed against his shoulder, he worked the trigger. The mercenaries returned fire, automatic weapons ammunition kicking up dust as the pieces of lead slammed into the ground around the big Australian. The gunmen adjusted their fire and riddled the man from Down Under. Jonathon fell to the ground with a dull thud, the M1 rifle dropping across his torso as he drew his final breath.

All was silent for a second or two. The soldiers were the first to react. Two of them began to examine Mr. Stick, while the fast attack vehicle barreled around the corner. Stick's features had taken on a grim expression. He was still alive, but his breathing was quick and shallow. Marty was lying still, as well. Elaine stared at first, at a total loss as to what to do. Other aid workers stumbled out of the buildings, wondering what had happened.

Stick pulled one of his men closer, giving him instructions. "Listen to me. Never mind my injuries. Continue to search this place until the briefcase is located, do you hear? Take the stubborn doctor lady and the fugitive to the jeep and watch them very carefully. Radio for the second team to meet us here." His voice began to lose force. "Once the reinforcements arrive, gather all these fucking aid workers together and take them back to The Plantation. Put them in the stockade. And execute anyone who fights back!"

Elaine tended to Marty's wound as best she could while sitting in the back of an old jeep under the watch of an armed thug. The second team had arrived and deployed themselves throughout the compound. Elaine could hear horrific screams and the crack of weapons.

Stick was sitting in the front seat of the fast-attack vehicle, slumped over with his head resting on the roll bar. Another soldier appeared, jumped in the driver's seat and took off, away from the station.

For the next thirty minutes, Elaine sat helplessly. If she moved, she'd be shot. She had no doubts about that. She was horrified by the murder of her Australian friend, and she had no clue what had happened to her teammates. The screams had been her last memory. Finally, the crew emerged from the building and took their places in their vehicles.

As they approached the gates of The Plantation's tall perimeter walls, the guard allowed access, nodding with a smile as they drove past. Elaine, terrified, looked around at the barrack-style buildings and felt impending doom. She put her head down and sobbed until a man struck her in the stomach with a rifle butt. She lifted her head to find herself in a large, enclosed garage.

Mr. Stick was being removed from the passenger seat of the fast attack vehicle. Men carried him to a door and then disappeared. Another soldier came around and dragged Marty away, leaving her alone with several other soldiers who avoided making eye contact with her. The remaining men lined up in a straight row in front of the row of fighting vehicles. What they were doing, she had no idea. So she sat and waited.

It wasn't long before an entourage of strangely-dressed men broke the silence in the garage. Two wore long white robes -- one a short, fat man with a bald head. The man walking in front was tall and thin. He moved gracefully. The third man was a hulk dressed in a military-style dark uniform. With his bristly hair and crooked nose, he looked mean.

"Well, well, what do we have here? You're the physician that works over at the aid station?" the thin one asked.

"Doctor Elaine Keller," she responded unsteadily.

"Such a noble cause you've taken on. I respect that. I assume you're from a wealthy family?" the Caretaker continued.

Although there were a few former doctors amongst his followers, by the time they reached The Plantation, their knowledge and skills were useless. The drugs and mind-control techniques turned them into automatons. The Caretaker relied on the medical facilities provided by the government of Capersdeed. If one of his flock fell ill, they had only the help of third world medical practices. If those failed, the sick or injured were disposed of. Only in extreme cases, and only for his inner circle, did the Caretaker arrange for transfers to offshore hospitals. A doctor on site would be a good thing.

"Your friend, the one we captured, he had a briefcase. Do you know what became of that?"

Elaine sidestepped his question and asked her own. "What are you going to do here? What's going to happen to me?"

The Caretaker smiled and forced a gentle tone. "You won't be harmed, dear, not if you cooperate. Now, back to the briefcase. Where is it?"

"There was no briefcase," she answered solidly. "He showed up on our doorstep injured and said that the police had ambushed him."

"On the doorstep you say? Like a little lost puppy?" Elaine remained silent. "I believe you, only because I trust the talents of my men. You were quite lucky my disciples thought to bring you back here. Several of your comrades were not as cooperative and my men were forced to...well...correct them."

That was when Elaine broke down, her body convulsing with grief. What about Batilda and Billy and Martin and Reggie? Were they lying dead, or screaming for help? Would anyone come to their aid? What about Pastor Tom and Robert? And Jonathan, poor, dear Kangaroo. She remembered him saying that the government of the island nation was never to be trusted and she sobbed at the thought of her friends.

"Well, I see we're not going to get much from you for now. I will need to call upon your services, though. My assistant has sustained an injury and I'll need you to look after him. The other man as well, the thief WITHOUT the case, will need some tending to as well. He's no good to me dead." The Caretaker issued orders to have Elaine removed from the jeep and escorted to the room where Mr. Stick now lay.

The short bald man and the hulk led the doctor, forced her, to the main door at the end of the garage. The Caretaker stayed behind to question his men.

After being pushed through the door, Elaine found herself in a small lobby with both an elevator and a wide spiral staircase. The room was roughly constructed, all the way down to a yellow caution tape marked with big bold black letters, 'PLEASE PARDON OUR DUST.' The walls, recently excavated, still displayed a rough, rock-like texture. In front of the elevator, the sand floor was absorbing a fresh puddle of blood.

## Caribbean Calling

As the elevator door opened, Elaine could see more blood inside. The three stepped into the small space and waited. After what seemed like an eternity to her, the doors reopened and they stepped out into a brightly-lit hallway constructed of white stucco and lined with several brown wood doors. The hall went on for at least a hundred yards and the ceiling was some twenty feet above her head.

The men continued leading her down the hall, hands affixed to her upper arms, until they reached the second door on the right. The small fat man twisted the handle and swung the door open, exposing a suite of rooms. Two robed individuals tended to their duties inside.

The suite was big and impressive. As they ushered her through the living room, Elaine was amazed to see a large entertainment system, along with a monstrous *LayzBoy* recliner, a couch, and a wet bar. A row of windows along one wall looked out on a courtyard. Down a hall, they passed a washroom on the way to a spacious bedroom suite. There, the big Black man lay on a king-sized bed, attended by a robed woman who held a towel, dark with blood, over the obvious wound site. The man didn't look too good -- in fact, he didn't seem to be breathing.

Elaine wanted nothing to do with it. This beast had perhaps murdered her friends back at the aid station. For a moment, she allowed herself to see Billy's face. Could it be true that she wouldn't ever see him again? Her medical training helped her to push the image out of her head. She had to compartmentalize. She had to concentrate on the matter at hand. She approached the bed and the woman with the towel moved out of the way. Thick, dark blood dripped onto the floor. The bed was filthy with bodily fluids. She picked up the man's wrist. His limb was heavy, lifeless, and cool to the touch. It was quite obvious that the man's soul was already standing before the devil.

"This man is dead," she announced. Back home, during her

residency, she'd treated all sorts of criminals and evildoers. Like she'd told Marty, it was part of the Hippocratic Oath. For a medical practitioner, everyone deserved equal treatment, regardless of what damage they'd inflicted on other people or things. There was a difference here, though. The crimes committed by her patients had never affected her. This was the first time she'd dealt, face to face, with a man that had caused the death of at least one person she had come to love.

"Is there nothing to be done? CPR? Anything?" the bald, pudgy fellow asked in a squeaky voice.

"What do you want from me, a miracle?" she snapped. "The man bled out. I don't have any equipment to revive him. No drugs, no intravenous supplies, no equipment at all."

The room was silent until the pudgy man ordered everyone to leave except for the robed woman. "Clean him up. Make him look good." He turned to the hulk. "Baron, we'll have to go to the Caretaker's room and speak with him."

Elaine was led back down the same hallway. When they entered the elevator again, the blood had been cleaned away. It smelled like bleach. The elevator ascended, and the doors opened onto a lobby, dominated by the spiral staircase. The Caretaker wasn't big on elevators. He preferred to use leg power. In this lobby, there was only one set of doors, made from polished, light-colored wood. The ceiling was constructed almost entirely of glass skylights, highlighting the night's stars.

After permission was granted, the three stepped into the Caretaker's expansive office. The thin man was sitting behind his desk, sipping on a tumbler full of rum and wearing a sleeping cap, giving him the look of Ebeneezer Scrooge. "Yes, Pusser. How is Mr. Stick?" His voice was smooth and mellow.

"I'm sorry, sir, so sorry. He is no longer with us," Pusser said quietly.

## Caribbean Calling

"Then the good doctor wasn't to be his salvation?"

Elaine had decided to take on a new tact. She spoke with respect, almost pleading. "I couldn't do anything for him. I didn't have equipment or supplies." She knew that she needed to prove herself valuable to these characters in order to have any chance of surviving this experience herself, which, at the moment, she didn't consider too high. They wouldn't let her go now. She had witnessed too much.

"Yes. You have a point," he replied. "Baron, I want you to assemble a crew and head back out to the aid station. Gather together all of the medical supplies and bring them back. Go tonight, before the local authorities get out there and take the items for themselves. Take anything else you see that may be useful, as well. And clean the place up a little." The giant remained silent. "Then go into the village and round up everyone there. And I mean everyone...and everything, the livestock, and supplies. Clean the place out. Secure the villagers in the stockade until I decide what to do with them. We can always use extra hands in the fields." The Baron turned on his heel and exited through the double doors.

"I'm afraid the Baron won't take the loss of Mr. Stick very well," the Caretaker commented. "They were long time friends. Keep an eye on him, Pusser." The Caretaker addressed Elaine. "Now, I have a proposal for you, Doctor. I believe the name was Elaine, Elaine Keller, correct?" Elaine nodded. "We could use a doctor of our own around here. I'd like to take you on. You'll be treated very well indeed."

Elaine made a conscious effort to keep her jaw from hitting her chest. "I...um...I can't do that. I have a job waiting for me back home. At a hospital. I'm...I...I'm not able to do that. I can't," she stuttered.

"Doctor, these people here are my flock. You could improve

their lives, continue your good works." He smiled and Elaine felt a chill run up her spine. "I'll give you some time to consider my offer." He leaned forward so that she could smell the rum on his breath. "Personally? I would take the offer. After all, we can't let you dance off into the night, can we? Pusser, get the doctor settled in. It's quite late, isn't it?"

Two guards outside accompanied them through a maze of corridors. Pusser was a rather soft individual, and the Caretaker didn't want any trouble. The doctor appeared to be a feisty one, capable of kicking his assistant's ass and making a run for it. The suite of rooms was modest but comfortable. The bedroom was furnished with a dresser, desk, and closet, and the bathroom was clean. A sitting area included a small kitchenette.

Pusser offered Elaine a bundle wrapped in a cotton sheet. After the men had left, she inspected the package, finding a white robe, a pair of thin lightweight pants, and a shirt made of matching material.

She thought to twist the door handle. Of course, it was locked. A grunt on the other side let her know that a guard had been stationed there. There were no windows in the room -- no pathways to freedom whatsoever.

After washing up in the shower, she dressed in the pajama-like clothing. She had no choice, as she saw it. She would have to wait to see what would happen next. She thought of her father. This would be second night that she hadn't checked in. Silently praying, she begged for his help.

caribbean calling

## **Chapter Twelve**

Eddie's first week had gone well. At least he hadn't gotten himself into any trouble. The most interesting assignment had involved a run down into the Everglades to deliver a package to a strange old hermit who lived in the middle of nowhere. It had been an all-day trip.

The morning started out as usual -- a trip to Starbuck's for a double shot of espresso. He'd met Rodger at the K and K building and found the man dressed casually. He looked to Eddie like Clark Gable going out on safari.

"What the hell are you dressed up like that for?" he'd asked.

"Didn't you get the message I left last night? I said dress for the jungle," Clark replied.

"No, man. I guess I was a little distracted."

"That girl's keeping you busy, huh?"

Eddie responded with a grin. The two headed out and made their way to Harbor Island, to Marci's place, so Ed could change into more appropriate clothing -- Khakis, Timberlands, a fire department tee shirt, and his trusty Mark Grace Cubs jersey. Mark Grace was one of Eddie's favorite players and he'd been pissed when the Cubs had let him go. It wasn't safari wear, but it was as close as he could come on a moment's notice. Marci had headed out already on a shopping run. She never seemed to tire of new shoes and handbags. She wasn't the type of woman Eddie had expected to fall for. She was a bit high-maintenance, and she was from a different world -- but their time together had been nothing but a pleasure.

He found Rodger kicked back, listening to *Master of Puppets*, by Metallica. "Jeez, I didn't take you for the head-banging type, Rodger," he said with a laugh.

"Dude, in my hey-day you wouldn't have recognized me. I had long hair, almost down to my ass, and a bong plastered to my lips almost constantly," Rodger grinned.

Ed shook his head in mock disbelief. "I guess we all have a past."

The trip down to the swamps had been a lot longer than Eddie had thought. They pulled the Lincoln into a parking lot. Muddy water had encroached upon both sides of the road for quite some time. In the clearing, a beat-up old wooden boathouse looked to be about the size of a garage. There was a padlock on the front door. Rodger slipped a key into the lock and the mechanism popped open. Inside, Eddie was surprised to find an air boat, a flat-bottomed contraption with a big fan on the back. He'd never ridden in an air boat before and the thought made him giddy.

"You know how to run one of these suckers?" he asked his partner.

"You could say that. I've been doing it all my life. During college, I worked for the Everglades National Park Service, running tours. Plus, I make this trip at least once a month."

Eddie looked at him with surprise. "Why? What's up with this gig?"

Rodger held up a fat envelope in explanation. "It's payday for an associate of K and K. He's sort of a strange old bird, a real recluse. I don't know the whole story behind it."

## Caribbean Calling

There were two seats on the boat. Rodger sat up top in the pilot's seat where the controls were located, and Eddie rode shotgun down below, where two single-barrel shotguns lay in the bottom of the boat. Eddie pointed to the weapons with raised eyebrows.

"Angry alligators, my friend," Rodger explained.

The craft skipped along the surface of the water, trampling reeds and other plant life in the way. Occasionally, Eddie noticed violent movements in the waters ahead. Rodger explained that it was alligators trying to get out of the path of the speeding boat. Eddie was horrified when Rodger ran one over, until he explained that they just dove underneath. The alligators weren't harmed.

The trip lasted about an hour before Rodger beached the craft on a patch of dry earth. The surrounding turf was overgrown and bright green. A narrow path leading deeper into the island disappeared into thick foliage. It was humid, dark, and mysterious, and Rodger indicated that they should each tote a shotgun, "for those angry alligators I mentioned earlier."

The path led to a large clearing, which had been meticulously tended to. Several small patches of bright flowers were surrounded by rock gardens. A hammock was suspended beneath the shade of two large weeping willows. Behind the trees, Eddie made out a strange little home. The sloped roof stood about six feet above the ground. The cottage itself was a mere thirty feet long and perhaps fifteen feet wide. The windows were small and round. The home was stick-built, its exterior walls painted the color of sand with deep green trim.

"Who lives here, Tattoo and Mr. Roark?"

"Fantasy Island? I think not. More like the Hobbit," Rodger answered as they approached the front door, which was more of a porthole.

## j. d. gordon

Eddie stopped and stared in surprise, thinking he had now seen it all. To the right side of the door, a very large alligator, twenty feet long from tip to tail, lay resting in the sun. Eddie was no expert on reptilian life, but he estimated the beast's weight to be every bit of a thousand pounds. The alligator wasn't the main attraction. Resting on top of the thing, between the bumps that formed the alligator's head, was a tiny hamster adorned with a little red bow tie and a baseball cap. The little guy was busy nibbling on himself, grooming the fur on his backside.

"What...what in the hell...what the hell is that?" Ed wondered.

"Yeah, amazing, isn't it? Those are his pets."

On a pole, sunk into the ground close to where they stood, was a large brass bell hanging from a thick piece of rope. Rodger pulled the rope three times and the bell chimed, echoing around the grounds. After a moment, the little round door opened and a small man, maybe four feet tall, stepped out, wearing a pair of denim overalls. His feet were bare. His chest was a scraggle of thick, bristly hair, and he was wearing a light blue ball cap with a Miami Dolphins insignia. His head, beneath the cap, appeared to be shaved.

"Oh, halloo, boys, come in, come in! I've made a fresh batch of hootch this morning." The man seemed friendly enough. Rodger stepped forward, unconcerned about the presence of the alligator and his little buddy. Eddie followed his lead. When they neared the reptile, its massive jaws opened a bit, emitting a quiet belch of gas. That was it, nothing else. The hamster looked up for a second, and then got back to grooming.

Inside the cabin, Eddie found a comfortable set-up. Although the visitors had to crouch in order to fit through the door, the ceiling was high enough for both men to stand straight up, their noggins just touching the surface.

## Caribbean Calling

Except for the john, everything was one big room. There was a little kitchen, a little table with four little chairs, and in the corner was a wide, king-sized bed, quite out of place considering the occupant and the rest of the surroundings. A sitting area with one little lamp and a coffee table made from two milk crates and a flat board all faced a little television set. The Fox News Channel was tuned in -- Eddie recognized Bill O'Reilly. In another corner of the room sat what appeared to be a still. A bunch of bottles marked XXX were set around it.

The old man demanded a little of their time. They all sat around the little table, Rodger and Eddie's knees almost up to their chests. He served them what he called his fresh batch of hootch, which was a fiery, clear liquid that left Ed with a nice little buzz.

"Do you have my package?" the man asked. Rodger handed over the envelope, which the man ripped open to reveal a big stack of one hundred dollar bills. Without apologies or excuses, he counted the money. Once finished, he moved his chair over, crouched down on his knees, and threw the bundle of cash into a hidden trap door. Eddie caught a glimpse of the space's contents. There were piles upon piles of similar stacks. The man was sitting on millions.

After the man closed the trap door and replaced his chair, the three spent a while chatting and sharing shots of the strong, strange brew.

The air boat ride back was as enjoyable for Eddie as the ride there had been -- perhaps more so with the hootch still running through his blood. It had been the most interesting assignment he'd been given so far, and he wondered whether he'd be back. Rodger had mentioned that it was a monthly assignment, but he hadn't offered any other information about the strange little man.

## j. d. gordon

It had been quite late by the time Eddie returned to the apartment and Marci. She had fallen asleep on the couch. He woke her and guided her to her bed. After a quick shower, he joined her, but didn't disturb her. They'd enjoyed each other that morning. As for the upcoming weekend, Marci had planned a kayak trip somewhere around the Tampa area after Ed checked in at the office. It had been a long time since Eddie had spent any time in a kayak.

Arriving at the K and K building on Saturday morning, Ed found a skeleton crew -- a few office workers trying to catch up, he guessed. He made his way up to Klein's office suite on the top floor, which was closed up. Thank god for air conditioning, he thought. It was damned hot already, almost too hot for that kayak trip Marci had planned.

Klein was sitting at his desk going through some papers. He was dressed casually, as usual. A serious looking man in a suit sat on the other side of the desk. "Come on in and have a seat, Ed," he said without looking up. "How's the first week been going?"

"I'd say there were some high points and some low points, and some interesting points, as well," he answered, sitting in one of the luxury leather chairs and nodding hello to the stranger.

Klein looked up and smiled appreciatively. "Oh, you liked the trip down south, did you?"

Ed nodded. "What's behind that fellow?" he asked, doubtful he'd get an answer.

"That's a family secret, Ed," Klein responded with a lackluster smile. Eddie left it alone. He'd find out eventually. "I've got a different sort of job for you today. It'll be an opportunity for you to get your feet wet...give you some experience with some of the things I intend for you in the future."

## Caribbean Calling

Ed felt his heartbeat increase a tad. Maybe things were going to start picking up on the excitement meter, after all. "Sure, sir. Whatever you need."

"This is Joseph Keller. We go back a long way." Keller extended his hand and gave Eddie a weak smile. "We have every hope that this won't amount to anything, but Mr. Keller has a daughter." Klein filed his papers in a drawer, removed his glasses, and looked at Eddie. "She's a doctor working with a relief organization, something like the Red Cross. Mr. Keller gave her a satellite phone so that he could keep in contact with her. She called him every night, up until three nights ago. He's tried reaching her, but she hasn't answered, nor does anyone answer at the facility she's working at -- an aid station of some sort. Naturally, he's very concerned."

Ed looked more closely at the man and could tell he'd been crying, or drinking, or both. His eyes were blood red. "He's gone through all of the official channels. The Caribbean Relief Corp has been trying to find out what happened, but it seems that the government of the island is proving to be of little help so far. They are investigating, but they have no answers." Klein stood up and moved around the desk to put his hand on his friend's shoulder. "So, Mr. Keller has asked for my help. It's very unusual for his daughter not to check in, no matter the circumstances. Are you up for a trip to the islands?"

Eddie didn't hesitate. His idea of heaven was cruising the Caribbean. "Absolutely, sir. I'd be happy to help." He looked at the broken man reassuringly. "I'll do everything in my power to find your daughter, sir."

"You won't be going alone," Klein continued. "I'm going to hook you up with a fellow I use from time to time. He used to work with Brighton. You remember Brighton, don't you?" Eddie nodded, aware that this job offer had been made in order to replace the dead man. "He goes by Mario, Mario Marino. He's in

Key West right now. I've got one of our planes waiting for you. You'll be flying out of Tampa tonight, so you'll have a couple of hours to get some things together. You won't need much at first. Mario will take care of most of the essentials. I've got you booked at La Concha…a little bird told me it's one of your favorites. Mario will be in touch after you arrive."

Eager to wrap up, Klein stood and handed Eddie a bundle of papers. "You'll find some information here, but Mario has most of it. Good luck, Ed. We'll talk when you return."

Keller looked up at Eddie. "Please find her. She's all I've got in this world. She's my baby."

"I understand, sir." That was all he could think of to say.

As he headed out, Ed thought that this would be the assignment that would help him decide whether to stay on or not. He'd have to arrive at the airport early. Though he was flying on a private company plane, there were still hoops to jump through in light of his firearms. Then there was Marci, but he wasn't too worried about that.

Marci was ready and waiting when he got back to the condo, wearing a smile and a bikini. She could tell right away by the look on his face that their day's plans had hit a snag. "Oh, Eddie, say it ain't so."

"Marci, I'm sorry. It's a last minute thing. The daughter of one of Klein's old friends has gone missing. He's sending me down to the islands to look for her. I'll make it up to you, I swear."

Marci gave him the evil eye for a second, and then smiled. "How come you're always off saving maidens in need of rescue? What are you, some kind of knight in shining armor?"

"I guess someone's gotta do it." Ed smiled sheepishly.

## Caribbean Calling

"Well, she better not get the idea that you're her prince. I've got first dibs on that." She walked over and kissed him. "Well, Katie is having a party tonight, anyway. I guess I'll drive down and spend the night. When will you be back?"

Eddie drew her back into his arms. "Faster than a speeding bullet, faster than the speed of sound, faster than…"

"Okay, I get it," she interrupted. Suddenly serious, she looked in his eyes. "You be careful, Mr. Heroics. I want you back in one piece."

Within an hour, he was packed and on his way to the airport. Although it was a private plane, it wasn't very impressive. Ed had expected a sleek Lear jet, what he found was a small, dual-engine Cessna. The pilot was a no-nonsense individual, seemingly upset to be pulled away from a day of golf in order to make the run down to Key West. It was late afternoon when they touched down, and Eddie was left standing alone on the runway a short distance from the small building that acted as the airport's terminal. He grabbed his bag and made his way over to the line of taxis waiting for fares.

The cabbie talked Eddie's ear off during the ride into town. He was a bona fide local, a "Conch," he termed it, born and raised on Key West. Eddie asked about the island and its culture and the cabbie told him the tale of the short-lasted and well-staged revolution. Eddie already knew the story, but listened politely. He'd been hoping for something more than the standard stories doled out to the droves of tourists that made their way to the southern-most point of the continental United States each year.

The lounge of the La Concha hotel had as much character as he'd remembered. He'd stayed a number of times before. The rooftop lounge had the best vista point on Key West. It was a perfect location for facing West and watching the sun sink

## j. d. gordon

beneath the horizon. Ed didn't understand why most folks seemed to prefer to head down to the pier at the end of Duval for the sunset. Sure, there was usually a festive crowd and a good band playing, but he thought the view from La Concha was about as perfect as you could get.

Eddie checked in at the front desk where an envelope was waiting for him. He carried it up to his room unopened. The room was a floor above the pool, which had a small tiki-themed bar next to it and was located on the third floor of the building, open to the sun. He had a great view of the pool's deck, where several bikini-clad, tanned women lay beneath the late Caribbean sunshine. Two men stood near the bar, looking down on the street. They were holding drinks and pointing at something below. Eddie figured them for Europeans. They seemed to be in their sixties, and had large stomachs, hairy backs, and the mandatory speedos. After pouring himself a beer from the mini-bar, Ed ripped open the envelope. He was hoping for enough time to stretch out a bit on the sun deck before meeting this Mario Marino fellow. The note was written in a heavy scribble:

*Fireman Ed,*
*Meet me after midnight at the Schooner Wharf Bar.*
*MM*

Wonderful, Ed thought to himself. How will I know who to look for? He'd leave that thought for later. For now, he was heading poolside.

When Eddie returned to his room, he was hungry. He hadn't had a chance to eat much during the day. Looking out the window, he noticed a new place on Duval that looked interesting. After a quick shower, he left La Concha, stepped out onto the sidewalk, and started heading in the direction of the restaurant. The sign above the entrance read, "Bald Jimmy's on Duval, Keywestern Establishment."

## Caribbean Calling

He cruised past the hostess, indicating with his index finger that he was headed for the bar, which turned out to be in an outdoor garden area. In all the years he'd been visiting Key West, Eddie realized that he'd never had a meal in a joint with a roof. With its multi-colored, exposed rough brick décor, Ed surmised that at one time, this piece of expensive Key West real estate had been nothing more than an empty lot between two buildings.

A young bartender approached and asked for his order. As he waited, he noticed that the walls were covered in items related to the fire service. There were antique fire buckets, leftovers from the days of the long-retired bucket brigades, old fire helmets, antique tools, and framed newspaper articles describing firefighting heroics. Patches from at least two hundred different fire departments were displayed on a long board behind the main bar. Ed noticed his own department's patch among the collection and beamed with pride.

He still had a few hours to kill before his meeting at the Schooner Wharf Bar. A band was due to play soon, so he decided to stay put until it was closer to midnight. It wasn't long before an order of conch fritters, a Corona, and a big plate of pasta arrived. He asked his server about the fire department items, eager to learn more.

"The owner, Bald Jimmy, he's a retired firefighter," the young man answered.

"Oh, yeah!" Ed exclaimed. "Do you know where he worked?"

"Not specifically, no. But I think it was somewhere up north. Maybe Chicago."

Ed asked if the owner was in and was disappointed when the waiter explained that Bald Jimmy had taken the night off to spend some time with his family.

# j. d. gordon

Ed took out his cell phone and began to dial the fire station's number back home, but he hung up after the second ring. How the hell would it look for him to be calling home like a little kid visiting Grandma for the summer? He was supposed to be living it up on vacation, after all.

The meal was delicious and the cold beer refreshing. Ed munched away as he watched the band set up on stage. B2B, they were called, a name which seemed somehow familiar to him, though he couldn't remember when he'd seen them before. As they struck their first notes, he remembered. A few years back, he'd attended a function in Key West known as The Meeting of the Minds, a national convention organized to celebrate the songs and writings of Jimmy Buffett. Ed was a huge fan of the singer and songwriter, and would see him if the occasion presented itself. Buffett fans were amongst the best fans in the world. They were a family, a network, devoted, and a lot of fun to hang out with. That's where he'd heard this excellent band before. They were so good, in fact, that he nearly missed his midnight appointment. It must be something about Key West, he thought. Every time he came to town, he was late for something.

Eddie collected the check from the booze-slinging woman behind the bar and paid the tab with a credit card provided by Klein for incidentals. He left her a fat tip.

Back out on Duval Street, people strolled up and down the sidewalk. Most of the stores were closed down for the night, but no one seemed to care. Eddie bummed a cigarette off a woman walking alone. The nicotine went straight to his head. He didn't smoke very often, relying on the advice that moderation is the key to a long life, so when he did light up, he caught a great buzz, especially if he was drinking.

Music drifted out of most of the bars and cafés along the way as he walked to the Schooner Wharf Bar, which was about ten minutes away. It seemed like the town changed, a little bit, each

155

## Caribbean Calling

year. Ten years back, he recalled, the walk to the Schooner Wharf Bar had been nearly deserted, and the path crossed through a shantytown of small retail stands and palm readers. Today, fancy restaurants, bars, and boutiques covered all available space. The developers had done a nice job on the area, but Ed sort of missed the panhandlers and the gypsies.

As always, a band was playing at the Schooner Wharf Bar. At least this place hadn't changed much over the years. Under the open sky, the garden area's floor was still crunchy with a mixture of gravel and sand. Boats and ships bobbed along the water, following the harbor waves. The air was salty, with the smell of diesel mixing in with spicy hints of the still-flaming grill.

Ed sat down and ordered a Meyer's Dark on the rocks. It hadn't been a year since he'd first run into Marci and her friends in this same bar. Tonight, a group of weekend bikers sat around the very same table they'd sat at that night. Ed thought about how much his life had changed in such a short period of time. In less than a year's time, he'd gone from foot-loose and fancy-free, without a care in the world, to, well, this.

Eddie surveyed the joint until another patron came over and sat down at the table across from him. The man looked familiar, a rough-looking type. He had three or maybe four days worth of stubble and his skin was a dark brown. With a wide-brimmed fedora hat, and a Hawaiian shirt, he didn't look so out of place here, though. Three scars cut paths through the jungle of black curly hair on his chest, sharing the rugged landscape with several strands hanging around his neck -- a gold chain, a collection of small round seashells, some turquoise beads, and a braid of multi-colored thread, similar to a friendship bracelet.

The two men sat looking at each other, one chewing on a cigar, until Eddie broke the silence. "So," he said. "What's up with you?"

### j. d. gordon

The man moved his cigar to the other side of his mouth. "Are you Eddie? The fireman, Eddie?" Eddie nodded. "I'm Mario. Mario Marino. No relation to the quarterback," he croaked in a rough, deep voice, extending his hand. Eddie shook his beefy paw.

A waitress came over and Mario ordered a Ketel One. "Anything with it?" she asked.

"Ice," Mario grunted in response. "So, when can you be ready to go?" he asked Eddie when she'd gone.

Eddie shrugged. "Just about any time," he answered.

When the waitress returned with the order, Mario reached into his pocket and pulled out a green bill with Grant's portrait on the front. He told her to keep the change. "Thanks," she said, grinning from ear to ear. "You give me a fifty every time and I won't leave your side."

For a while, the men sat in silence. It seemed to Eddie that his new partner was thinking, considering his options. Finally, he spoke. "We'll leave tomorrow night, then."

"Yeah," Mario drained his glass.

"Let's get some rest then," Eddie said.

Mario beckoned to the smiling waitress lurking near the door. "How about a round of shots?"

Eddie shrugged. "We need to get some rest."

"Sure we do," Mario grinned. "Just not quite yet."

Eddie shrugged as the waitress pranced up to the table to take Mario's order.

Caribbean Calling

## Chapter Thirteen

The hidden stockyard behind the main building of The Plantation was all cleared out. Some of the Caretaker's followers were standing by the overhead garage door, accompanied by several of the ranch's soldiers, two in each corner. No one worked the fields. Everyone was tucked away, drugged up and sleeping in the barracks. The sound of a helicopter's blades chopping through the thick morning air could be heard in the near distance.

The soldiers looked to the sky as the vehicle approached the landing zone, which sat in the center of the stockade. The men held their hands up to their faces as it began to touch down -- dust, stones, and other debris whirled in the wind. The chopper was a large model, designed and built by Boeing for the United States military. This particular aircraft was owned and operated by an organization with much less honorable goals in mind.

Lester Crow sat inside, behind the cockpit. He'd been able to make it in person after all. The job that had ended up killing his father had been a simple one. A standard kidnapping -- hold a girl for ransom, and kill her after receiving the cash. It had turned out to be a fiasco. Now, he was cautious with security.

This trip to Capersdeed, an island nation that would be lucky to be included by Rand-McNally, didn't cause him to fear for his safety too much, although he normally would have sent one of his lieutenants or captains.

## j. d. gordon

When Lester had received the phone call from his new business associate, though, he had been very angry indeed, and wanted to attend to the matter personally. This Caretaker, Reese was his name, had been referred to him by a man the Crows did a lot of business with -- the commandant of Capersdeed, who was a small-time corrupt public official with his hands in a lot of pots around the Caribbean. He had made the Crows a lot of money.

Several days ago, however, the Caretaker had called to complain about a shipment of fake merchandise and the theft of money by one of Crow's underlings, Robert Crane. When Crow's attempts to reach his employee failed, he'd made the decision to investigate the matter himself. Crow wanted no more slip-ups. Because of mistakes that had been made in the Klein kidnapping, the Crow operations had almost been discovered. It would have been difficult for Lester to start over. He'd only known one way of life, and one home, since he'd been a child. His father's secluded island served as their base of operations.

The inside of the helicopter was luxuriously-appointed with wall-to-wall carpeting, six captain chairs, a wet bar, a computer system, and a television and sofa in the space the military would normally use to store troops or cargo. The rear-loading hatch was kept operational, but never used. Lester preferred the side doors.

On the outside, the craft was simple. There were no markings whatsoever, but the chopper was armored to protect the vehicle and its occupants from most ammunition, short of anti-tank or ground-to-air missiles. It could bite back, too. A twenty millimeter Gatling gun and forty millimeter cannon, operated by the aircraft's pilots, were situated in a hidden nose cone. If needed, the shielding cone retracted to expose the armament.

Today, the helicopter carried six individuals -- the pilot and co-pilot, Crow's two bodyguards, Crow, and his right-hand man, Hector. Four of them were dressed in Italian suits and carried concealed handguns. The bodyguards also held submachine guns.

## Caribbean Calling

The landing gear touched down and bounced once, before coming to a stop. The pilots motioned to Lester that it was safe to leave the craft. Both bodyguards stepped down into the dust and the heat first, then Hector, and then, finally, Lester himself.

A small group of robed individuals acted as a greeting party while one short and rotund man approached Lester and his comrades. "Gentlemen, welcome to The Plantation. I am Mr. Pusser. The Caretaker is waiting inside for us. If I may escort you to his suite, please follow me."

Lester was a bit peeved that the Caretaker hadn't met him personally, there in the stockyard. They passed through the garage, with its fleet of military vehicles, and entered a construction zone, where an elevator waited. They were joined by a fellow introduced as the Baron, a huge, strange-looking man with eerie eyes of different colors. All piled into the small space, and Lester had a good look at this rather evil-looking individual.

Hector broke the silence by addressing Pusser, his right index finger extended. "Pull my finger," he said.

Pusser gave him a queer look.

"Ah, Hector, not everyone appreciates your sense of humor," Lester said, shaking his head.

The Baron chuckled and obliged the man's request, whereupon he passed a torrent of gas.

"How juvenile, really," Pusser chided as the doors opened, bringing the relief of fresh air.

Behind the doors at the end of the corridor they traversed, the Caretaker was seated with a beautiful young woman. At first, Elaine had been defiant, and had attempted to revolt. There were points during the second day of her captivity, when she was locked in her room, that she suspected her food or drink was being spiked with something. She refused to consume anything at all. After several hours, though, the Caretaker had ordered her strapped down, and one of the robed ones had given her a shot of something in the buttocks.

By that evening she'd begun to feel a strange sense of calm, as if she'd been tranquilized. She'd thought to herself that perhaps she was in a state of shock. She knew from being a doctor that the mind and body coped with stress in often unexpected ways. After some time, she had stopped thinking about her aid station coworkers and had begun to feel almost robotic. She didn't question it. She was incapable. Although she'd entered a hazy, almost dream-like state, it felt normal to her. It felt pleasant, even.

On that day, the Caretaker had set a space aside for her, within the main building, with instructions for her to create a clinic and small surgical area with the medical equipment the Baron had retrieved from the aid station. The tools looked and felt familiar, but the source of that feeling was something she pushed back into the recesses of her mind.

She also found herself giving in to the Caretaker's demands, which were frequent, and sometimes included intimate acts. A little voice inside her tried to break through, but she ignored it. Instead, she began to find the Caretaker somehow charismatic. He spoke kindly stroked her hair. Often there were hours of time spent with him that she couldn't recall the details of later. Whatever the case was, she was falling in line, and quickly.

She spent a part of each day with the Caretaker now, usually one of her daily meals. Today, it had been during the morning tea break that the Caretaker had enjoyed her company.

## Caribbean Calling

Lester couldn't take his eyes off of the lovely young woman. The Caretaker didn't much care for this, so he ordered her back to her clinic after a mumbled introduction.

It was time to get down to business. With no intention of calling this man the "Caretaker," he asked, "So, what is the problem here, Reese?"

"Well," the Caretaker snapped his fingers and Pusser turned to leave the room, "your man seems to have pulled a fast one on us. I would like to be compensated for my loss."

Pusser returned, carrying four weapons -- two grenade launchers and two assault rifles. Lester examined them. "Yes, yes, the AK-47 and the M-79 grenade launcher. I'm familiar with both weapons."

Pusser handed Lester one of the AK-47s. He toyed with the various mechanisms and declared it to be a perfect weapon. Then Pusser handed him the second weapon. It didn't take long for Lester to realize it was a fake. After examining all of the weapons, he was satisfied with Reese's complaint. "I must say, I'm disappointed. Shocked, really. Have you recovered the missing funds?"

"We have not, despite great effort. The money must be out there somewhere, though. We captured one of the men responsible and questioned him. He was hiding at the aid station. He told us he had hidden the money near the site. We searched the wreckage, but couldn't find the case," the Caretaker explained.

"Have you brought the man out there to the site with you?" Lester asked.

"Unfortunately, the man is dead." Reese paused, and then admitted, "I'm afraid we are novices when it comes to the art of interrogation."

## j. d. gordon

Lester held his hand up as if to ask to be spared the details. "Don't worry about the money. We'll refund it immediately. I would like to find that briefcase, however. We wouldn't want it to fall into the wrong hands. I haven't brought enough staff with me to aid in the search, but we'll be sure to do a fly-over of the site on our way out. I'll have a team here by tomorrow," he promised. "How about the locals? Have they had any access to the site yet?"

"Of course, I contacted the commandant with that concern in mind. The aid station and the crash site have been sealed and left alone, with the exception of a staged investigation. Apparently, the director of the aid station returned from an off-site trip and called the local police. The commandant has…well, let's just say that the director has been taken care of, along with the station's pastor. They'll be cooling their heels for at least a week. The commandant will deal with the Caribbean Relief Corp's representatives. He's quite handy that way, as you well know."

Lester sighed and rubbed his temples. "I'll be in touch with the commandant as well, concerning this situation. We have a very cooperative relationship. The CRC is nothing to worry about. The left hand rarely knows what the right hand is doing."

Reese stood. "Well, Mr. Crow, I do appreciate your concern and your help. I would like to encourage a mutually-beneficial relationship with your organization in the future."

Crow remained seated. "I do have a proposition for you, Mr. Reese." The Caretaker crinkled his brow in anticipation. Crow continued, "The woman, the one who was here earlier. I find her…engaging. May I make you an offer for her?"

"Our new doctor?" the Caretaker shook his head and chuckled. "You know, I've grown quite attached to her. She's quite remarkable."

## caribbean calling

"Perhaps five hundred thousand would give you reason to find another fish in the sea?" Lester questioned.

Taken aback, the Caretaker took a moment to consider the offer. "Well, she's very beautiful and very talented. I'm just not sure…"

"One million dollars," Lester interrupted.

The Caretaker smiled. "I'll have her get her things ready. Shall I have her escorted to your helicopter?" The deal was closed.

The morning tea had elevated Elaine's mood to near euphoria. She'd been on her second cup when a strange crew had entered the Caretaker's office. She recognized Pusser and the Baron, but the others were new to her. She'd been disappointed when the Caretaker had ordered her back to her room, which had been upgraded to a luxurious suite. She had planned to spend the morning getting settled into her clinic. That she hadn't seen any patients yet didn't cause her any concern.

Back in her room, as she gazed out the window, she was drawn to a large woman in a dirty flowered dress and red bandanna, huddled in the stockade with a crowd of natives. The woman seemed so familiar, but her mind was so foggy, she couldn't grasp on to the thought for long. She felt very sleepy and lay down on the sofa in the sitting room, falling asleep immediately, as she usually did after spending time with the Caretaker.

She was in a much different world when she woke up.

While she lay on the floor of the helicopter when Crow and

his men returned, a man in a robe informed her that they had given her something so that she would sleep for at least a few hours.

Lester was overjoyed by having acquired this new possession. He wasn't sure what he was going to do with her. He would make at least double what he'd paid if he sold her. Perhaps he would keep her around for a while as his little sex toy, though, like some of the other girls he'd purchased. Eventually, she'd be killed, or sold into one of the black market prostitution rings he did business with, or put to work on the island. They were half-way through the trip back to Crow Island when Elaine came to.

Crow Island could not be found on any modern map. Blackwell Crow had come across the island when his dynasty had still been in its infancy. He'd been trafficking drugs when a posse from the United States Drug Enforcement Agency had begun tailing him. He and his partner had managed to stay a manageable distance from the agents, three boatloads in all. With the certainty that it wouldn't be long before they were taken down, Blackwell knew that they would have to take out his pursuers.

In the near distance, in a remote part of the Caribbean, he'd spied a small chain of undeveloped islands. Cruising his boat into the lagoon of one of the small islands, he'd found himself between two tall, stony mountains. His plan had been successful. Not only had they managed to elude their pursuers, they'd found a strategic paradise. As his criminal corporation had grown, Blackwell had set up camp on the island.

Today, the place was like Xanadu. Expansive manicured gardens and lawns surrounded the main building, which had been styled after the old southern plantations. Blackwell's favorite attraction on the island, prior to its development, had been the ruins of British encampments located on the island's highest point. During colonial times, the island had been used as a stop-

## Caribbean Calling

off for British convoys into the Caribbean. The now ruined encampment had been used to garrison infantry and artillery. Before his death, Blackwell had often visited the ruins. Old cannons still lay in the rubble.

Lester didn't make a habit of exploring the site. His favorite part of the island was the underground docks that his father had constructed during the early years, including a large, flooded cavern off the lagoon.

Lester wasn't Blackwell's son by birth. He'd been adopted as an infant, though not legally. Lester had been the son of a family who had been cruising on their private yacht. Blackwell had hijacked the vessel and tossed the family and crew overboard. After taking a liking to the feisty young boy, Blackwell had decided to raise him as his own. He'd sent Lester to the best schools money could buy, and Lester had received military and combat training from the best soldiers, from the ranks of the best armies in the world.

Elaine lifted her head up from the couch where Lester had ordered her secured. "Where am I?" Her voice was groggy.

Lester walked over to the couch and stood above her. "I'm Lester Crow. You'll be my guest for a while." Then he turned away and rejoined his men, who were gambling around a small table.

Elaine attempted to stand and say something in her defense, but she found herself bound. The best she could do was lay there and struggle.

## Chapter Fourteen

Eddie returned to the Schooner Wharf Bar a few minutes before sunset, just as his new co-worker had suggested. He sat down and was tempted to order a Corona, but there were two problems with that. First, he was nursing a vicious hangover. He'd tried to sleep it off by the pool during the day, but it was still with him. He had been successful, however, at frying himself to a crisp under the Caribbean sun. He'd even been forced to toss his protective vest and shoulder holster into the duffel bag with the rest of his items rather than strap it over his tender skin. His Colt was resting in the waistband of his shorts. He cinched the belt a little tighter. The gun wasn't going anywhere.

Secondly, he thought it would be wise to use a little common sense this time. He wasn't sure what he was getting wrapped up in, so a clear head was a must. It was hard as hell to separate business from pleasure in this part of the world.

"Eddie! You made it!" Mario was smiling. "I wasn't sure how you would be feeling after those many shots we enjoyed last night."

"Some influence you are as a boss," Eddie teased. "I'm alright."

"First of all, I'm not your boss. Second, you've gotta have fun while you can in this business."

## Caribbean Calling

Eddie thought about that for a moment, weighing the relative danger of this work versus fighting fires. He was of the mind that all things worked themselves out in the end. Klein had described this job as a cakewalk, so he figured he didn't have much to worry about.

"You ready to go?"

Eddie nodded in the affirmative and followed Mario down onto the docks. A catamaran was heading out on a sunset cruise. A soft glow emanated from the western horizon. He wasn't sure what kind of watercraft to expect. When he'd hooked up with Brighton, they'd used an old, souped-up fishing boat -- a sleeper, so to speak. The inboard engine had been a real monster, though, and stashes of weapons, including a rocket launcher, had been hidden in various locations throughout the boat. Ed wondered if Mario's boat would be any safer.

As the two men neared the end of the line, Ed saw a massive cigarette-style boat with bright orange and red flames painted on the side. The craft was all waxed up and shining beneath the light of the lamps that were posted on the docks.

"Whatever happened to going undercover?" he said out loud, staring at the flashy craft.

"What could be better cover than posing as some rich Italian guys in an expensive custom speedboat? I think it's quite brilliant, really."

Ed was happy to find that there were, indeed, weapons on board. Mario didn't stash them in secret hiding places. He left the items, which included rocket launchers, rifles, and an M-60 machine gun, lying around the cabin, which Ed thought was sloppy housekeeping. "You keep a nice, clean house here, Marino," he said, shaking his head.

"I'm not having the ladies over tonight," Mario answered,

standing by the ship's controls. He was wearing a sleeveless tee shirt, a stub of a cigar clenched between his teeth. The hair on his back waved in the breeze.

Mario maneuvered the craft away from the dock while Eddie tied down all of the lines and secured any loose items on deck. It wasn't long before they were slipping past the sunset pier at Mallory Square and the islands off the coast of Key West. Upon closer inspection, Eddie noticed that some of the islands were great mounds of earth boasting large, luxurious homes.

"I'll be damned," he commented to Mario. "Where do people get the money to maintain something like that?" He pointed to one of the homes.

"I'm not sure. But that one, there on the right, is mine."

"Are you fuckin' kidding, man?" Eddie's jaw gaped. Mario didn't answer. He simply smiled and pushed the cigarette boat's throttle to its limit.

Eddie loved being on the open water at night, although the Caribbean couldn't really be considered open water. For Ed, open water meant nothing in sight, and these days, it seemed no matter where you were in the Caribbean, something was out there with you, even if it was a deserted island, or a light in the distance. Regardless, he found the view beautiful. The stars were clear in the night sky, providing enough light for Eddie to enjoy the sight of dolphins frolicking.

After a five hour journey, Mario powered down the boat's engine to a near idle. They were approaching their destination after a long ride. Ed had spent a portion of the trip checking out the weaponry, and then he'd joined Mario on deck, where the two had lounged around smoking sweet-flavored cigars. Swearing he'd caught a buzz, Eddie chalked it up to the fresh sea air.

Mario pulled the vessel into an alcove on a small island. The

## Caribbean Calling

perimeter was dotted with scrub brush and large mounds of sand, but the island's interior was quite different. Ed could see that it was lusher, with dark green palms that sported clusters of large coconuts. Down the shore, he could see a long white sandy beach. It was a hidden gem of an island oasis, the only thing out of place being an old Albatross seaplane sitting in the darkness of the cove. He knew that the famous seaplanes had been used during World War II as submarine chasers and for reconnaissance. They were rugged, sturdy planes.

A man had been sleeping by a small fire on the beach. He was up now, and rubbing the sleep from his eyes. They dropped anchor several feet from the shoreline, and Eddie jumped into the surf, which he found to be almost over his head. He swam until he was able to stand on firm sand below.

Mario popped open a collapsible raft, the kind that springs to life with the pull of a cord. "No reason to get wet yet, rookie," he croaked as he paddled past with the raft's small oar. The stub of his cigar was still hanging from his lips.

Eddie tiptoed onto the sand, soaked from head to toe. Immediately, he recognized the man sitting on the beach by the fire. "Ay, mon, eets de firemon from up nort', mon!" Marvin, a pilot who ran his own small transportation company near Miami, laughed heartily. The Jamaican also moonlighted for Klein.

"Marvin! Man, it's good to see you again! Is this your antique?" Ed motioned toward the seaplane.

"I wish she was mine to own, mon. Eet belong to Mista Klein, mon. I fly it fo' him, though. I guess dat make eet mine in a way, mon!"

While Eddie and Marvin caught up, Mario kept busy unloading and deflating his little raft. When he was done, he joined the others in front of the fire in a different outfit -- safari wear -- like what Rodger had worn the day he and Eddie had gone to see the weird old fellow in the swamps. He set a similar set of clothing on the ground for Ed to change into -- tan pants and a white cotton shirt. Eddie recalled Brighton issuing him a similar costume when they had headed to Crow Island to rescue Jennifer Klein.

"Alright, enough chitter-chatter, guys. I don't want to spend all month on this project." Mario's cigar stump wasn't much longer than an inch, but it stayed right where it was. "This should be easy. Marvin, land us close enough to Capersdeed so we can paddle in. The law isn't too friendly here, so pick an out-of-the-way spot, okay?"

Eddie cut him off. "Hold on a second. Did I hear you say that we're going to Capersdeed?" He'd spent the night in jail the last time he'd visited the island nation.

"Yes. And I'm familiar with the trouble you met there last year. The government of Capersdeed is as crooked as a dog's hind leg. By the way, do you speak any Spanish?"

"Um...adios?" Eddie offered.

"I thought so. I've had a Canadian passport and credentials prepared for you," Mario explained. "As for me, I'm from Cuba now, and I'm your personal tour guide. You're a rich Canadian banker who's been transferred to the Caribbean. You're out scouting future business locations. Hopefully, the small-fry police force here will buy the story. If not...if they want to drag us in... we'll have to go to gun." Mario patted his pistol, a Smith & Wesson .357 magnum revolver, like the one Eddie had back home -- only Mario's was gunmetal blue rather than stainless steel. The weapon was stashed in what looked like a fancy photographer's vest with pockets and pouches down the front and sides. He even had a camera to add authenticity to the disguise.

Thinking he was going to have to bear the pain of the

## Caribbean Calling

shoulder holster on his fried skin, Ed was surprised when Mario handed him a similar vest. There was no need for the protective gear, either. This new addition to his wardrobe was constructed with a thin layer of Kevlar -- not as impenetrable as the vest, but offering some degree of protection. Eddie thanked his partner and began suiting up. There were still a few hours before daybreak, but Mario wanted to be on the shores of Capersdeed before sun-up, so the trio boarded the old Albatross.

"This thing is awesome, man," Eddie commented as he entered the belly of the craft. There wasn't as much space as he had imagined. He had only seen the planes in books and History Channel documentaries. It had an old musty smell, which added to its character. Two seats up front were for the pilot and co-pilot, with a third seat behind.

Eddie and Mario sat in the back, in the old storage compartment, as Marvin operated the controls. Using the first portion of the flight time to go over the particulars of the mission, they discussed who they were looking for. Mario had some photos Klein had provided which he extracted from a thick file folder.

After the plans were laid out in some detail, they relaxed a bit. Mario asked Eddie a lot of questions, which Ed was fine with. He figured his veteran partner wanted to find out what kind of novice he was working with. The same thing happened back at the firehouse when a new guy started. Eddie thought again about his buddies in Chicago. He missed them. He missed the routine and the camaraderie. He missed Hank.

The flight was short, but they were still running a bit behind schedule. Streaks of sunlight began to spread out in the distance. When Marvin dropped the old Albatross until it was almost skimming the surface of the sea, Eddie was reminded of how clear the waters were around the island of Capersdeed.

## j. d. gordon

Marvin and Mario had done a nice job selecting a landing site. It was a flat, wide, sandy shoreline, white and beautiful. The sea that lapped up onto the shore remained shallow for quite a distance. Eddie was relieved that some corporation hadn't bought up the real estate to build some cheap stucco buildings and called it a resort.

The landing seemed a bit rough to him, but it was, after all, his first time in a seaplane. He watched out of the side window until the propellers came to a standstill. The plan was simple. Marvin was to wait, Ed and Mario were to row to shore, find the girl, say hello, and then return to the plane. Simple enough.

Mario popped open another of his inflatable rafts and the two men began rowing. Even in the early morning light, Ed could see straight to the bottom of the sea. A conch shell rested below and Ed wondered if the little slug was kicked back in his little house, reading the morning paper.

In a short time, they made it to the beach. Mario deflated the raft and tucked it under some bushes. Making their way into the island by way of a small footpath, Eddie asked if they were going to wander around until they ran into the woman.

"I have a plan," Mario answered with some irritation. "I'm breaking you in slow, kid. There is a huge amount of preplanning that goes into any operation, large or small. I sat over a map for several hours getting familiar with the layout here. I've arranged for a vehicle," he explained.

As the words exited his cigar-deprived mouth, the path opened up into a clearing where an old Range Rover was waiting. A man sat there, his back leaning against the front tire. A little campfire smoldered a few feet in front of him and a thin stream of smoke climbed up into the ring of trees that surrounded the clearing.

A skinny stick that was stuck into the sandy soil stretched

## Caribbean Calling

over the fire with a black, gnarled chunk of something sticking off the end. Ed assumed it was a forgotten hot dog, and, sure enough, a pack of sausages, covered in sand, lay at the man's side.

Mario nudged the sleeping gent with the heel of his boot. The fellow woke up with a start. "What, man? I'm having a little picnic here..." He stopped speaking for a moment when he noticed who the boot heel belonged to. "Aw, hey, Mario. Dude, I must have dozed off for a while."

The man had a slow way of speaking. His hair was long, brown, and curly, and was held up in a makeshift bun by a frayed headband, making it seem longer than it was. He was wearing a tan tweed vest over his otherwise bare torso and his chest and belly were soft. A tattered old pair of bell bottom pants and a pair of sandals completed the outfit. Ed thought he looked like an out-of-place hippie.

"Hey, TC, I'm glad, and surprised, that you made it here on time," Mario offered in way of a greeting.

"Dude! I always try to come through, don't I? I'm a busy guy, you know. Who's your friend?"

"Don't worry about that," Mario replied brusquely. "The less you know, the better." Ed wondered why there was such a need for secrecy.

"Um, do you have my payment, man?" TC asked timidly. Mario nodded and rummaged through a duffel bag he'd brought along. He pulled out an envelope and handed it over. TC ripped the edge open and counted through the bills contained inside. "Okay, dude, looks good. I'll be waiting here." He resumed his place near the fire and looked around for his opened package of dogs, muttering about having left the last one on the fire too long.

"TC, you forgetting something?" Mario asked.

"What's that, man? You wanna get high before you leave?"

"No," Mario shouted like an impatient father, "my information?"

"Oh, yeah, right, right!" TC stood up and dug around in his pocket, coming up with a crumpled piece of paper. "This is a map with directions out to that aid station. I swung by there yesterday. The place was trashed and looked picked over. The local police were out there. I didn't have any money on me, so I couldn't get any more information." He unfolded the paper and showed it to Mario. "See this spot? Watch out for that. There's an over-turned truck there. There are some bloodstains on the ground around the area, and I found a few spent shell-casings. There were also some tracks made by other vehicles that someone had tried to cover up. But they didn't do a very good job." TC sounded very professional all of a sudden. Then, "You guys sure you don't wanna get high before you leave? It's primo, dude."

"Maybe later," Mario answered. "We gotta run. Thanks for the info."

They jumped into the utility vehicle, and the motor started right away. Mario shifted into gear and drove down the dirt path. Soon enough, the path led to a road, but it wasn't much of an improvement.

Mario was silent, as if deep in thought, until Eddie asked, "What's that guy's story?"

Mario waited a moment, then gave him a brief rundown. "He's a character, that TC. I know that at some point he was in the military. Special ops, I think. Anyway, after he got out, he was recruited by the DEA, but the politics got to him. He had some kind of a breakdown, so he stayed where they'd stationed him. Capersdeed. Can you imagine?"

## Caribbean Calling

"How did you get involved with him?" Eddie asked.

Mario paused, then changed the subject. "This information about the aid station and the over-turned truck -- I'm not sure what to make of it." He reached into an inside pocket of his vest and pulled out a long, thick cigar. He bit the end of the big joint off and spit it out the window. Out of a different pocket, he fished around for a silver Zippo lighter. Steering the vehicle with his knee, he used both hands to light it up. Stoking the cigar, smoke billowing from the sides of his mouth, he looked over at Eddie. "I think this job might be more interesting than we had anticipated."

j. d. gordon

## Chapter Fifteen

Elaine was escorted to a cold, cavernous dungeon. It was noisy, and still in a drugged daze, she couldn't quite come to terms with what was going on. She ran her hands across the stone walls and shivered in the damp air. A single wooden bench with a soggy old mattress provided the extent of comforts. A dirty, green wool blanket lay on the floor in a heap. In the corner, a smelly pit full of filthy water served as a toilet. Steel bars prevented any thought of escape.

After the iron gate had been slammed shut and locked, she was left alone to ponder her fate. She cried herself into a restless sleep. The robe she was wearing over her cotton suit did little to keep out the cold. She didn't even want to touch the blanket.

She assumed it was morning when a guard arrived and ordered her to get up. When he let her out of the cell, she found herself in a large flooded cave. She could see docks above her, and the space was a constant drone of the noise of power tools. Three impressive watercraft bobbed on the waves by the docks. Two were covered with workers in blue jumpsuits, sanding, painting, and altering the appearance of the boats. The other vessel was being ignored, for now, but it was a work of art, an antique, most likely. The wood was polished to a high sheen, the paint without defect. The owner must spend much time and sweat of laborers keeping the ship looking so fine, considering the environment. Elaine noted that the ship's name was El Presidente.

## Caribbean Calling

The guard prodded her to a wall marked by a large spigot and a hose. A dockworker stood there, nozzle in hand. "Get undressed," the guard demanded. "You're going to see the boss. He wants you cleaned up." He was a mean looking man, but the gun he held looked, to Elaine, even more sinister. She did what he asked. The man with the hose squirted something thick onto her skin from a clear bottle -- some sort of soap, she guessed. Then the worker turned the stream on. The water was freezing. Elaine screamed at the force of the water and its temperature, and the men laughed, continuing to hose her down. When the soapsuds were gone, they made her stand there, naked, for what seemed like an eternity, making lewd comments. Eventually, they threw her an old towel. Once dried, she was given a pair of socks, an orange shirt, and a matching pair of pants. She shivered, from fear and from the cold, as she dressed. Her wet hair was left hanging on her neck and shoulders. Then, she was escorted to a much more pleasant location on Crow Island.

Lester hadn't been in the mood to deal with his new acquisition, the female doctor, when he'd returned home. After landing, he'd told Hector to have one of the men stash her away in the cells down by the docks. Before anything else, he needed to plan the search for the missing item left behind on Capersdeed. He put Hector in charge of the operation. There was a lot of money in that case and he wanted to make sure it was recovered.

Hector selected six men for the job. He briefed them, and then had them pack up their equipment. By morning, their weapons were cleaned and they all appeared in the Crow standard issue uniform, tan and military-style, ready to go. Nylon suspenders and web belts were used to tote most of the weaponry and other tools.

Hector would lead the expedition. He inspected the soldiers

and was satisfied with their appearance. They looked official, clean-cut, and hardcore, all battle-seasoned veterans. The Crow organization drew their men from all walks of life, and from many different countries. They were, after all, very well financed.

They left a little before dawn in a helicopter similar to the one used by Lester Crow, but not as luxurious inside. The armed men lined the aircraft's wall in their battle gear, communicating through earpieces and microphones wired into their helmets. When the craft landed, the soldiers would be deployed through the automated rear hatch.

The pilot notified Hector that they had arrived at their destination, and the helicopter settled near the site of the overturned truck. The rear hatch lowered and the men flooded out. Hector walked down the rear loading ramp and stamped one of his booted feet on the dry earth. The appendage had fallen asleep during the flight and the tingling sensation had spread its way up into his calf, irritating him further. He'd been the one to hire Crane in the first place, and it was his personal mission to fix this mess.

Crow's general surveyed the area surrounding the crash site, his keen eyes taking in the landscape and the variances in the terrain. He began to issue orders and his men spread out in a wide pattern. Along with the battle gear, the party had brought tools to aid in the search. Each soldier operated a different type of inspection device -- an infrared camera, a metal detector. Anything that would help them find the lost case.

During the search, the soldier Hector had appointed as a lookout alerted his boss to a foreign vehicle. Hector raised a pair of binoculars to his hazel eyes and noted a four by four resting at a crest on the road in the distance. Two men dismounted from the vehicle and established eye contact, or, more accurately, lens contact, as they gazed at each other through similar devices.

## Caribbean Calling

Hector studied both individuals. They seemed harmless enough. One of the men had a long cigar sticking out of his mouth, but Hector didn't notice any weapons. He wondered why they were so curious, and why they didn't approach if they were so interested in what was going on. Hector ruled them out as government officials from Capersdeed. he was familiar with most of them. The area was supposed to be closed off to anyone not with the government, though. For a moment, he thought one of the men looked familiar. He zeroed in on him and tried to recall where he'd seen him before. His thoughts were interrupted when one of his men presented him with a black case. It was beaten-up, having spent nearly a week in a rocky crevasse filled with standing water. The place where they'd found it was home to a colony of very large, disease-ridden mosquitoes, which was why no one had run into the cash-filled case.

Hector opened it. The cash was still there. The bills would need some time hanging on a clothesline, but they would be suitable for circulation again soon enough.

Pleased with the mission's success, Hector returned his attention to the strangers on the hilltop. They were still peering at the scene through binoculars. They seemed interested in the spectacle. Never mind, he thought to himself, the show is over. Then, rethinking the situation, he spoke briefly to his pilot.

He ordered his men to load up and the soldiers took their places in the belly of the flying beast. The rear loading hatch returned to its closed position, the pilot fired up the turbine, and the propellers began to spin. The aircraft lifted into the air and ascended to above treetop level.

Then, the nose cone dipped down and rotated in the direction of the vehicle sitting alone on the roadway. Sitting up front in the co-pilot's seat, Hector could now see that the men were, in fact, armed. He saw the two men speak to each other, and then scramble out of sight beneath the thick jungle canopy that lined the roadway. He now felt sure he recognized one of them. After his orders, the weaponry located on the nose of the aircraft bellowed forth, the forty-millimeter cannon and the twenty-millimeter Gatling gun blowing the land vehicle into small pieces. The pilot continued to pepper the area for several minutes.

Hector never did anything half-assed. He ordered the pilot to land the machine. He wanted to see the dead bodies of these two men with his own eyes, and he wanted to know who, exactly, they were. He had a suspicion that one of the men was his old nemesis, Eddie Gilbert, the young fireman from up north, the man who had disrupted the Klein kidnapping job and caused the death of Blackwell Crow. It was something in his gut, and he never ignored his intuition.

## Chapter Sixteen

Eddie and Mario sat in silence, taking in the surroundings. The air conditioning was on the fritz, and the day was getting hotter and hotter as the sun plotted along on its course. The going was slow. In the boondocks, far away from any settlements or towns, the roads were ridden with potholes, gouges, and endless tree limbs. The roads in the towns and villages weren't much better. There were still the same potholes and gouges, but the tree limbs were replaced by ox carts, ancient cars, free-roaming livestock, and roadside markets.

According to TC's map, the crash site was a short distance from the main city, along the same route. After leaving the congested rat-trap referred to as a city by TC, Mario and Eddie kept their eyes peeled for any sign of the wrecked truck. The road beyond civilization was abandoned. Apparently, local authorities had denied access to civilians. At the end of the town's stretch of road, an old Bronco blocked the way. The top of the vehicle had been removed, and in its place, a heavy machine gun had been mounted. Strands of belted ammunition hung from the side. There were four officers in all. Mario approached and stopped.

"Hello, gentlemen. How are you on this glorious day?" He smiled and waved as an officer walked toward them.

"What's yo business here, mon?" the officer demanded.

"My name is Carlos Fuentes and this gentleman is James

Graham. He is a banker from Canada here to investigate investment opportunities. We've been given permission to explore the beauty of the island."

The officer looked skeptical. "I din't get no message about no Canadian bankah, mon. Anyway, da road ees closed, mon."

"Well, good sir," Mario continued, "Mr. Graham here is rather pressed for time. I think he would be very happy to compensate you for your trouble, wouldn't you, Mr. Graham?" Mario turned to Eddie and eyed the duffel on the passenger side floor. Ed got the message and extracted a wad of bills from the duffel pocket. It was Canadian currency. Mario took the stack of bills and handed it out to the officer. The man put the money in his pocket and waved them through without any further ado. Mario knew the officer would phone the incident in as soon as the two men got on their way, and he knew that they would now have to work very quickly.

They didn't encounter a soul until they reached the crest of a tall hill, where Mario came to a stop. The crash site could be seen in the distance, but unexpected activity was taking place there. A large black helicopter sat on the ground and a squad of well-armed men appeared to be searching for something. They were spread out in an organized formation, marching back and forth scouring the brush. One man stood, issuing orders. He was clearly the head honcho.

Eddie and Mario stepped out of the vehicle and Mario tossed Eddie a pair of generic binoculars. His own set was more impressive. After a moment, Mario lowered his eyepiece and swore. "Shit! We should have backed off. Now we've been spotted." Raising the binoculars again, he added, "Let's see what happens. The jig's already up. Maybe they'll think we're tourists."

"Looks like they found what they were looking for," Eddie

## Caribbean Calling

commented when one of the searchers displayed a black case to his boss. He couldn't tell what was inside.

Moments later, the crew packed up their gear and re-boarded the helicopter. When the aircraft ascended and began to turn towards them, Mario saw the nose cone transform into a nasty looking weapons turret. It was obvious what was going to happen next.

"Get away from the truck, Eddie, hit the ground and..." Mario never finished his sentence. Even if he did, the words would have been inaudible above the sound of the helicopter's ammunition. They jumped into the thick foliage for cover and waited. Mario was pissed at himself. He'd seen this coming and he'd been in the business too long to have become so complacent.

TC's truck disintegrated into pieces as a cascade of shells hit it. Then, the gunner turned his weapons toward the area surrounding the vehicle. The high-powered ammunition was merciless. Everything that called the roadside home was decimated by thousands of rounds. The fact that not one shell pierced skin was a Hollywood miracle. A large boulder, seemingly placed there by God for the purpose of saving lives, had protected Eddie's body from being shredded. Suddenly, he heard a voice out of nowhere. It was Mario's voice, close, yet muted, on the satellite radio. Eddie pulled the device from his side pocket and pressed a button to respond.

"Eddie," the voice on the radio squawked. "The bad guys are landing. These guys gotta be heavily armed. If we want to get out of this, we need to hit them as they dismount. Get back up to the roadway and don't be stingy with the ammo!"

"Roger," Eddie answered simply. He pulled the Colt out from the inside of his vest, slid the action on the pistol, and made sure there was a round in the chamber. This was no time for a misfire. He stuck a spare magazine in the front pocket of his vest.

## j. d. gordon

Nervous as hell, he took a couple of deep breaths, and then crawled out from behind the rock. The helicopter's landing gear was barely touching the road and it was difficult to see what was happening. The spinning rotor blades were creating a virtual sandstorm. He whipped on his sunglasses to help shield his eyeballs.

Eddie could make out the rear loading hatch lowering. He raised his weapon and pointed it toward the rear of the helicopter as soon as he saw movement. A soldier was exiting the loading ramp and Eddie pulled the trigger twice. The man fell to the ground. He didn't know where Mario was, but he knew his partner had nailed the enemy's point man. He saw his two slugs slam into the helicopter's tail.

When two more soldiers emerged from the rear of the craft, Eddie let loose. He pointed the weapon at his target and pulled the trigger until the magazine was empty. Then he hit the release button on the side of his trusty Colt. The depleted magazine fell to the ground near his feet while he slammed a fresh clip into the bottom of the pistol.

Looking up, he saw his assailant lying on the ground. The second man had almost made it to the foliage on Mario's side of the road. Now he was in the road on his back -- Mario had laid him out. Another soldier stuck his head out of the rear of the helicopter. Mario and Eddie both opened up on him and he retreated.

The machine powered back up, the rotors picking up speed, and the chopper rose to treetop level once again. There, it twisted about, again aiming the deadly front turret in the direction of the men on the ground. After a downpour from the automatic weapons, the aircraft hovered, changed directions, and headed in a southerly direction.

Eddie lay still, having taken cover by his God-sent boulder.

## Caribbean Calling

"You okay, Ed?" It was Mario on the satellite radio, again.

"Yeah, I'll meet you up top," Eddie responded.

Both men emerged onto the roadway, slowly at first, and then more confidently as the sound of the rotors chopping through the air diminished. The incident had caused profound devastation. Beyond the destruction of TC's truck, there were dozens of large indentations in the road. The plant life on either side of the road was ripped apart and tossed around like a giant salad, and smoke still hung in the air. Mario began rummaging through the possessions of the troopers left behind, searching for anything they could use. Eddie joined in.

"Mario, this one is only wounded." There were three in all.

"Is he conscious?" Mario asked as continued checking the pockets of the dead.

"Yes, he's conscious, but he's not going to make it. He's floating around in an ocean of blood over here. His pulse is weak and he's barely breathing." It was second nature for Eddie to assess the condition of any injured person. Like all firefighters and paramedics, he carried parts of his job with him wherever he was.

"There's not much on these guys. No cash, no identification. One guy had a couple of Tootsie Roll in his pocket, but that's about it. They're all armed with AK-47s. I don't think they were expecting trouble, though. They're not carrying very much ammunition." Mario dropped everything in a pile by Eddie's feet. Eddie stood after closing the now dead man's eyes. He couldn't bear the man's expression.

In all, they collected three AK-47s, six magazines of ammunition, three fragmentation grenades, and three small 22-caliber automatics, which the men had been carrying in ankle holsters.

## j. d. gordon

"Let's each take an assault rifle and three extra magazines. Here's a grenade for you, you know how to use that?" Mario asked. Eddie nodded. "Okay, good. Might as well take one of these 22s, too. I'll take these two Tootsie Rolls, you sure? I don't need both of them."

"No, I'm good, really," Eddie chuckled, amazed by Mario's composure. Mario unrolled the treats and chucked them into his mouth.

Ed secured his new pistol and holster around his own ankle, and then helped Mario drag the dead men into the jungle. The insects would have a feast. When the task was done, they sat on a log to assess their options. Mario stuck a fresh cigar into his mouth, bit the end off, spit it out, and lit the log with his Zippo. "Well, it seems we have a situation here."

Ed felt exhausted. "I'd agree. No car, far from home, not equipped very well, and the locals are bound to be on our tails soon."

"You may turn out to be pretty good at this job, Fireman Ed," Mario said with a chuckle.

The first action decided upon was to attempt to reach Klein with the satellite radio. The attempts were unsuccessful. Mario was able, though, to reach Marvin back at the landing site. Ed could hear him trying to update the pilot until he disconnected in frustration. "Fuckin' guy is stoned out of his gourd. He's got TC with him. He said he'd keep an eye out, whatever that means." Mario paused and looked at Ed. "Well, you ready to hoof it? Let's find this aid station."

The two made their way down the road. It was hot and humid and they had no water, no provisions for the long walk. After a mile or so, they came to the end of the rain forest, the thick jungle foliage changing to wide and rocky fields. It was mid-afternoon, and both of them were exhausted. Once they made it to the top of a hill, another was waiting. Finally, they saw, in the distance, their objective. At the crest of yet another hill, they found themselves looking down on a small village. Fields surrounded the developed area, some flooded, some dry, but there wasn't a soul to be seen.

Mario lifted the binoculars to his eyes. "Why the hell isn't anyone out there? You'd think they'd be out working the fields. I don't see any movement in the village, either." Mario consulted his map. "I think that's the aid station on the far side."

As they began their walk into town, the most notable thing was that the place was deserted, not a dog, cat, cow, or even a simple chicken was around. The place was a ghost town.

"I don't like this at all." Mario voiced what Eddie had been thinking.

The two decided to separate, one on either side of the road. They held their weapons at the ready, safety switches disabled and bullets in the chamber. Their hike to the aid station on the far side of the village remained quiet. Birds chirped and sang as if nothing was wrong.

When they reached their destination, the two went about searching the site. The well was still working and there were still some scraps of food left in the dining room. They poured themselves a couple of large pitchers of water and scooped some peanut butter out of a previously unopened jar. Fearful of eating anything that had already been opened, the pickings were slim.

The nourishment and water helped to clear their heads, and they decided to try Klein again. This time they were successful. Klein was out on the golf course, taking a mulligan at the box on hole nine. The conversation was only moments along when Mario broke it off. A vehicle was approaching the aid station by way of the road through the village. Mario spotted the dust being kicked up before either man heard it coming.

# j. d. gordon

"Oh, shit," Mario said, looking out the window. Eddie turned to see the armored vehicle lumbering along toward them. It was a half-tracked vehicle, tires in the front and treads in the rear, and it moved slowly. Four soldiers rode in the rear, which was open, but which provided protection to anyone sitting or crouching in a firing position. One soldier was leaning against a large machine-gun mounted there. Eddie could make out only one person sitting in the driver's compartment. The armor plating designed to protect the windows was on a hinge so that it could swivel up and out of the way when the vehicle was not under attack. That's where it was now located. Except for the soldier leaning against the gun, the men looked to be smoking and joking, as if they were on a scenic tour.

The armored vehicle rolled to a stop in front of the main building. Eddie looked to Mario with questioning eyes.

"Okay. Here's the plan," he answered, reading Eddie's mind. "We're going to capture that rig, take a prisoner, and get down to the bottom of this mystery."

Eddie's heart dropped to his stomach. "Oh sure, that sounds pretty simple. The two of us will take on an armored vehicle full of men that are, most likely, armed to the teeth."

Mario nodded and smiled.

As Capersdeed's finest began to drop from the side of the half-track, the driver stayed in his seat and the man standing by the machine gun remained still. The barrel of the heavy weapon was tilted, pointing up to the sky, and the man smoked a cigarette. Obviously, they weren't expecting any trouble.

The soldiers spread out and began searching the area. First, they entered the camp houses, sticking their heads in and then moving on to the next. One soldier made his way to the pole barn in the rear of the compound, his path taking him past the kitchen where Eddie and Mario crouched. As he passed the kitchen door,

## Caribbean Calling

Mario pounced like a tiger, grabbing the man and dragging him into the room. Eddie knocked him over the head with a frying pan, ensuring that he'd be out cold for some time. After using towels to bind and gag the soldier, they dragged the limp body under the long dining table.

"Eddie," Mario whispered, "I want you to stay here. I'll take care of these guys. They're amateurs. Anything happens to me, stay low and get back to Marvin, then report everything to the boss." Eddie gave Mario a thumbs up. It didn't seem like the right time to second-guess anything Mario said.

Mario clutched the assault rifle with a firm grip and moved out into the compound. Eddie was surprised at how swift and silent the crusty old Italian could be when he needed to. Mario made his way to one of the camp houses at the end of the row. The screen door on the front of the structure emitted a squeak as he entered, inviting the attention of a nearby soldier. The man circled the building prior to entering.

Seconds later, Mario exited the house through the front again with a knife in his hand, blood dripping from the blade. He sprinted across the clearing in the direction of the pole barn. By Eddie's count, if one soldier was in the kitchen with him, and one was laying dead in the cabin that would leave one more roaming about and two more in the car. When his attention was distracted by his prisoner's struggles, he conked him again on the head, quieting him down. Then he turned around to look out the door and found himself staring into the barrel of a shotgun.

"Hey, mon, what the hell you doin'? Back up and untie my man or I'll take off yo stinkin' head!" His tone was vicious, but he paid for his lack of hospitality. With Mario's arm wrapped around the fellow's melon, the soldier was taken down to the wood planks of the floor in one swift motion. Mario plunged the blade of his knife up into the man's chest, beneath the breastbone. The tip of the blade punctured his heart and he was dead before he knew what had hit him.

"Jeez, Ed. I leave you alone for a coupla minutes and look what happens."

Ed's own heart was pounding. He was lucky, he thought, that he hadn't shit himself when he'd come face to face with the business end of that shotgun.

"You're doing fine, kid, keep it up. You're taking to the business just fine." Mario's encouragement steadied him for the time being.

After Mario explained their next move, Ed ran around one side of the main building, and Mario the other side. Holding on to the shotgun that had, a moment before, been stuck in his face, Ed adjusted the accompanying bandoleer he'd wrapped around his torso. The Capersdeed military must have a small budget, Eddie thought. The shotgun was single barrel model, a 12-gauge. He popped open the breach. The guy hadn't even loaded the damn thing. He'd been staring into an empty weapon. He slipped a shell into the gun and secured the breach. One round would suit his purposes.

Separated, Mario and Eddie had their communication devices in hand. When they each reached their prearranged positions, they made contact. A single word kicked off the action. "Go!"

Both men took off running. The half-track was in front of the main building, and the distance each of them had to cover was about equal. Eddie focused on the front end of the vehicle. As he jumped up onto the hot, solid surface of the engine compartment, he could read the shock on the driver's face. Then he heard the clatter of Mario's AK-47.

Mario had targeted the man standing near the heavy artillery. He'd waited to open up until the very last moment,

## caribbean calling

when the soldier had caught Mario's charge out of the corner of his eye. Turning in disbelief, the man attempted to target Mario with the big gun, but the AK-47 cut him down in no time flat. He fell backward, slamming into the short wall on the side of the truck before falling over the side and landing heavily on the ground.

Eddie was successful as well. After surprising the driver, he stuck the barrel of the shotgun through the window, made eye contact, and then waited before pulling the trigger. This business of killing folks, bastards or not, went against Eddie's grain. He couldn't help his hesitation. The driver yelled out and went for his side arm, and that's when Eddie pulled the trigger. It was over. The only sound was that of singing birds. Acrid smoke drifted about.

Mario spoke first. "Well, we've got someone in back we've got to speak with. You stay out here and keep an eye out for any surprises. I'm sure if these guys don't report in, more will be coming along soon." He trudged around the side of the main building, out of sight.

Ed checked out the rear end of the half-track. There was some pretty heavy firepower on board the old contraption. Extra boxes of fifty-caliber ammunition for the machine-gun were stacked against one of the truck walls, covered in blood. On the other side, mounted in brackets, were two collapsible light anti-tank weapons, both American made. He'd learned how to use these types of weapons during his time in the Navy.

Next, he wanted to check out the driver's compartment. He pulled the lifeless body of the driver out and was getting ready to jump in when he noticed the blood and brain tissue splattered everywhere. He jumped when Mario snuck up behind him.

"Clean that shit out of there, will ya? We're taking this pig with us."

"Did he tell you anything? Did you get anything out of him?" Eddie tried to mask his nervousness.

Mario looked at him as if he'd just fallen off the turnip truck. "Did I get anything out of him? That's why I make the big bucks, Eddie. Jeez." Mario inspected the inside of the cab again. "And just so you know, I don't slaughter people who don't threaten me. They'll find the guy before the day's over and he'll be back out wreaking havoc in no time. Anyway, apparently, these folks were rounded up and taken to some compound known as The Plantation. It's some kind of cult or something. It's supposed to be right down the road a bit."

"Did he say anything about the Crows?" Eddie asked.

"The Crows? He mentioned that they were here. Why?"

"Those guys in the chopper. They were dressed like the Crows. I visited their tranquil island to pick up Klein's daughter last year." Eddie mentioned the time casually, as if Jennifer had been rescued from a bad blind date.

"Yeah, he mentioned the Crows. He didn't know if they picked anyone up, though. I don't have any reason to believe they have the doctor we're looking for. Do you?" Mario asked.

"No...I mean, I wonder what they have to do with all this shit. They're real bad news, those guys."

"Well, I have a feeling the answers to our questions will be found at this plantation. Let's saddle up, kid."

"You have a plan?"

"Not yet. I figure we'll come up with something when we get there."

Eddie thought for a moment. Sticking his index finger in the air, he indicated to Mario to hang on for a minute. Darting into the main building, he exited five minutes later with an IV pole,

## Caribbean Calling

some medical tape, and a bundle of white material.

Mario had found a garden hose on the side of the porch and was cleaning the inside of the cab when Eddie returned. "It'll be wet, but it'll be clean," he said, as if the material he'd just cleaned up was a spilled ice-cream cone. He didn't ask about the equipment Eddie was holding.

"I take it I'm driving this wreck?" Eddie asked, placing the gear in the back seat of the truck.

"I figure you're the most qualified. You drive fire engines, don't you?"

Eddie took a closer look at the driver's compartment and shook his head with doubt. There was a lever for the throttle. A long stick protruded from the floor between the two seats. A button was marked "ignition." Three large pedals were situated in a row above the floor board, which still showed traces of blood. The vehicle was ancient.

"I'll tell ya one thing," Eddie said, scratching his sunburned head, "a modern fire engine is a hell of a lot easier to work with than this. It's got an automatic transmission, a turbo-charged engine, anti-lock brakes...this sucker has to be double clutched, for crissakes."

Sitting in the driver's seat, he ground a few of the teeth in the transmission's gear box down, and eventually got the awkward machine moving, albeit backward at first. After a moment, he got it going in the right direction, a little rough, but in the right direction.

"Hang on, Mario, the speedometer on this baby goes all the way up to forty miles an hour," he said as he slammed the shift into the next gear.

Cruising along, the old needle behind the smeared glass sat at the thirty mile an hour mark. No one bothered them on their way. At the peak of one of the endless hills, the primitive road wound about in a haphazard manner. Eddie depressed the brake pedal and slipped the vehicle's transmission into neutral. They were overlooking a wide, deep, green valley. It would have been breathtaking under more relaxed circumstances. Dozens of people in long white robes tended various crops with antiquated tools. Some even worked plows powered by horses and oxen.

In the background, Eddie and Mario could see an expansive compound surrounded by tall and thick brick walls. A guard shack prevented unwanted guests.

"It looks like a fortress from medieval times," Eddie said in wonderment.

"Sure enough," Mario answered, cigar in place. "So, what's your plan, kid?" The sun was now high in the sky, and little beads of sweat formed on the swarthy man's forehead.

"Funny you should ask," he responded, exiting the truck's cab and grabbing the materials he'd collected back at the aid station. "The way I see it," he continued as he stuck the IV pole into the soft roadway, "we don't have a beef with these folks. We need information on the woman."

Eddie unfurled the white cloth, which was a large cotton blanket, and wrapped one end around the top of the pole. "And if I know Lester Crow, and I think I do, Lester has her. I feel it in my bones, man."

Mario watched with amusement as Eddie wrapped tape around the cloth to secure it. He knew where Eddie was going with this. "In the old days, armies used to wave a white flag and call a truce. Or, sometimes it was to collect the dead and wounded off the battlefield. Sometimes, it was to socialize, believe it or not."

Eddie completed taping down the bottom portion of the

blanket and then stood back. The white flag of truce waved in the warm breeze.

"A white flag, that's your plan." It wasn't a question. "You're fuckin' nuts, kid, but we'll give it a try. I'll go in and see if it works."

Eddie shook his head again. "Not you, friend, me. If anything happens and I can't get out, that doctor will be depending on you. I'm expendable in this situation."

Mario cast a serious expression across his mug, an unusual action for a usually jolly fellow. "If anything, Ed, you are noble." The two were silent for a minute or two. "Well, let's roll, as they say."

Eddie jumped back into the driver's seat, the makeshift flag propped up next to him. He shifted gears and they were on their way, following the winding road. They stopped fifty yards short of the breach in the compound's tall walls. Eddie checked his pistol in the holster inside his vest and checked to make sure the .22 automatic was in his ankle holster. Then he exited the vehicle, flag in hand, and approached the main entrance.

"Wait a minute," Mario rasped in a loud whisper from the truck. Eddie turned back. "This might be useful." He tossed Eddie an envelope stuffed with US currency, Grants, mostly. Eddie stuffed the wad into his waistband.

A guard stepped out as Ed approached. The man was wearing the same long robe that the people in the fields were wearing. Ed was sure there was a firearm somewhere in all those folds of cloth. He could see a large group of people huddled in the middle of an open space beyond the gate and wondered if they were the folks from the deserted village and aid station. They looked miserable, dirty, and scared.

"Is there something I can help you with?" the guard asked in a curious tone.

"I'd like to talk with the person that runs this outfit," Ed answered with well-acted confidence.

"About what?"

Eddie decided to go straight to the heart of the matter. "I think your organization may have, or may know the whereabouts of a female physician I am looking for."

"Wait there." The guard hesitated for a moment, and then disappeared behind the wall. Soon after, he returned. "The Caretaker says he will see you. Someone will be down to escort you."

Eddie waited in the heat and the dust, the flag still in his hand. After about ten minutes, a golf cart pulled up with a giant of a man behind the wheel. He stepped off, and the little vehicle wobbled, attempting to maintain its suspension. There was something familiar about him, but Eddie had no idea why.

"You're here to speak with the Caretaker?" he asked. "And you think the white flag will ensure your safety?" Well, it worked back in the old days," Eddie answered with a straight face.

"Yeah, I'm familiar with the custom. But are you honorable enough to live up to the standards?"

Eddie hesitated. He knew what the giant's next question would be. "I am."

"May I have your weapons please?"

Eddie reached into his vest, pulled out his Colt, and handed it over. Then he reached to his ankle and displayed the .22 pistol. The big man collected both weapons and ordered the gate guard to pat down the visitor. The search produced no other hidden weapons.

## caribbean calling

"Okay. Get in the cart. You can leave the flag here."

"If it's not a problem, custom dictates that I keep the flag with me," Eddie replied.

The man thought about it and shook his head, but then submitted. "Okay, whatever."

The little cart sputtered and leaned to the right as it crossed the yard. Along the way, Ed watched families, huddled into small clusters. Uniformed men stood watch over them. A small young white woman with short brown hair, big black spectacles, and a braided anklet crouched in the group. The man parked the cart and led Eddie into a modern, air-conditioned building. The hallways were wide and bright. Ed felt proud carrying the flag, taking part in a long-standing tradition of warfare that had been effective, even in the most dangerous circumstances. Ed felt an eerie calm. He didn't question it.

On the far side of the room, an elevator took them to the top floor, number six. At the end of the hall, they entered a spacious office suite. A thin, handsome man sat behind a large desk. He had short gray hair, buzzed to the scalp, like Eddie's.

"So, may I ask your name?" The man had a soft, comforting voice.

"My name is Edward, but please call me Eddie."

The man made no invitation for Eddie to sit. "I'm the Caretaker. What brings you here, Eddie?"

Eddie stood with his flag, erect and confidant. "Well, sir, I've been employed to find someone. I think you may know where she is."

"She must be very special, this woman."

"I'm looking for a doctor. Her name is Elaine Keller. She was the physician at the aid station not far from here."

# j. d. gordon

"Yes, Doctor Keller." The Caretaker smiled. "I know of her. What is your business with the young woman, may I ask?"

"The person I work for has asked me to find her. I didn't think it would be a difficult task. It seems to be turning into that, though."

The Caretaker stood and inspected Eddie. "You know, if you're in the 'business,' I could use a man like you here, Eddie."

"Mr. Caretaker," Ed spoke with the utmost respect. "I have an idea as to what type of organization you have here. It may be a life for some, but not for me. I'm here to do a job -- a job I intend to complete. I have no issue with you or your lifestyle. I respect you, honest. You've got a hell of a deal going." Eddie paused for a beat. "Please, don't disrespect me."

The Caretaker looked Eddie in the eye, never blinking. Eddie remained defiant, he returned the glare.

"Why should I take to your cause, Eddie?"

Eddie reached into his waistband and tossed the envelope of greenbacks onto the desk.

The Caretaker didn't reach for the package. Instead, he looked to Eddie's escort. The man reached over, opened the envelope, and fingered through the bills inside.

"It's a nice figure, sir," he reported.

"Nice? How nice, Baron?"

"Very nice, sir."

Baron. The name struck a chord in the recesses of Eddie's mind. He studied the giant's features, and then it hit him. One brown eye and one blue. He couldn't believe it. How had this happened? That person...here? In the middle of the Caribbean? In this crazy situation?

## Caribbean calling

The Caretaker folded his hands on the desk and sighed. "I'm afraid I don't control the fate of the woman you are seeking. She is in the hands of the Crow organization." It was the answer Eddie had anticipated, but it didn't make it any easier to hear. "That's the most I can offer you. Unless, of course, you would reconsider signing on with me."

"No, sir," Eddie answered, still in shock, although he disguised it well. "Thank you for accommodating me. I'll take my flag and continue on my mission."

"Good luck to you, Eddie." The Caretaker didn't look up. "Baron, please return our visitor to the main gate."

It wasn't until they were riding down in the elevator that the Baron spoke. "You handled the Caretaker well. I thought for sure I was going to have to take you down."

Eddie looked at him. "So, Baron is your name?" The man nodded. "Well, that's a contest I'm glad to have avoided."

The men walked in silence to the golf cart. It struck Ed as silly, two grown men, warriors of a sort, driving around in the little leisure vehicle, like two retired gents out for an afternoon round of golf. The Baron deposited Eddie at the front gate and returned his weapons. Ed checked. Both were still loaded. He looked at the Baron, straight into those crazy eyes. "We've met, you know." The Baron cocked his head to the side, as if the action would loosen a memory in his big noggin. "The last time was many, many years ago, in a small playground, beneath the shade of an old gray stone school building in Chicago."

The Baron's features changed. "Eddie? Eddie Gilbert! Holy shit! I told you I would get you, Eddie Gilbert, didn't I?" Eddie was sorry he'd brought the subject up. The Baron, for a moment, looked very pissed. Then his expression softened. "Aw, hell. That was a long time ago, Eddie. Things change."

## j. d. gordon

"Yes, they do, Bartley." Ed used the Baron's given name. "They sure do." He turned his back to the Baron and walked away, dropping the white flag on the ground.

As Ed headed for the truck, the Baron stepped forward and picked up the white flag. He took a last look at his old schoolyard adversary. "Good luck, Eddie Gilbert. Maybe we'll meet again." Ed didn't answer.

Mario noticed the confidence in Ed's gait as he approached. "Well? How did it go?" he asked.

"Mario, we're going to Crow Island."

## Chapter Seventeen

A guard escorted Elaine to a large, much more comfortable room in a different area of the Crow complex. Round white columns stretched from the polished wood floor to the white-planked ceiling, where large Casablanca fans stirred the air. On the far side of the room, French doors led to a large veranda. Elaine could see mountains in the distance, and a beautiful blue lagoon. In front of the veranda, a man sat behind a massive desk sifting through papers.

"Sir, I brought the girl, like you asked," the guard reported.

The man looked up from his work. He had sharp features, enhanced by his slicked-black hair pulled back into a ponytail. He was dressed in a cream-colored cotton shirt. Elaine recognized him as the man who had visited the Caretaker back at The Plantation. "Thank you, Juan. You may leave us alone. I'm sure I can handle her."

"Yes, sir." The guard bowed his head and retreated from the room, closing the door on his way out. Elaine was left standing in the center of the room. Her hair was still wet.

"Well, Doctor, I see they cleaned you up a bit. I do hope you're feeling better?" His tone was kind, hospitable, even.

"It wasn't the most pleasant experience," she answered quietly. She was very frightened.

"Have my men done anything they should not have?" Elaine

didn't answer. "I didn't think so. I'm reserving that pleasure for myself," he laughed. As if confused by her lack of appreciation, Lester motioned for her to sit. Two low-backed chairs sat in front of the desk. Elaine walked over and heeded his command.

At first, Lester ignored her, thumbing through more papers on his desk. Although afraid, Elaine was aggressive by nature, a common trait amongst people in her line of work. Her head hurt, she was shaky, and she knew she was beginning to go through withdrawals from whatever they'd been giving her at The Plantation. After several minutes, she worked up her courage.

"Excuse me, but what is going on here? Why am I here?" Lester continued to work, not answering her. Fear began to manifest itself into anger. "Hey, asshole! What the fuck is going on here?" She slammed her open palm onto the desk and a couple sheets of paper scattered across the desk.

Lester sat back and studied her for a moment. "Well, I must say, I like that in a woman. A bit feisty, are you?" He smiled. "What's going on here, you ask? Why don't we step outside for a while and talk. I've got a little surprise for you."

Lester stood up and moved towards the veranda, while Elaine stayed put. He motioned for her to follow, and seeing no alternative, she gave in. The view from the veranda was spectacular. A landscaped garden featured meandering brick paths and planters filled with colorful flowers and plants. People in tan uniforms moved about in the garden, pruning bushes and watering. A small dock sat on the edge of the lagoon by a speedboat, a restored Criss Craft.

What she saw in the distance, on a small white sand beach, marred the beauty and horrified her. A man's body, nude, was lying there, arms and legs stretched apart and staked down on pegs sticking out of the sand. His flesh was burned. Next to him was a bucket with a brush sticking out of it.

## Caribbean Calling

The expansive veranda was decorated with latticework, white and clean, covered with green vines sprouting small white flowers. It provided excellent protection from the sun. A table with a green cloth over it was set for two, with crystal glassware, sterling silver, and fine china. A vase in the center was filled with an arrangement of flowers.

"I've taken the liberty to arrange a lunch for us. I chose the menu for you. I do hope you enjoy it." Lester pulled Elaine's chair out for her and she sat down. After placing a napkin on her lap, he helped her to slide the chair toward the table. "You asked what this is all about. I'll do my best to explain. First, though, let's enjoy this delightful meal together."

He served the lunch himself -- rare shark steaks, beans and rice, a casserole of vegetables, and large freshly baked rolls, butter glistening on the surface. Then he poured them each a glass of chilled white wine.

Faint at first, the sound of a helicopter could be heard in the distance. The noise became deafening as the chopper flew over the building, as the surrounding mountains created an echo.

Lester waited until the noise lessened, and then addressed his guest. "What is this all about? Well, Doctor, that depends on you, really. I am something of a ladies' man. I enjoy the company of beautiful women. Perhaps you will be a willing participant. In that case, in the end, and it will end when I find a fancy for another, it will be much better for you. If you resist you will find yourself in much the same position as that poor fellow down on the beach." He shook his head as if to indicate that it was a nasty sight. "There are other unfortunate endings as well. It depends on my mood when the time arrives."

Elaine tried to swallow the food before her. She took a sip of wine, hoping it would calm her nerves. "And if I accept your advances?"

# j. d. gordon

Lester smiled with what he perceived as victory. "Well, there are a couple of options, then. The Caretaker at The Plantation mentioned that he would have you back. Or perhaps I could put you into service, in the laundry room or something similar. Perhaps in the gardens. They're lovely, aren't they? That way, if I feel like it, you'd always be available." He paused then, and his face and tone took on a more sinister aspect. "I will promise you this, though. You will never escape, and you will never return to your old life." Elaine let him continue, her mind racing. "You've seen the faces on the milk cartons back in your country? Well, I know where many of those people are...or were."

"Certainly this is a lot to absorb. So, please, eat your meal. I'll have the guard take you back to your accommodations when you're finished. Go ahead and sleep on it, dear. Give me an answer in the morning." His tone and body language indicated that the conversation was over. The two continued to eat in silence.

Elaine's stomach threatened to expel its contents as she processed the man's demands and threats. Questions whirled about in her mind. How big is this Island? Is there a hope of escape? What about Daddy? How the hell did I get caught up in this?

Her thoughts and the meal were interrupted when another man walked out onto the veranda. He carried a briefcase.

Lester beamed. "Ah, Hector! I see you have been successful, yes?" He motioned to the table. "I'm sorry I don't have a place set for you. Please sit down. Pour yourself a glass of wine."

"Gracias, Lester. I could use it." Hector approached, ignoring Elaine. He was accustomed to Lester's dalliances.

Lester opened the case and examined the contents. Once satisfied, he shut the case and secured the locking mechanism.

"Lester, allow me to apologize for the situation with Crane. I am ashamed to say that he fooled me for all those years. Truly, truly ashamed." Hector lowered his head in deference.

"Hector, the greed of men never ceases to amaze me. I paid him well. He had a generous pension plan to boot. It's very unfortunate, but these things happen. I don't blame you. I blame my own lack of…direction. Please, have another glass of wine." Hector eyed Elaine. "Oh, pardon my bad manners. This is Dr. Elaine Keller. You remember her from our trip to The Plantation."

Hector nodded appreciatively. "A beautiful piece. Are you going to share her?"

"We'll have to see about that. Perhaps, once I've finished with her." Elaine was disgusted, but kept her mouth shut. She was nothing but a piece of meat to be bargained over. "In any case, let's hear the news. Were there any complications? And, by the way, I'll need you to arrange for replacements for the Caretaker. What a ridiculous title that is. What is his name, anyway? Reese, isn't it?"

Hector poured himself another brimming glass full of wine. "Yes, I believe so. I'll arrange for that right away." Hector drained his second glass and went to reach for more, then reconsidered after catching Lester's eye. "We did run into a little trouble, though."

"Trouble?" Lester seemed surprised.

"Yes, a little." Hector looked at Elaine. He knew Lester didn't like to discuss business, particularly unfortunate incidents, in the company of outsiders.

"Hector, please ask the guard to take our guest back to her quarters. Elaine, I'm sorry to have to cut this short. My humble apologies. I'll wait to hear from you in the morning." He stood, as any gentleman would, as she was led away, back to her room, or cell, as it were.

"Well?" Lester said when she was out of earshot.

"Unfortunately, we lost three men. We had some unexpected visitors, I'm afraid."

"Unexpected visitors? The commandant assured me that the area would be sealed off." Lester's neck began to redden.

"Yes. The area was under heavy guard. I don't know how these two men slipped through."

"And who were these meddlers? Government troops? American drug enforcement?"

"That's the interesting thing. I viewed them from a distance, but I think I recognized one of the men."

"Who was it? Did you deal with them? Take them out?"

"We tried. We hit the area and destroyed their vehicle, an old SUV. They took off into the jungle, so we landed. They returned fire as we were off-loading. After three of our men went down, and a fourth was injured, I called off the action. I figured we had what we'd come for. I didn't think taking any more losses was worth the trouble."

"So who was it you say you recognized?"

"I think it was Eddie Gilbert."

The comment came down like a ton of bricks for Lester Crow. "Eddie fucking Gilbert? What the fuck would he be doing on Capersdeed? Do you suppose he's on Klein's payroll, now, looking for that bitch?" The memories of the fireman still haunted Lester. He had often thought of sending a team up to Chicago to take the man out. He'd thought he'd had him at Spike Island, until the U.S. Coast Guard had made an appearance and fouled things up. In quiet moments, usually late at night, Lester dreamed of going back in time. If he'd had a larger force, he'd have been able to deal with the Coast Guard bastards as well. "Hector, go get the doctor. I want to speak with her again."

"Yes, sir," Hector answered respectfully. He could tell his boss was furious.

He returned with Elaine in less than five minutes. She was beside herself. She'd been about to make her move. She didn't need to sleep on anything. She'd already made the decision that she'd rather be hunted down on the island like an animal than give in to this creep's plan for her. She hadn't gone to medical school all those years to snip bushes or wash clothes. No man, no matter how powerful he thought he was, was going to control her. Now, here she was, standing once again on the veranda.

Lester looked distressed. "Are you familiar with a man named Eddie Gilbert?" Elaine shook her head. She'd never heard the name in her life. Lester raised his voice. "I want the truth! I'll have you moved to more comfortable quarters if you cooperate."

Hector was surprised. It was unusual for Lester to bargain with anyone.

"I'm sorry," Elaine replied. "I have never heard the name before."

Lester sat down and drained the wine in his glass, then poured another. "What about Bruce Klein?" he asked, in a calmer tone.

Elaine didn't answer right away. "That name doesn't ring a bell." She paused again. "Isn't he a politician or something?" In fact, she knew Bruce Klein very well. He was one of her father's closest friends. They had served together in the military. At this point, she saw no reason to lie, but on the other hand, she didn't want to give her captor any benefit of her knowledge.

"Take her back to her cell," Lester ordered.

"You said if I was honest, I wouldn't have to go back to the cell," she protested.

"Take her back to the cell," he repeated. There would be no deal. The conversation was over.

After she was led away again by the guard, Lester and Hector continued their discussion. "Hector, I want you to contact Reese. I also want you to tell the commandant that this man is on his island. I want to find out everything about Gilbert's recent whereabouts. I want him, do you hear me? I want him alive, if possible, but dead would suit me fine as well."

Hector nodded and assured his boss that he would deal with the situation effectively.

Lester sat angry and alone on his veranda, finishing his now cold shark steak, dreaming of revenge.

This time, Elaine thought, Lester had seemed very angry. She was relieved to get away from him. Eying the lone guard, she tried to think of a plan. If she were going to do something to help her situation, it would have to be now. Even if it meant braving the jungles of the island's interior, she wanted to avoid spending another moment in that stinking hole.

The guard was walking behind her. He didn't look threatening, except for the fact that he carried a small machine gun. She now wished she had taken up her father's offer to teach her about using firearms. She'd never had any interest whatsoever. She was a doctor, on the earth to heal, not harm.

## Caribbean Calling

On the first trip to Lester's suite, she had noticed a passageway. She guessed, by the layout of the building, that the exit led to the front of the building, on the opposite side of the veranda. What she would find there, she didn't know. She would have to trust her gut instincts.

As the pair passed the hallway that, with any luck, would lead her to freedom, she stopped suddenly, causing the guard to bump into her. Trying very hard to behave calmly, so as not to alarm the guard, she turned around and faced him. He began to speak, but never had the opportunity to finish his thought. Elaine kneed him, hard, in the family jewels. The man bent over in agonizing pain, his gun bouncing off his torso. That's when it hit her. She wanted that gun. Kicking the man repeatedly, the force of the blows hurt her foot, which was covered only by a cheap slipper they'd provided her with earlier, after the shower. As the man rolled around on the floor, she removed the strap from his shoulder. His hands were busy clutching his aching genitals. The hallway remained empty.

Taking off running, she pushed open a door at the end of the hall and found herself standing in front of a landing pad with a large black helicopter in the center. One man leaned against the far wall, and saw her run from the building. She was hard to miss in her bright orange outfit. Reaching to his side in an attempt to draw his sidearm, Elaine surprised him, and herself, by leveling her weapon and pulling the trigger. The weapon coughed up its deadly contents, riddling him with lead. Even after the man fell to the ground, Elaine kept her trigger-finger depressed until it stopped bucking in her hands. She'd used up the entire clip. She dropped the weapon on the ground, ran to the lifeless body, and grabbed his pistol. Then she disappeared beneath the surrounding jungle canopy.

"Perhaps this may be to our advantage," Lester said to Hector, as his meal lay cold and half-eaten on the table before him.

"How's that, Lester?"

"If he hasn't yet been picked up on Capersdeed, I'm sure the fireman knows by now that we are involved in the doctor's disappearance. He'll show up here, and when he does, we'll be waiting."

"And what if he brings the power of the United States with him?"

"I'm not worried about the United States. If they were going to extend their influence to our operation, they would have done so by now. They've been aware of us, and our location, since the Klein incident. If they didn't strike then, they won't now. They've got their hands full with the Middle East and terrorism right now, anyway." Lester gazed out onto the calm blue Caribbean water. "As far as the fireman is concerned, he'll wander right into our clutches. It's his...and my destiny." He backhanded the now empty bottle of wine, sending it flying to the ground where it smashed into a thousand pieces.

Caribbean Calling

## Chapter Eighteen

Back in the old Albatross, Eddie replaced a blood-soaked bandage that was wrapped around his upper left arm. Mario was up front, communicating with Klein. Marvin was in the pilot's seat. The wound had stopped bleeding.

A half hour earlier, Mario and Eddie had hunkered down in the half-track. Eddie had been sure to reposition the armored shield over the front window for protection -- they weren't expecting to make it back to the plane without being harassed in some way by the local armed forces. After having dealt with the commandant in the past, Eddie knew where the leader's sympathies lay.

Without the heavy shield above, Eddie could feel the sun beating down on his brow. The narrow slit cut into the shield provided a minimal view of the road ahead. Mario was standing behind the driver's compartment manning the heavy machine gun.

They passed the aid station and drove through the nearby settlement, and then through the acres of farmland. That's when Eddie applied the brakes, bringing the old beast to a standstill. In front of them, what looked to be the entire island's forces stood spread out on the edge of the rain forest. Eddie had to poke his head out the top of the truck to get a better view of what they were up against.

"Maybe you should've held on to that white flag, kid." Mario's rough voice had a sarcastic, almost comic tone.

Barring the roadway was an interesting and formidable mix of military might. Two small tanks flanked the road that disappeared into the thick foliage. They were old, but they were tracked vehicles with small cannons protruding from the turrets. Several other vehicles included four by fours with chopped tops, armed with heavy machine guns. Two jeeps sat smack-dab in the middle of the road, acting as barriers. In front of, behind, and on top of all the vehicles were hoards of infantry with an array of small arms trained in their direction.

Eddie stood up on the driver's seat, almost level with Mario, who handed him a pair of binoculars. "This ought to be a doozy, huh?" the Italian asked.

Eddie tallied up the number of soldiers waiting for them. He counted at least thirty that he could see, and that wasn't counting the crews working in the bellies of the armored vehicles. He shrugged. "Shit, I don't know. What are you thinking?"

Mario pulled two fresh cigars from his front breast pocket. "You want one? They're my last two."

"What the hell," Eddie answered without hesitation. Taking the Zippo, he set the tip of the cigar to the blue and yellow flame, took a few puffs, and passed the lighter back.

"Well, Ed," Mario said between puffs, "we have three choices, all with similar endings, I think. We can try and bust through here, or we can take an alternate route. I'm sure that's guarded as well. Or, we could surrender."

"I don't think the latter is an option with Mr. Commandant."

"Right. I see your point." Mario gave a heavy sigh. "Then I say we bust through."

## Caribbean Calling

Ed scratched his head and resigned himself. "Okay, Mario, what's the plan?"

"See that spot barricaded by those jeeps, between the tanks?" Eddie nodded. "We'll head for those jeeps as fast as we can and push them out of the way."

"What about the tanks?" Ed asked, bewildered.

"I'll take care of them. Our friends left a couple of rockets back here for us."

Eddie said no more. He turned around in his seat, cigar clutched between his teeth. After taking the time to check his weapons, he stashed a shell in the barrel of the shotgun and sat the weapon on the seat next to him. The .22 automatic was loaded and in his ankle holster. As for the Colt, it was loaded and sitting beneath his shoulder holster. Finally, Eddie pulled the magazine from the Russian-made assault rifle. The AK-47 was ready to go, sitting next to the shotgun. He slammed the vehicle into drive and the heavy vehicle lurched forward.

As the vehicle gained speed, Eddie worked the gears. The little orange needle was only up to the thirty mile an hour mark, but Ed felt like he was hurtling down the road at an amazing rate, adrenaline complicating his perception. Through the small slits in the driver's plate he could see the soldiers begin to jockey for the best firing position. Puffs of smoke and flame jumped from the barrels of the two tanks and an explosion rocked the ground on either side of the half-track.

Muzzle flashes in a long row were visible as the enemy began to pour fire in their direction. Ed could hear pieces of metal bouncing off the hull of the truck. Approaching the jeeps lined up across the road, Ed could make out the heavy, banging sound of Mario working the machine gun. A jeep in their path was decimated as he raked the enemy line with the large rounds. Tracers streaked over Eddie's head. Then he noticed soldiers running about in panic. Distraught officers were pointing, directing the men where to go and how to react. It seemed to Ed that there was a lot of chaos amongst the ranks, considering the half-track was their only adversary.

The enemy tanks fired again. One shell veered off, missing the gunner's intended target. The second tank's round landed home, though. The projectile slammed into the front of the half-track, slamming Eddie forward into the steering wheel with its impact. Momentarily, he lost his breath and saw stars. The next thing he knew he was shaking. He took a deep breath and realized that the shaking was Mario, pulling on his arm, trying to get him out of the driver's seat.

Eddie nodded to let his partner know he was all right. His first action was to pick up the assault rifle, leaving the shotgun behind. As he stepped out of the vehicle, he noticed a group of soldiers coming their way, though still at a distance. Both men let loose on the approaching figures. Several of them fell to the ground.

"Come on, let's move that way. Here, take this." Mario threw Eddie one of the light rockets that had been stashed in the back of the half-track. Extending the weapon to its full length, Mario put the weapon to his shoulder and lined up the sights on one of the armored vehicles. When he depressed the trigger, the missile screamed from the barrel, flames following its flight. One of the tanks exploded, leaving nothing but a smoking shell behind.

Eddie saw an officer redirect a squad of soldiers away. Another pack took their place. He expended the magazine in his AK-47 and reloaded. As he was lifting the weapon to his shoulder, he felt a searing pain in his right arm. He twisted and tripped, falling to the ground, dropping both the rifle and the rocket launcher. He could hear Mario let another volley go from the assault rifle.

## Caribbean Calling

When he rolled over, he saw yet another group of soldiers approaching. They were close, and gaining ground fast. He reached into his vest and gripped the Colt. Leveling the weapon, he began pulling the trigger, sure that he and Mario would soon be dead, or sitting shackled in the commandant's little dungeon. From there, they'd be handed over to Lester Crow.

A small-framed vehicle with large knobby wheels careened past. One man drove while the other operated a machine-gun, lighter than the fifty-caliber on the half-track, but with rapid firing, similar to an M-60. The gunner released the weapon's fury as the vehicle circled around the band of infantry approaching Eddie and Mario. The group scattered, several of the men falling to the ground. Eddie recognized the gunner. It was the Baron. His old schoolyard nemesis had come to drag him from the clutches of the commandant's forces.

After Eddie and Mario had pulled away from The Plantation, the Baron had returned to the Caretaker's office. The leader had already begun putting his plan in motion.

"Our coup d'etat is about to begin," he said, patting his associate on the shoulder. "The island is in chaos and the commandant's forces are unorganized."

The Caretaker's on-site army had already been assembled. The shore teams had been dispatched and were on their way to a fleet of stashed-away gunboats. The Baron headed down to the garage after reporting to his boss. Another team was mounting up their vehicles. They would be deployed to prearranged attack sites all around Capersdeed.

The Baron knew that Eddie was heading into a trap. The commandant had been forewarned of Eddie's presence by the Crows, who had contacted the Caretaker, as well. Reese hadn't made any promises. He'd already built a strong respect for Eddie's up-front tactics.

The Baron took his place on a vehicle and headed off to the larger of two roadblocks, which had been set up by the commandant to find Gilbert and his partner. He didn't know why he felt an alliance with Eddie, but he chalked it up to hometown ties. Whatever the case, the Baron had made it to the fireman's aid in the nick of time.

Marvin and TC were surprised to see the old half-track, steam pouring out of its smashed up front end, pull up into the small clearing in the jungle. The Albatross floated on the water a short distance away. TC was the first to stand up. "Hey, man, what happened to my ride?"

"We, uh, ran into a little trouble. Don't worry, you'll be well compensated," Mario assured him.

"What am I supposed to do now for wheels?" the half-baked hippie complained.

Mario looked at him for a moment and then pointed to the half-track. "Take that pig!"

TC was elated. Hollering goodbyes, he jumped into the truck, fired up the diesel, and drove away. Eddie could hear him crunching and grinding the gears as he beat a path into the jungle.

Minutes later, the high-pitched sound of an engine approached. Through the trees, the Baron appeared, leading a team of four fast attack vehicles. The Baron had a smile pasted on his big mug and his thumb was extended skyward. "We got 'em good, huh, Eddie?"

Eddie wasn't sure what to make of it. His arm hurt like hell,

## Caribbean Calling

and here he was, miles upon miles from home, looking into the face of an old childhood enemy who was working in a cult for its loony-tunes leader. He wasn't comfortable with the cult and its ideology, but he was grateful indeed for the strange alliance.

The Baron dismounted and walked over to Eddie, still smiling from ear to ear. "What's your plan now, old pal?"

"Well, Bartley…"

"Please, Ed, it's Baron, okay?"

"Sorry, Baron."

"Well, I'll have to defer to my boss, but I think we're heading to Crow Island."

"Would you guys like a little help?"

Eddie was amazed by the unexpected offer.

j. d. gordon

## Chapter Nineteen

Lester was unhappy when the nearly crippled guard presented himself. He and Hector were still lounging on the veranda discussing their plans for capturing Eddie. They had already contacted the forces on Capersdeed and given them a head's up.

"What do you mean she got away?" Lester did his best to keep his composure. The guard's punishment was swift and severe. Lester shot him on the spot. Then he ordered Hector to call in a crew to clean up the mess. The second order issued was to find the escaped doctor. "Find the bitch! She can't have gone far. The island's not that big."

There were five men in the posse, all wearing the standard Crow island uniform, tan on tan and equipped with automatic pistols and sub-machine guns.

Elaine had a difficult time moving through the branches and thick brush. The critters and creatures that call the tropics home didn't help either. She wasn't sure how much time she had, but she knew she was being hunted. She had no clue where she was going, or what she would do. All she knew was that she had to get away somehow.

She pushed forward until she came to a long, rocky ledge.

## Caribbean Calling

There, she could see a small clearing in the distance, a small beach surrounded by large boulders. Flying down a rock-strewn path, she reached the beach. There was nowhere else to go. She spied an island in the distance, but it seemed awfully far away.

Her mind raced through various options. She could try and swim for it. She'd probably drown in the effort. Perhaps a passing boat would pick her up. That seemed unlikely. Nothing of the sort was in sight. She could wait and hide, but that could last an eternity. How would anyone know where she was? She could wait to be found by Lester Crow. Who knows what that would bring? He'd kill her, no doubt about that. She thought of the man nailed to stakes on the beach. Dolphins had been known to save wayward souls lost at sea. She could wait and hope for that. Minutes passed. That was that. Elaine decided to swim.

Hector and his crew made their way through the thick foliage quickly. Elaine Keller wasn't the first of the Crow's guests who had managed to slip away. This group of men knew every hiding spot on the island. As in the case of Alcatraz, almost no one had ever escaped captivity on Crow Island.

Their prey had gotten a head start, but Hector knew where she would end up. They all ended up in the same place. The trails through the jungle all led to the little beach on the back side of the island. As soon as Hector and his men stepped out on that beach, they could see her in the distance, maybe five hundred yards out. It was a long way -- most never made it out that far before turning back, drowning, or being attacked by sharks. The Crows stocked the waters around the island with an abundance of the dangerous creatures.

Hector grinned as Elaine tried to breaststroke her way to freedom. "Call for the boats to pick her up. Lester would be disappointed to hear this one had turned into sushi."

# j. d. gordon

Elaine was becoming exhausted. The little voice in her head was screaming for her to turn back. Her arms and legs ached. Off to her right, she noticed a shadow out of the corner of her eye. Instinctively, she turned her head in that direction. A dorsal fin broke the surface of the water, only for a moment, and then disappeared, leaving behind a trail of white bubbles. Then, she felt something brush up against her leg, it was slick and smooth. She stopped and treaded water, panic setting in.

She thought of the movie Jaws, which she hadn't seen in over a decade. She remembered a scene where a little boy had escaped an attack by the aquatic marauder by remaining still. The boy had been in shock. With all the control she could muster, she kept her body as motionless as she could. She could see the monster twenty or thirty feet away and began to cry.

It got nearer. She waited for the pain of its razor sharp teeth to puncture her skin, and the force of its jaws to drag her under.

Instead of going for her leg, though, the creature's body broke the surface of the water. Airborne for a moment, the animal arced over her head. Elaine let out a shriek. It was a dolphin, a beautiful, wonderful, adorable, friendly, dolphin. Bouncing about in the waves, the ocean mammal almost seemed to be smiling. He had found a new friend to splash with in the warm water.

Elaine was too exhausted to play, though, and after the dolphin swam and jumped for a few minutes, trying to coax her into some fun, he lost interest and moved on. Though relieved, Elaine couldn't help but regret that the legend of dolphins saving unfortunates at sea wasn't accurate.

She treaded water for a few minutes, trying to find strength, and noticed a group of lobsters scurrying around the sea floor.

## Caribbean Calling

Raising her head, she could now see a group of figures standing on the beach she'd escaped from. Most of them were toting weapons, but they didn't seem to be in attack mode. Then, from behind the cove, she saw two boats racing toward her. Elaine's attempt at escape was about to be aborted. She had no strength left to struggle as she was dragged into one of the boats. In the distance, she heard an airplane, and then she passed out.

## Chapter Twenty

"Klein says we're on our own. He's going to try and arrange for some kind of support, but it's very short notice. He did give us the option to call the mission off, though. What's your feeling on that, kid?"

Eddie considered the suggestion. On the one hand, it would be easy to take the out. This was a dangerous situation, and one he'd found himself in too recently, to boot. On the other hand, he couldn't see leaving this poor woman behind with the Crows. God knows what they'd do to her. Besides, they already had some help on the way in the form of the Baron, though the plane they were in would cover distance much more quickly than the Baron's gunboats. They'd be about two hours behind.

The Baron had assembled a team of thirty men, piled into three boats, which were armed with heavy machine guns and cannons. While Eddie didn't approve of the cult and its practices, the added help was essential. He would deal with the situation at The Plantation when, and if, he came out of this alive.

Their rendezvous site was to be a small island ten miles from Crow Island. Marvin landed the aircraft on the side facing away from the enemy's camp. A large clearing nearby would serve as a perfect spot for the Baron's gunboats to make a temporary landing. After what felt to be a long wait, the Baron waded to shore, his men and three gunboats waiting in the shallow water for orders. The Albatross was anchored in the water, as well.

## Caribbean Calling

Eddie, Mario, and the Baron held counsel on the beach. The Baron had brought a case of Red Stripe along with him. The bottles were ice cold, and Eddie drained a few bottles of the Jamaican brew while they made their plans. They would wait until nightfall, and then set out.

Eddie enlightened the men about Crow Island as best he could. Although he'd had the relative pleasure of visiting the island once before, he didn't know much about its layout. His penetration, at the time, had been minimal at best.

It was just before midnight when they deployed. Mario grabbed another one of his inflatable rafts, and Eddie teased him about buying stock in the company, as they boarded one of the Baron's gunboats. In a short time, Eddie, Mario, and three of the Baron's associates jumped out into the raft about two hundred yards from the same little beach that Brighton and Eddie had visited during their last foray. After it drifted onto the sand, they stashed the raft behind a grove of palms. The full moon hung in the night sky, round and bright. Eddie wondered whether that was a good thing or not. The tension was broken when a gust of wind blew a coconut from its lofty perch, hitting Mario right on the noggin. "Okay, shut the fuck up, you guys. We're supposed to be professionals here," Mario said with a smile.

Ed surveyed the scene, which he found eerie, but interesting. The Baron's men were not cult members. They seemed more like ex-military, all lean, mean, and well trained. Communication took place through nods and simple replies. All of the men, including Eddie and Mario, were uniformed in black combat fatigues. Vests, attached to their suits, were packed with an assortment of knives, pistols, and grenades. Eddie carried his .22, as well, in his ankle holster. The Baron had swapped out the AK-47 Eddie had nabbed for an M-16. The American assault rifle was fitted with an M-203 grenade launcher beneath its breech. Eddie also carried a supply of forty-millimeter grenades in a bandoleer wrapped about his torso.

Mario stuck with his trusty AK-47. He borrowed a pair of night vision binoculars from the Baron, and another man carried a sniper rifle outfitted with a night scope. All in all, the small team was very well equipped.

It would take some time for the other teams to reach their deployment areas. Until then, they lay quiet.

Elaine was hurled to the floor of the boat. No one said a word to her as the craft jetted around a pair of tall cliffs to the lagoon. The body she'd seen on the beach from the veranda was still there and Elaine wondered if he'd had the good fortune to die.

Sadistically hauled from the boat, she wasn't returned to the prison cell. She was pulled by the hair to Lester's suite. Two guards waited with her there until Lester returned after several minutes. Ironically enough, he apologized for making her wait.

"Well, now that you know that escape is impossible, perhaps you'll reconsider your position," he said, as if offering her a job at a Fortune 500 company. Elaine didn't give him the dignity of an answer.

Several other men entered the room and were offered cocktails. Then, as Elaine sat silently, shackled in a corner, they sat down to dinner. Dining on rare steaks, Caesar salad and rice pilaf, the men drank and smoked and laughed as if they were at a Saturday night country club dinner.

Elaine was ignored as the bunch of modern day pirates discussed increasing security, and then changed the subject to the ex-congressman named Klein, and the firefighter named Eddie Gilbert. Lester had an enormous amount of disdain for both men, but especially Gilbert. His neck turned red and he swore when he spoke of him. As for Elaine, she wished Lester's bitter enemy would show up. At least it would distract him from her.

Around midnight, things began to change. The party was in full swing and Lester and his guests leered at her diabolically. Then, from the direction of the lagoon, an engine screamed, followed by a series of cracks. It sounded like the Fourth of July out there. The drunk and stoned men on the veranda became very serious, and Hector exited with two men. Lester remained behind, holding a radio to his ear. He looked very, very angry.

"Mario!" Eddie heard the Baron's voice crackle on the radio's miniature speaker. "We're in position."

Mario was in command of the small team. At first, the Baron had wanted to report to his old schoolmate, but Eddie had explained the situation back on the beach.

"So this is a new gig for you, huh, Ed?" the Baron had asked as they shared a Red Stripe. If not for the mercenaries checking and rechecking their equipment, the group could easily have been mistaken for happy campers. "Are you going to leave the fire service?"

The Baron had shared his life story with Ed. He'd spoken about his father, and everything he'd been through since their days back at William P. Gray Elementary School in Chicago. He'd been sent off to military school after fourth grade. Eddie had, in turn, related the story about his time with the military, college, and the training for the fire service.

Eddie decided to broach the subject. "So, how in hell did you get involved with The Plantation?"

The Baron shook his head and smiled awkwardly. "Man, that is another story for another day." The two shared a brief silence.

"Seems like a million years ago, huh, Ed? Since we were kids hanging out in the schoolyard? What was it, again, Ed, that we almost tangled about?"

Ed remembered it like it was yesterday. "It was Jonny Tackle, Baron. Remember? You were picking on a small fry. I stepped in and stopped you."

"Yeah, yeah, that's right. I remember now. What happened? I remember you being dragged away and I was shakin' my fist at ya."

"I caught hell from the school counselor and you got hauled off to the principal's office."

The Baron paused in thought. "So, what happened?"

"My folks and I moved to Elmwood Park that summer. You lucked out, Baron!"

"I lucked out! Man, I would've kicked your ass!"

Eddie smiled and looked at him. He was huge, and as many scars covered his arms and chest as tattoos.

"Let's call it a draw, Baron," Eddie said with a wink.

The Baron chuckled. "Okay, Ed, we can call it a draw, but I still would've kicked your ass."

Eddie didn't have any problem giving him the last word. "Okay, buddy, that's probably true."

Over the next hour or so, the two men sat on that beach talking about their old haunts, the pizza place on the corner, the candy shop, and the old schoolyard. Eventually, it was time to saddle up. They shook hands and patted each other on the back. It was possible it would be their last meeting, if things went awry.

Not long after, the fight started with two of the gunboats

running into the lagoon at high speed. Riddling the area with heavy machine gun fire, shells from the cannons slammed into the body of the main house. The first attack team could see figures running about a large garden. There, the Crow men organized into teams and returned fire.

Lester knew the time would come, but he didn't think it would be tonight. Otherwise, he would have held back with the drink and smoke. Standing on the veranda, he watched as the gunboats laid fire into his sprawling garden. Then he saw a sizable force of dark-clad men jump from the boats and onto the land surrounding the lagoon. If he was glad about anything, it was that he had doubled up on the guard for the night. Once the exploding shells started bouncing off his luxurious home, Lester stepped off the veranda into the relative safety of the building.

After closing the French doors, which were sturdy and reinforced with thick steel and bulletproof glass, he sat down behind his desk with a loaded automatic pistol within reach. Guards stood by the main doorway, which was also reinforced. Small vertical slits were built in to allow firing from inside. In a pinch, a stairway led down to a small lobby, which exited onto the helicopter pad.

"Well, Doctor," he said with venom, "it seems as though the fireman has come to your rescue."

Elaine wondered who this fireman was that Lester kept speaking of, and, for that matter, why he would come to rescue her. She said nothing, eyes closed, listening to Hector's reports as the battle raged on. Apparently, the news wasn't good. An unexpectedly large force had come aground, and things weren't working out in the Crow's favor. At this point, any and every Crow employee was being ordered to join in the fight.

"Lester!" Hector's voice screeched from the hand-held radio. "Pull back from the office!"

"Repeat?" Lester maintained an eerie calm.

"I think you should you pull out of the main building. I've got the bird warming up on the secondary pad, just in case."

Lester massaged his temple with his free hand. "Are you suggesting things aren't going well?" His tone was one of disbelief, though gunfire could be heard in the background.

"That would be correct, sir," the voice on the radio crackled.

After a beat, Lester responded. "I'll be along soon."

Lester sat silent at his desk, gripping his pistol. The guards looked very uneasy, though they remained quiet. Lester tallied how many soldiers he had stationed on the island. It had been a busy week and his men were spread too thin, many of them scattered around the globe, maintaining his crime business. He wondered if Hector had sent out an emergency message telling his off-site crews to report to the secondary base of operations. That would be a first. The secondary location, Gangplank's Island, had never needed to be utilized. In the past, his father had vacationed there from time to time, for a change of scenery. It had never been used in an official capacity.

Finally, nervously, one of the guards spoke, "Sir, perhaps we should go."

Lester grabbed Elaine by the scruff of the neck and dragged her down the stairway. In the lobby, they were forced to stop. A group of men were moving down the hallway, where a firefight had broken out between the invaders and the Crow guards. Lester ordered one of his guards to join in. Because the enemy forces were attacking from the main helipad, he would have to make it to the secondary pad and helicopter with the woman and the remaining guard. They wouldn't shoot if she were his hostage.

## Caribbean Calling

Mario moved his team forward through the tangle of bushes and plants toward the main building. The helipad in front of the building was empty. Through the night scope, he could see six men laying low behind the pad, next to a doorway that seemed to lead to the bowels of the building. From his last visit, Eddie remembered that the door led to a lobby where a stairway climbed to the Crow's personal office suite. That's where he had found Klein's daughter, Jennifer. Automatic weapons blasted away in the background, and a sniper in their midst opened up on a target.

"Hold steady," Mario ordered. "The rest will show their positions in a minute."

Sure enough, the sniper let a second round fly, and the area behind the helipad exploded in muzzle fire. Eddie guessed they were facing four defenders now."Eddie, toss a grenade into the pad. Smoke it, and follow it up with a couple of frags," Mario growled.

Eddie searched the bandoleer for the frags, and then laid the grenades on the ground in front of him. Pushing the trigger on the launcher, Eddie felt the discharge. The round bounced onto the pad, smoke billowing from the shell. Then he pushed the loading mechanism back and plopped a fresh forty-millimeter round into the chamber. As soon as the expended shell fell, he repeated the action. The explosions rocked the ground. Now he placed a scatter round into the short barrel. The deadly piece of ammunition would spread a murderous hail of buckshot.

As he performed these actions, the other men in the team opened up with full force. Eddie couldn't hear much over the sound of the automatic weapons, but he could smell the sulfur. Mario ordered the team to move forward and the five men started off in the direction of the pad and the building beyond.

One of the Baron's men fell to the ground, holding his gut, where one of the enemy rounds had penetrated his protective vest.

Eddie fired off his M-16, the selector set on automatic. The rounds in the magazine were expended and the empty clip fell to the ground. His arm protested in pain from his earlier wound as he stuffed in a fresh magazine. He could feel fresh blood flowing from the rip in his skin. He stopped for a moment to check on the Baron's injured man. The man pushed him away, signaling him to keep going. It was not in his nature to rush past an injured person, but he heard Mario shout and he moved on.

"We're playing soldier today, kid, not paramedic!" The same stinking, soggy old stub of cigar was still planted between his teeth. It had gone out hours before.

A Crow guard appeared to the right of them. The man lifted his weapon, but was cut down by a blast from Mario's assault rifle before he could fire. Eddie rushed right by this man, feeling no regret.

Now that the area was clear of defenders, Mario and his crew assembled near the doorway leading into the main building. Only one of the Baron's men was still in action. Two others had been left behind on the pad and in the jungle. Eddie didn't know whether they'd been injured or killed in action. He hoped the money the men had made for their services was worth the price of life and limb.

The last man left standing was the man Eddie had stopped for. He could see a copious amount of blood flowing from his wound. The man's thigh was split open, and the strap from the man's weapon was wrapped around his leg. The makeshift contraption did little to stem the flow of blood.

Mario glanced down the hallway beyond the wide doorway. "We've got some bad guys down there. I can't tell how many, though." After another look, his question was answered by the rapid click of a sub-machine gun. He let loose with his assault rifle, then changed magazines in one smooth motion. "Alrighty, then, let's earn our paychecks."

Mario jumped into the hallway, Eddie right behind him. The Baron's man made the turn and caught a burst from one of the sub-machine guns. He fell to the floor in a heap. Eddie's response was to push the trigger on the grenade launcher again. The gunman hit the ground amidst the casings littering the corridor's carpet. Seconds later, two more men went down. Eddie could see four people trying to make their way down the hallway through the smoke, a hundred yards away. One of them was a woman. "That's got to be her, Mario," he said. And Lester Crow, he thought to himself.

"Give 'em everything we got, kid, but place your rounds carefully. Don't hit the girl."

Eddie slammed another smoke round into the hallway, and was about to pull the trigger on the launcher when he realized that filling the narrow corridor would hinder the operation. The fleeing enemy would be given cover by the smokescreen. Instead, he snatched the rifle that the Baron's man had been using. Lifting the weapon to his shoulder, he lined up the cross-hairs and pulled the trigger. Bingo. The high-powered shell slammed into one man's rib cage.

Two remaining men dragged the girl along. Eddie knew which one was Lester. It was the greasy-looking one with the ponytail. The three were nearing a turn in the corridor and would be out of sight in seconds. Eddie's mind raced. Should he pull the trigger and chance hitting the girl? If they got away, would he and Mario be able to find them again? He didn't know the layout of the joint, and was afraid that they would dash down a secret hallway. If he and Mario made a left instead of a right, it would be a disaster.

If Eddie had learned anything in his years of service as a firefighter, it was to go with your first instinct. He pulled the trigger. The man he'd targeted fell and lost his grip on the girl. Immediately, she scrambled, kicking to get away. The second man, Lester, stopped, pointing his weapon down the hallway. Eddie hit the ground hard, trying to avoid being hit. He lost his breath for a moment with the impact from the fall. Lifting his head, he saw Mario firing off the AK-47 as he ran down the hall in the direction of the girl, though Lester managed to throw himself out of a nearby door.

With every ounce of strength he had left, Eddie stood up and followed his partner, joining him at the end of the corridor. A puddle of blood surrounded the girl, who was sitting on the floor in a heap crying, her head in her hands, between her knees.

"Are you Doctor Elaine Keller?" Mario asked gently, the ever-present cigar sticking out of his mouth.

Shaking and panting, she lifted her head. "Yes, I am."

Caribbean Calling

## Chapter Twenty-One

Eddie sat at the Schooner Wharf Bar reading the latest edition of the *Key West Citizen*. The sour lime floating in his cold Corona caused him to purse his lips. It was evening time, and he was beyond exhausted. A short story on the third page caught his eye. CROW FAMILY CRIME SYNDICATE TAKEN DOWN. The account made no mention of what had happened. It didn't matter to him. He knew the story and he had the stitches to prove it.

What bothered him, though, was that the reporter had failed to mention the most important part of story. Lester Crow had managed to escape, like a bank robber slipping away into the darkness after a big heist.

Below, a paragraph was devoted to the rescue of a number of Caribbean Relief Corp workers from what was called an agricultural commune. According to the report, they had been either sent home or reassigned to another relief station in another devastated country. One man, a Billy Stang, had stayed behind on Capersdeed with a woman, Batilda Washington, and a Pastor Tom Northrup, to set about reopening the medical clinic. The director, Robert J. Moore, had been relieved of his duties.

## j. d. gordon

Eddie had flashed on the idea of hunting down Lester Crow himself while standing in that corridor on that horrible night. He had, in fact, made a move to rush past Mario and the devastated young doctor.

"Where the hell do you think you're going, Rambo?" Mario had shouted.

Eddie had been in an adrenaline-induced frenzy. "I'm going to get that bastard Crow."

Mario had held him back by his shirtsleeve. "Eddie, fuck that. We're heading out. We're done. We've got what we came for. Look at yourself, kid. Your arm's bleeding again, your head's bleeding. Are you nuts, man?"

A slap in the face would have had the same effect. Looking down at himself, he'd noticed his bloodstained sleeve and he could feel blood trickling from his forehead from a bullet that had grazed him moments earlier. He had to admit, the old soldier was right.

Eddie and Mario had retreated with Elaine back out to the helicopter pad. The area was clear, but they could hear the continuing sounds of battle coming from two different directions. Mario replaced his handset and contacted the Baron, who reported that things were wrapping up on his end. Still involved with the party attacking the main building off of the lagoon, he said that resistance was light, and they were pushing the Crow forces back into the complex. With that situation under control, Mario changed frequencies and contacted Marvin with orders to pick them up back on the beach.

On their way out, Eddie looked up and saw a black Crow helicopter overhead. Lester stared out from the front window. He looked pissed. "Goddammit," Ed muttered. "The fucking guy has nine lives."

## Caribbean Calling

Elaine, who had until then been too dazed to speak, found her voice, "Who are you guys, anyway?"

Recovering from his anger at watching Crow escape, Ed looked right into her eyes and spoke softly. "I'm sorry. I'm Eddie Gilbert, and this is my associate, Mr. Mario Marino."

"No relation to the quarterback," Mario added.

Shakily, she went on. "Who sent you here?"

"Mr. Klein. He's an old friend of your father's. Do you know him?" Emily nodded her head in recognition.

The three found their way back through the bushes and came to rest on the beach. Elaine collapsed in the sand, although she had regained her composure rather quickly, considering the circumstances.

Mario sat down on a large stone and felt around in his pocket.

Eddie shook his head in amazement. "You ran out, remember? We smoked the last two this afternoon."

"Damn, that's right," Mario cursed. "You know, if I'd thought we were going to make it past that road block back on Capersdeed, I wouldn't have shared."

The Albatross could be seen in the near distance. Marvin was banking the old seaplane in for a landing.

Elaine raised her eyebrows in concern. "We're going to get out of here in that thing?"

Eddie reassured her. "Yeah, don't worry. We'll be fine -- a bit tight, but just fine."

The old seaplane landed in the water and Marvin could be seen sticking his thumb up, a big smile displaying his pearly white teeth. Ed retrieved the little raft from the bushes and they stashed their weapons and rowed out to the plane, whose

## j. d. gordon

propellers were still spinning. Marvin wasn't sure how quick their take-off would have to be.

Once inside the belly of the old plane, Eddie stripped off his vest and shirt. Mario tossed him a first-aid kit and told him to clean himself up, then went up front to give Klein the good news.

"Let me take a look at that," Elaine said, sifting through the materials in the first-aid kit. "There's not much here, but I think I can do something for you." Eddie winced as she poured peroxide over his wounds. Then she patted it dry with some gauze sheets and applied a dressing.

"I'm used to being on the other side of this kind of thing," Eddie commented.

"Oh yeah, how's that?" she asked, gauze clenched between her teeth. There were no scissors in the first-aid case.

"Well, in real life I work as a firefighter and paramedic up north. I'm, uh, trying out a new line of work. It's a long story."

Elaine looked at him with surprise. "You're that Eddie Gilbert? The super-hero fireman?"

Eddie blushed. "Yeah, that's, ah, me."

"Lester mentioned you," she said. "He doesn't like you very much."

"I don't imagine he does," Eddie agreed.

Mario joined them in back. "So, Klein came through. It was a little late, but it was help." Mario started looking around the back of the plane, under cushions and inside cabinets.

"Does he know?"

"Yeah, I radioed him. He seemed pretty happy." Mario let out a hoot, and Eddie gave him a questioning look. "Someone will have to deal with the whole Plantation deal. You know, we owe your old buddy, the Baron. I let Klein know how helpful he was."

Elaine's eyes widened. "You guys know about The Plantation?"

Mario chuckled. "Jesus. Not by choice, honey. Ed threw them for a hell of a loop. That's how we learned where you were."

"I was there for some time, drugged up on something. But my friends, my co-workers at the aid station, and the villagers I think...God, I was so out of it, but there are people at that plantation who need help. Batilda and Reggie and Martin...I don't know who else. You've got to...we've got to go there and get them. Please." Tears welled up in her eyes. "They're such good people. And Jonathan...charming, lovable Kangaroo. They slaughtered him in front of my eyes. His body should be sent back to his home. And Billy! What happened to Billy?" The tears became a torrent running down her cheeks.

Mario sat next to her and put his arm around her shoulder. "Listen, darlin'. You're exhausted. We're exhausted. We'll get help for them, I promise, okay? But we can't do it tonight. Tonight we've got to get to safe ground."

Eddie had worked seventy-two-hour shifts back home. He was exhausted, but he was used to pushing himself to the very limit. "Mario, if there are hostages at The Plantation, we've gotta get 'em out. I don't know how the hell we'd do it, but somebody has to do something."

"What're we gonna do, Fireman Ed? Is Marvin gonna land on the roof and we'll swing down on ropes? Klein's guys are out here." Mario looked at Elaine. "We'll get them out, okay? I swear it on my grandma's life. When we land, I'll get Klein's men on the radio and explain the situation. You can talk to them... explain what happened and who they are. Is that okay?" He spoke gently and sincerely.

Elaine threw her head back and took several deep breaths. "Okay. As soon as we land. I love them, ya know?"

"Cross my heart. They'll get 'em out."

Eddie knew in his heart Mario was right. Capersdeed wasn't his problem to deal with. But he'd make damn sure himself that the doctor's friends would be let go. The Plantation was creepy, and the Caretaker was a wing-nut. But they weren't in the habit of killing regular folk. They took everything they had. Klein would know how to deal with it.

"I found one!" Mario stood up and displayed his treasure. The front of the cigar was smashed, and the rest crinkled, but he was able to get it lit. Marvin lectured from up front about the dangers of smoking in an aircraft, but Eddie never found out if the words of caution had any effect. Within a minute, he was fast asleep, Elaine's head in his lap.

A while later, Marvin landed near Mario's sleek cigarette boat with the flaming paint-job. "Well, mon, will you be stayin on wit Meestah Klein?" Marvin asked Eddie as they shook hands.

"Honestly? I'm not sure."

"Well, you keep in touch, mon."

Mario sparked up the boat's engine and they headed back to Key West. Klein had arranged for a plane to take them back to Tampa, but Eddie declined the ride. Calling Klein on the boat's radio, his boss's first words were, "Hey, Ed, I sure hope you're not calling to tell me that you're no longer interested in the job."

Eddie hadn't expected that subject to come up so quickly. "You know, Mr. Klein, I'm going to take a few days to kick it around. My first stop is at the ER. I'll need a few stitches before anything else." He handed the phone over to Mario, who, with Elaine's help, informed Klein of his men's next mission.

## Caribbean Calling

Klein arranged for a car to take Eddie to a local medical clinic. A taxi picked him up at the airport and raced him to a clinic on Stock Island. Though he wondered how Klein arranged these things so quickly, he never asked.

Mario was headed with Elaine to a plane out of Key West International. The two men nodded their goodbyes, and gave each other a hearty handshake. Elaine gave Eddie a warm hug and a kiss on the cheek. She had tears in her eyes. "Thank you, Fireman Ed. I'll never forget you."

It was late evening when a cab deposited Eddie back onto the doorstep of the La Concha. Though they were a bit wrinkled, Eddie had changed back into some decent clothing at the clinic. Tomorrow, he'd treat himself to a new outfit, though there was $15,000 worth of suits back at Marci's -- and more to come if he stayed on.

After placing the 'Do Not Disturb' sign on his door handle, he lay back on the bed and ordered up some room service -- a pizza and a couple of tumblers of Myers, with extra ice. Flipping through the TV channels, he made it through half the pizza and one glass of the dark rum and then drifted off to sleep.

It was late in the afternoon when he woke up. A slip of white paper had been slipped under the door. Horrified at first that it was another of Mario's notes inviting him to go on another job, he sighed in relief when he read that the maid service had at least attempted to clean his room. He showered, shaved, ironed his clothes, and headed up to the roof for the glorious sunset. The event was still an hour or so off, so he ordered a cocktail and set about considering his future.

For one thing, there was the job back home. He wanted to call. He missed his buddies and the daily routine a lot. Maybe he'd write a postcard. That would give 'em something to laugh about. Then there was Marci, who had begun to steal his heart.

As the majesty of the sunset began, he reveled in the cheers of the other rooftop bar patrons. Damn, it was beautiful here.

For now, a stroll seemed like a good way to end the evening. By tomorrow, he would feel all of the bumps and bruises from his recent adventure. He rode the elevator to the lobby and headed in the direction of the main door. A copy of the *Key West Citizen* sat on top of the front desk.

"May I take this?" he asked the woman working the desk. Ed grabbed the newspaper and headed out onto Duval, walking in the direction of his favorite Key West watering hole. It was always the Schooner Wharf Bar.

The walk along the strip was pleasant. He passed a palm reader in a doorway and considered getting a glimpse into his future, but then decided against it. A trio of street musicians mimicked a version of Buffett's *Margaritaville*, and delectable aromas drifted into the street from the sidewalk establishments. It was a typical night in Key West.

Eddie took a seat at the bar and ordered up a Corona with a slice of lime. A band was setting up for the night. Ed opened the paper and started skimming it. The story about the recent take down of the Crows dominated his attention. The band was about ready to play, but Ed was thinking he should head back and get some more shut-eye. Marci would be meeting him in the morning, and Ed wasn't sure what was going to happen with that.

Using the dim bar lights to flip through the classified section, an ad caught his eye.

> Key West Fire Department seeks applicants to test for the position of professional firefighter. Apply in person at 123 Ocean Lane, Key West, Florida 33040.

Eddie looked up from the page -- the Key West Fire

## Caribbean Calling

Department. That could be an interesting option. But what would he do for cash while he went through the process? The sweat on the outside of the beer bottle dripped down its sides, soaking the cardboard coaster beneath. Eddie bummed a cigarette off a guy sitting next to him. He lit it up with a borrowed match and called out to the guy behind the bar, "You guys wouldn't happen to be hiring bartenders, would you?"

The End

# More Great Books from Red Engine Press

**Losing Patience** by Joyce Faulkner
ISBN(10): 0-9745652-4-5
ISBN(13): 978-0-9745652-4-8   $15.95

These tales remind one of classic episodes of the *Twilight Zone*.

**In the Shadow of Suribachi** by Joyce Faulkner
ISBN(10): 0-9745652-0-2
ISBN(13): 978-0-9745652-0-0   $15.95

Fictional story of the battle for Iwo Jima.

**They Came Home: Korean War POWs Tell Their Stories**
by Pat McGrath Avery
ISBN(10): 0-9743758-6-1
ISBN(13): 978-0-9743758-6-1   $14.95

True stories of three soldiers who were prisoners of war in Korea.

**Have Poem Will Travel** by S. Dale "Sierra" Seawright
ISBN(10): 0-9745652-3-7
ISBN(13): 978-0-9745652-3-1   $9.95

Reminiscent of the rhythms of Loretta Lynn, Woody Guthrie and Pete Seeger.

**The Complete Writer: A Guide To Tapping Your Full Potential**
by Walton-Porter, Lawrence, Avery, Faulkner
ISBN(10): 0-9745652-6-1
ISBN(13): 978-0-9745652-6-2   $17.95

Great tips on writing, publishing and promoting your literary masterpiece.

# Children's Titles from Red Engine Press

**Miller the Green Caterpillar** by Darrell House
Illustrated by Patti Argoff
ISBN(10): 0-9663276-9-1
ISBN(13): 978-0-9663276-9-4    $16.95

A tale of determination, vision and the belief that sometimes wishes do come true. Ages 3 – 8.

**The Path Winds Home** by Janie DeVos
Illustrated by Nancy Marsh
ISBN(10): 0-9743758-0-2
ISBN(13): 978-0-9743758-0-9    $16.95

A must read for a child in today's diversified and multicultural society. The book is in hardcover. Ages 2 – 8.

**How High Can You Fly?** by Janie DeVos
Illustrated by Renee Rejent
ISBN(10): 0-9663276-2-4
ISBN(13): 978-0-9663276-2-5    $16.95

A story about self-esteem and acceptance of others. Ages 2 – 8.

**Tommy's War** by Pat McGrath Avery
Illustrated by Eric Ray
ISBN(10): 0-9663276-8-3
ISBN(13): 978-0-9663276-8-7    $5.95

Tommy and his friend each have a parent that leaves home because of a war. Ages 4 – 7.

These book are available from your local bookstore, on-line supplier or Red Engine Press (www.redenginepress.com).

## About the Author

Firefighter and paramedic-turned-author, Jimmy (J. D.) Gordon was born and raised in Chicago where he developed a keen appreciation for the finer things in life: pan pizza, live blues and the Cubs. Jimmy loves spending time in the Florida Keys and in the Caribbean. He lives with his family in Glen Ellyn, a suburb of the "Windy City".

Readers may contact Jimmy via JimmyGWrites@aol.com.